King of the Golden Valley

King of the Golden Valley

Alan
Scholefield

St. Martin's Press
New York

Library of Congress Cataloging in Publication Data

Scholefield, Alan.
  King of the Golden Valley.

  I. Title.
PR9369.3.S3K5   1986   823   86-1827
ISBN 0-312-45507-0

First published in Great Britain by Hamish Hamilton Ltd.

First U.S. Edition

10 9 8 7 6 5 4 3 2 1

For Penelope Hoare

CONTENTS

PROLOGUE

Chinese Turkestan

On a Spring day in 1939 Musa Ahun, a post-runner attached to His Britannic Majesty's Consulate in Kashgar, was approaching the top of the Baltek Pass on the edge of the Karakorums where he would take his noon halt. He would make a fire in the *serai* and he would smoke. He would not eat. That pleasure would be saved, God willing, until the end of the day.

He rode a Kirghiz pony and carried the leather post-bags over the animal's withers. He had been on the road for one week and would continue for a second, until he reached the Indian Postal Service's most northerly depot at Sarikol. There he would hand over the post-bags, collect another set containing mail for the Consulate staff and the few other sahibs in Kashgar, such as the Swedish missionaries and the Russian count who drank too much and the personage who lived in the place called the Golden Valley. Then he would make the journey in reverse.

It was a bitter, lonely road of ice and snow, howling winds and heavy mists. Occasionally he would meet Indian merchants with their caravans of yaks, bringing spices and Manchester goods to Yarkand and Kashgar, and sometimes Turkis, like himself, going the other way with their loads of gold, jade, Khotan carpets, Kirghiz felts and, above all, *nasha*. To reassure himself, he touched the cotton bag in his pocket and felt the dry, brittle, tobacco-like leaves; there was still a reasonable quantity left, and if he was careful it would last him to Sarikol where he could buy more. Praise be to God for *nasha*. It was better than food, better than lying with his wife, or even with the boys from Urumchi who had skins like

3

apricots. It took the tiredness from his muscles and gave him visions of paradise; it also made him less afraid.

Musa Ahun was a small, moustachioed man who had been born and raised on the plains. He found these great mountains inhospitable and frightening. Gods and devils were said to live among the crags. He made sure he said his prayers five times a day, stopping no matter what the weather or how exposed the place. Sometimes he muttered additional prayers as he rode along, talking to God to keep his spirits up. Sometimes, too, he saw Buddhist prayer wheels in rock niches, and he would give them a turn with his hand as he passed; where was the harm in additional allies?

He had made this journey many times but had never become used to it. He did it because it paid well, because he had a family of six to feed and clothe and because one day he would have the money to buy a small piece of land and grow millet and mulberries and sit in the shade and let his daughters attend him. He could not go on for ever. Already he was thirty-five years old and, like many born in Yarkand, he had a goitre at his neck. There were people there whose goitres touched the ground. He hoped, God be praised, this would never happen to him. He knew, too, that his lungs were going. He approached each pass now with apprehension. On this particular day in March he could feel, as the air thinned and the pony struggled upwards, the burning in his chest cavities, the grey sickness and the giddiness of altitude. Added to this, there was the problem of the sun. He liked dull days. But the Spring sun burned brightly and the mountain slopes shone with melt-water so that his eyes ached.

Musa Ahun rode on. Every hour or so he would dismount and walk for a while before remounting. He knew of travellers whose legs had frozen stiff from sitting in the saddle all day. He knew of a post-runner who had died of the rotting sickness because this had happened to him.

He steered his mind away from such thoughts and rearranged the post-bags to get a better balance. A lammergeyer, looking for bones to shatter, sailed overhead on great spread wings. 'Not here', Musa Ahun said out loud to the bird. 'Not this time'. As though hearing him, the lammergeyer began to rise on the morning thermals until it became a tiny black dot in the cobalt sky. Musa Ahun's eyes followed it until he lost sight of it.

But the bird could still see the horse and rider as slight inconsistencies in the landscape. Below it, spread farther than even its telescopic eyes could see, were the great peaks of the Karakorums and the Pamirs, and to the north the linking ranges of the Tien Shan. In this wild and little-known region, five countries met: China, Afghanistan, Tibet, Russian Turkestan and India. Few, except cartographers, could even guess at the exact frontiers: the lammergeyer, of course, had no interest in frontiers.

Musa Ahun continued up the pass. The track was squelchy with snow, mud and running water. It was the worst time of year; the time he feared most. To take his mind off his troubles he thought of his wife and his children, and then his mind wandered to the day he had left the Consulate with the mail. He had been given the letters and had wrapped them in oilskin and had put some in one pouch and some in another and then, just as he had finished, the *munshi* had brought out a parcel to the courtyard and handed it to him. It meant that he had had to repack the rest of the mail to get the balance right. And he had not got it right. The parcel was heavy and pulled the pouches down on one side. He did not often carry parcels to Sarikol; they all seemed to come the other way, from England by way of India. Ten years before a postrunner had died on the road back from Sarikol. The English sahibs had gone to look for him but it had been late in the year and the snow had come. When they found him in the Spring the wolves and the bears and the lammergeyers had got at his bones, but the mail pouches were safe. Apart from letters, they contained tins of sweet cake and sausages made from pigs. The sahibs had eaten them. It was not much to die for.

The *serai* at the top of the Baltek Pass was no more than a small hut built of stone with a roof of wooden beams, on top of which had been laid a covering of felt. It was said that if one stood on the snow slope above the *serai* one could see three countries. Like the lammergeyer, Musa Ahun had little interest in views and when he reached the top he dismounted stiffly and gave his pony several handfuls of fodder. The wind

5

blew keenly here and he took the post-bags and went into the *serai* for shelter. He squatted inside the room with its filthy dirt floor and blackened fireplace, and rolled himself some of the *nasha* in the special paper he found in the rubbish bins at the Consulate. It came all the way from London and people squabbled over who was to read it first, or so he had been told. For smoking, the paper was better than other newspapers, especially the ones from Russia. He lit the *nasha* and squatted against the wall, letting his arms fall forward over his knees. The drug began its work. First it took away the cold and then the soreness in his head. He felt himself float slightly away from his body. He had sought paradise and to a certain extent he had found it. So that when he became aware of the roaring noise he wondered if it was only in his ears. He was not afraid.

The avalanche buried the *serai* and the pony and it buried Musa Ahun. At one moment there had been a building and a worn track, outcrops of rocks, a prayer wheel and the evidence of many fires. When the ice-dust had settled it was as though none of these things had ever been. The whole top of the pass had changed. Part of the side of a mountain now lay on top of it.

Musa Ahun was not to know any of this. He had died in the first few seconds. As the avalanche had hit the *serai* he had been flung forward, then the roof had come down on him, then the walls, and finally nearly forty feet of snow.

No one came to rescue him, because no one knew exactly where he was. A caravan of yaks was stopped at the pass the following day and the merchants had to go back almost to Sahr and start again by a different route. The Baltek Pass was closed for good.

A search was made for Musa Ahun but after a week it was stopped. The Spring avalanches made it too dangerous to continue. People in the Consulate remembered him for a while then he was forgotten. His wife was given a small pension and took her children to her family in Yarkand. Another post-runner was taken on in Musa Ahun's place and a different route to Sarikol was found. The post *had* to get through. Musa Ahun would have seen the irony in this; he had never received a letter in his life.

BOOK ONE

The Letter

1

'Mr. Winter?' The young woman ticked his name off in her diary. 'As in summer and . . . ?'

She was attractive, pert, in her early twenties, and Daniel, thirty-two and out of breath from running from the Tube, realised that to her he must seem elderly.

Instead of answering her smile with one of his own he said. 'No. Wynter. As in of discontent. . . .'

The look in her eyes changed. There was a hint of confusion which was replaced by irritation. 'Mr. Blacker was expecting you at three,' she said.

'There was a bomb scare on the Underground.'

'Would you take a seat and I'll see if he's free.'

He lowered himself onto the uncut moquette of a small sofa and picked up one of the magazines on the low table. It was the *Shipping Journal*. He looked for *Punch* or *Country Life*, but could only see more shipping magazines. He sat back. If he got the job and was expected to read them, he would, but not until then. He looked round the office of the Koriakis Steamship and Navigation Co., which lay off Fenchurch Street in the City of London. There was a model of a small coaster in a glass case along one wall, a portrait of King Constantine above the door, and a framed photograph of a Homburg-hatted gentleman in his sixties with hooded eyes and a thin mouth who he guessed might be Mr. Koriakis himself.

'Mr. Blacker will see you now.'

He was shown into a small office whose window had a view of a dusty grey building. Blacker was a nondescript man and must have known it, for he dressed to give himself personality:

his shirt was dark blue with thick white candy stripes; he wore long grey sideburns, a heavy gold ring.

'Winter.' He came briefly to his feet and shook hands. 'That's the name for today all right. Freezing out.' A large gold digital watch on his wrist went bleep-bleep. 'I'm running late,' he said.

'I'm sorry,' Daniel said. 'There was a bomb scare on the Tube. We had to change trains at Embankment.'

'Oh, well . . . sit down. It says here that you read Anglo-Saxon at Edinburgh.' Blacker tapped Daniel's C.V. 'Why?'

'It seemed like a good idea at the time.'

'What were you going to do with Anglo-Saxon?'

'I thought I might teach.'

'And did you?'

'No. I took a short-service commission in the Navy.'

'Another good idea at the time?'

'I suppose so.'

'And then . . . you were in the Falklands?'

'Yes, sir.'

'Bloody silly affair that, if you ask me. Who needs half a dozen peat bogs and a hundred thousand sheep?'

Daniel thought of *Sirius* bursting open like a paper bag when the Exocet hit her; he thought of the blazing oil, the men whose hair was alight, the blackened faces, the bodies face-down in the water.

He said, 'You were there?'

'Course I wasn't there. But I can read.' Bleep-bleep went the Blacker watch. 'I've got to get to Basingstoke. Look, we're not a big company. But we're expanding. Mr. Koriakis has ordered another ship for the fleet. . . '

'How many will that make, sir?'

'Three. I told you we weren't big. But Mr. Koriakis thinks the coaster trade is picking up. We may be needing officers. Savvy?'

'Yes, sir.'

'It's not the Royal Navy. We work in places you people never heard of.'

'I see, sir.'

Blacker rose. 'Right then, Winter. We'll let you know.'

Daniel stood over him. 'By the way, it's Wynter with a y, not Winter with an i. I just thought I'd tell you.'

The same confusion crossed Blacker's face as earlier had crossed that of his secretary, then was replaced by the same irritation. 'All right, Mr. Wynter with a y, we'll be in touch . . . if we can find a place for you.'

He stopped off at Sainsbury's in Swiss Cottage on the way home to Richmond Crescent. He had promised Julie he would pick up a steak if he got the job, something cheaper if he hadn't. He bought the steak anyway – to celebrate never having to work for Mr. Blacker – and a couple of litres of *rioja.*

The flat was only a few minutes from the Finchley Road station, part of a large house that had been split up into smaller units. When they had first moved there, not long after they had started living together, each had bought a separate flat. It was in keeping with the independence they had agreed on. Daniel had taken the garden level and Julie the ground floor, just above. At first they had stuck rigidly to their agreed life-style, but then he had found himself more or less permanently in her bedroom and they had compromised. He would sleep upstairs with her, she would use his sitting-room, which was bigger than hers, in exchange. Give and take. Quid pro quo. Even-Steven. Start as you mean to continue. . . .

She had looked at him with that faintly amused air of cynicism which sometimes unsettled him and had said, 'It will make things easier when we split up. No fighting over the pictures.'

He opened the door, heard the typewriter above him and knew she was working on a T.V. script. Sometimes she worked at home, sometimes at the television company's offices in Soho.

The typing stopped. 'Daniel?'

They had put in a Victorian spiral staircase to link the two flats. He climbed it and came into her sitting-room, which she used as a study-cum- . . . he was not sure cum-what. It was the untidiest room he had ever seen. An ironing-board stood in one corner next to a basket containing some of his shirts. Under the house rules he should have sent them out to a laundry, but he couldn't afford it. 'I'll iron them myself,' he had said. 'All naval officers know how to iron.' But she had been firm. 'I *like* ironing,' she had said. He had been grateful for that. There were two old desks and a table. On one of the desks was a sewing-machine, on the other a large electronic typewriter.

'Hi,' he said, rising up from his neat and spartan naval quarters into the room which, if it had been discovered in any of the naval establishments to which he had been attached, would have meant someone's instant court martial.

He could hardly see her for the manuscripts, papers and books spread about in confusion. Sometimes he found her general lack of organisation and care irritating, but now, as she turned to greet him, he knew the irritation was insignificant. She had inherited her genuine ash-blonde colouring from her Danish mother. She was a few years younger than himself, big-boned and generously proportioned, and was almost as tall.

He kissed her, smelling her skin.

'I was going to ask how it went,' she said. 'But I can see.'

'If they say yes, I'll say no.'

'As bad as that?'

'Worse. Digital watch. Bleep-bleep. Must go to Basingstoke.'

'Oh, dear. Tell me about it later. I have to finish this. Did you get something to eat?'

'Steak. To celebrate not working for them.'

'Marvellous. Just what I feel like. Write it up on the board.'

'No, this is on me.'

'Write it up or I won't eat it.'

He started descending the staircase, but she stopped him. 'I want to ask you something. If you were going to stab someone, to make absolutely certain of killing him, where would you aim for?'

'The heart?'

'What if the knife-blade turned on a rib?'

'Look, I don't really. . . '

'I thought men were supposed to know things like that.'

'Not this man.'

'I read somewhere that you should hold the knife low and stab upwards under the rib-cage.'

'Sounds super. Try it that way.'

'Don't make fun of me.' She turned back to the typewriter. 'Oh, by the way, I nearly forgot. The Foreign Office phoned.'

'What for?'

'I didn't ask. Did you apply for that Vickers job in Dubai? Wouldn't they have to vet you?'

'But that was ages ago.'

'Anyway, I thought you'd decided against it.'

Her fingers attacked the typewriter keys with an angry rattle. She doesn't want me to take it, he thought. His own flat was dark and gloomy. Evening was coming in fast. He went out into the garden and stared at the jumble of flowers and weeds. Sometime he'd have to do something about the garden. In a corner was a summer-house which he had turned into a work-shop. He went into it and switched on the light. At one end of the hut was a bench with a vice and above it, in neat racks along the walls, his tools: chisels graduated in sizes, drills, spokeshaves, T-squares, planes – including three wooden box-planes which he loved – cross-cut saws and rip-saws and tenon-saws. Most had belonged to his uncle, who had taught him how to use them. Daniel was making Julie a set of cupboards for her work-room and one of the doors was still held in the vice. Automatically, he picked up a sheet of fine glass paper and began rubbing a rough patch. The work-shop was a refuge on days like today.

He had no wish to go back to sea, but had applied for the Koriakis job because he had to be realistic. After his short-service commission had ended, he had decided not to stay on in the Royal Navy. It had never been what he wanted. He had joined from university because he had felt his life lacked direction. The Navy had changed that; it had directed is life with a rigidity for which he had not been prepared and he soon found that there were few aspects of it over which he had complete control. He had also found that he did not like to be cooped up with other men, did not like his life to be regulated like a chronometer. He discovered that he was something of a loner, a man who liked to make his own decisions, good or bad, but to make them himself. He disliked committees, he disliked memos, he disliked all the bureaucracy so beloved of the naval hierarchy: in short, he disliked the Navy.

The Falklands War had changed that briefly. During that time he had known what he was doing and why, and when it was over he had been strangely pleased he had taken part, and survived. But later disillusion had set in. Fortress Falklands and the endless patrols had worn him down until he became morose. When his short-service commission ended, he left the Navy without regrets.

But what was he to do with the rest of his life? He had no skills of value to a civilian. There were, of course, organisations whose sole function was to place retired Naval officers in work. But what kind of work? In Britain? In the 1980s?

His first position was selling photo-copying machines to stationers and bookshops. In four months he sold three. Then he tried selling advertising space for a company that published girlie magazines, and finally he joined a shady organisation that arranged charity events – until the managing director arranged his own event and absconded with the profits.

It was at that point his marriage broke up. When he had come home from the Falklands to the house that he and Joanna had bought on the Downs near Emsworth in Sussex, things had at first seemed much as they had been before he left. Jo was, as always, part of the landscape. She still spent most of the day in corduroy slacks, gumboots and heavy sweaters, still mucked out the pony's loose box, still grew her own vegetables, still talked of buying their own calves or lambs to fatten, still kept chickens . . . sometimes he thought that the word self-sufficiency had been invented for Jo.

It might not have been the perfect life he would have chosen for himself, but the house was near the Portsmouth Naval Base, which meant that he could spend the nights at home when he was ashore. And anyway, what kind of life *did* he want?

'What do you want to be when you grow up, Daniel?' his aunt used to ask. He hadn't known then, he didn't know now.

And then, suddenly, his married life had come to an end. He had been on a Ministry of Defence course in London for several months, living up in town five days a week and seeing Jo at week-ends. One week-end she had introduced him to Rex. He was a solemn man, much older than Jo, wearing self-conscious country tweeds and a watch and chain over a comfortable belly.

'This is Rex,' she had said. 'He wants to marry me.'

When Daniel had recovered enough to regain speech he had said to Rex, 'Would you excuse us for a moment?'

'I'm awfully sorry,' Rex had said. 'Is this *very* inconvenient?' He had reminded Daniel of a walrus, heavily moustached and rather hairy.

Daniel and Jo had gone into the kitchen. He remembered that the new eggs had been collected and were in their little wire basket.

They had talked for a long time. Although it was only ten in the morning, he had found himself drinking whisky. After a while Jo had taken a cup of coffee to Rex, who was reading *The Times* in Daniel's favourite chair.

He had gathered that she had met Rex at a pheasant shoot in Sussex. She had gone to stay with a school-friend and he had been another guest. He farmed a thousand acres in Wiltshire.

'But what about us?' She had remained silent. 'And all this?' He had swept his arm around to encompass the house and the three acres of land. 'And what about the dogs?'

'I know all that.'

'You can't *love* him! He's old enough to. . . '

'Excuse me. I'll find out if he wants some more coffee.'

His pride hadn't allowed him to believe it. He had thought she would get over it and everything would return to normal. Yet even at his lowest ebb, in some deep place within him, he had been aware of an unfamiliar excitement. At first it was slight, but it grew into a secret hope that things would never return to 'normal'.

And they never did. He left the Navy. They agreed to a divorce.

Then had come the division of the spoils and Rex's shrewd bucolic sense had influenced Jo in ways he could not have foreseen. She had fought over almost everything: whose was the fridge, the washing-machine, the vacuum cleaner, the book-cases he had made for the living-room? If the horse was hers to dispose of, what about the car, the carpets, the light fixtures? Even his tools: the box-planes were collectors' items which might go well at auction, she had said. This had finally triggered his anger.

That day, nearly three years ago, when he had taken his personal belongings and left the house, had been the last time he had seen her. The divorce had gone through and he had tried to forget her, but it had been difficult to dismiss from his mind a large chunk of his life.

He finished rubbing down the cupboard door and stacked it against the wall with the other one. He'd give them an undercoat sometime.

He wondered what the Foreign Office wanted. He had applied for the arms supply job with Vickers the previous summer. That was before he had decided he didn't really want to leave England. Now things were different.

He showered and changed and by then it was nearly seven. The typewriter was still clattering above him and he called up the stairs: 'Do you want me to bring you a drink?'

'No. I'll be down in five minutes.'

He poured himself a glass of wine and stood staring from the window. It was below street level and all he could see of the passers-by were legs; some in trousers, some booted, occasionally a shapely calf. But mainly he saw his own reflection. Just over six feet tall, with dark hair worn longer than when he had been in the Navy. Widely spaced brown eyes which had a good deal of humour in them but which now regarded their owner solemnly. The reflection changed as Julie came down the staircase.

'Where's that drink?' she said. 'I've just killed off my lover and I need it. I decided not to use a knife after all. Too messy.' She drank half her glass of *rioja* at a gulp. 'So I shot him instead.'

She had changed into jeans and a blouse and there was nothing under the blouse except Julie. The shirt was made of blue silk and clung to her breasts, emphasising their high curves and the nipples that stood out like tiny pistol barrels. She sat on the sofa, curling her long legs beneath her. She

16

had come down in bare feet and the nails on her toes were freshly painted. 'Tell me about today,' she said.

He sketched in briefly what had happened.

'To hell with them,' she said. 'You don't need them.'

'I need someone.'

'You'll find someone.' Then, by association, she said. 'Did you write up the price of the steak?'

'No.'

'Darling, if you don't it'll never work. We said at the beginning that everything was to be split down the middle.'

'I know what we said.' He poured her another glass. 'Let's have some real frites for a change. Steak and frites. Pretend we're in France.'

They went into the kitchen. As she peeled the potatoes he slipped his hand under her blouse and held her breast. 'Shall we have an orgy?' he said.

They ate their steaks in a small breakfast alcove where the space was so confined that they were almost touching. The sexual tension was like static electricity. He could feel the contraction of his own skin and could almost see, through the thin silk of her blouse, the hardening of her breasts.

The steaks were excellent but he hardly tasted his, and because of the way she looked at him, the way her eyelids half hid her eyes when she was excited, he knew it was the same for her.

It was sexuality that had first attracted him to her and, he was soon to discover, her to him. Pure animal sexuality, and they had made no bones about it. There was none of the pretence: I love you for your sweetness and the nobility of your mind.

He had met her at a dinner party in Twickenham. Although there had been six other guests, they had been very aware of each other. At the end of the evening they had stood on the pavement outside the house chatting with their hosts, then she had tried to start her car. The starting motor had turned the engine over without success, churning away in the still night. There had been a strong smell of petrol and then the unmistakable sound of a dying battery.

'Would you like me to try?' Daniel had said.

17

'No, thanks. It needs a new battery. I'll find a cab, then pick it up tomorrow.'

'I'm going into Central London, if that's any good to you.'

He had driven her back to her Notting Hill Gate flat. They hadn't talked much in the car. She had offered him coffee. He had accepted, but had not got to drink it. They had not even gone into the bedroom, but had fallen on each other like gladiators and had finally moved from the sofa to the floor. Clothes had been scattered over the furniture and the carpet as though burglars had gone through a set of drawers.

He had lain with her in his arms, stunned. The experience was new. His sex with Joanna had been regular, restrained, unexciting. Not that she was cold. It was as though she was unmoved by sex, as though she could take it or leave it without being distressed or overjoyed either way. With Julie, it was explosively different. There was no question of regularity, of a habit-forming pleasure. It was more like an eruption that could take place any time of the day or night. That first night had been heightened, if that was possible, by her confession that she had deliberately flooded her car. 'You didn't think I was going to let you get away, did you?'

At that time she was a script editor for an independent television company, but was already starting to make a transfer to creative writing. She had adapted Wilkie Collins' *The Woman in White*, and then she had written a six-part original thriller set in the Algarve. Both had been successful and she now had more work than she could handle.

'Coffee?' she said.

'Why don't we finish the wine upstairs?'

They lay on her big double bed. 'This is the time I'd like a cigarette,' she said. 'A real orgy. Sex. Wine and a Gitane.'

'Me too. Don't think about it. You should have other things on your mind, anyway.'

He stroked her long body, running his hand over the swelling curves of her buttocks, up to her shoulders and over her breasts, and could feel the reaction-shiver ripple on her skin. 'Psychiatrists say that everyone needs skin-contact,' he said.

But there was something missing and afterwards as he lay

with his glass of wine balancing on his naked chest he wondered what was happening between them.

At first their love-making had been so intense that there had been no room in their lives for questions; it was enough that they had each other to devour. But slowly the questions had appeared, at least for him. Did they love each other? They said so, but did they mean it? He knew she'd had a long affair with an actor and had been badly scarred when it had ended. Was she capable of pulling down her defences and making herself vulnerable again to the extent that true affection demanded? For that matter, was he? And if not, what would happen to them? Would they drift on like this until, as she said, they began to squabble over the pictures?

'Would you go?' she said suddenly.

'Go where?'

'To the Gulf. If they offered you the job.'

'They won't.'

'But *would* you?'

'I don't know.'

There was a short silence. 'Daniel?'

'Yes?'

'You'd tell me, wouldn't you?'

'Tell you what?'

'If everything was over between us.'

'Christ Almighty, what are you talking about?'

'Remember what we said at the beginning? No strings, no entanglements.'

'That was at the beginning.'

'Yes, I know, but I want to be sure.'

'Would *you* tell *me*?'

'That doesn't arise.'

'Well, it doesn't arise with me, either.'

But neither was content. It took them a long time to relax and even then they did not fall asleep as they usually did, with her bottom pressed firmly into his stomach, his left arm holding her close. They slept together, yet separately, on either side of the bed.

2

Daniel followed the ancient messenger down a series of gloomy corridors. They reached a door and the messenger knocked. 'In you go, sir. Mr. Rowse, Asian desk.'

Even sitting down, Mr. Rowse seemed to be one of the tallest men Daniel had ever seen. His head and chest were well above the big desk, while his feet stretched out in plain view under it. He rose in a series of unfolding movements. 'Mr. Wynter? Do come in.'

He wore his thin, greying hair shorter than was usual and his glasses sat on top of his head. Daniel would have put his age at forty-five.

'Did you bring any identification, Mr. Wynter?'

'I didn't realise. . . '

'Didn't my secretary. . . ?'

'I wasn't told.'

Daniel went through his pockets and brought out scraps of rather grubby paper and old envelopes.

'A passport or a driver's licence would do.'

'I haven't brought either.'

'Would you mind answering a few questions then, just to confirm the identification?' Daniel nodded and he said. 'What was your father's name?'

'Richard.'

'And the rest?'

'Richard Coles Wynter.'

'Your grandfather?'

'Harry Coles Wynter.'

'Is your father still alive?'

'No. He died in 1954.'

'How did he die?'

'In the Comet crash. What's this all about, anyway?'

Rowse looked at a sheet of paper on the desk, made a mark on it, and nodded.

'And your grandfather died. . . ?'

'In Central Asia. But what's all this got to do with the Gulf?'

'The Gulf? Nothing whatever.' He paused, then added, 'Our Mr. Meaker in the post-room will be extremely pleased. It took him some time to put it together, but it's all down here. Names. Places. Your mother's sister lived in Blythburgh, I believe.'

'She and my uncle brought me up. But what. . . ?'

'Something rather odd has happened.' Rowse unlocked a drawer in his desk, brought out an envelope and passed it to Daniel. It was what used to be called a 'large standard envelope' of reinforced paper. Once it had been white, now it was discoloured with age and the address had been almost obliterated by what might have been water stains. But the name was clear. It was addressed in flowing copper-plate to his father, Richard Coles Wynter, Esq., then there was the indecipherable address and at the bottom was part of a word ending . . . IRE and the faint outline of ENGLAND.

'Where did you get this?' Daniel said.

'It was handed in to our Embassy in Islamabad about six weeks ago by an official of the Pakistan Postal Service and came to us in the Diplomatic Bag. If the address had been clear they would probably have sent it on in the usual way. One does come across anomalies like this occasionally. You've probably seen items in the press: letters turning up twenty or thirty years after they've been posted. Caught in a Post Office drawer, fallen behind a filing cabinet. Then the office furniture is sold or moved and they're found again. That sort of thing.' He pointed to the envelope. 'This one's been franked at the British Consulate in Kashgar. If you look closely you can even make out the date.'

'It's 1939!'

'What do you think the address might have been?'

'Hampshire? We lived in Hampshire when I was a baby. Near Alton.'

'That's what Mr. Meaker thought. Spent days in Somerset

House. Voters' rolls. Clubs. It took him three weeks to trace you.'

He looked at the envelope expectantly and Daniel realised that he wanted him to open it.

'Is that all?' Daniel said.

'I'm afraid so.' Rowse was still looking longingly at the letter. 'If you want to find out anything more about how it was found, you could speak to Sonny Desai at the Pakistan Embassy. I mentioned it to him and he said he'd look into it.'

'Thank you.' Daniel stood up.

His disappointment undisguised, Rowse said crossly: 'You have to sign for it.'

[3]

Daniel left the Foreign Office and found himself in Petty France. The letter was in his inside jacket pocket and every now and then his fingers touched it, subconsciously making sure it was still there. He was torn between an eagerness to open it and, at the same time, a feeling of unease. It was something from the past and he was suspicious about raking up the past. He could not recall any instance when something good had come to him that way.

He took the Tube home. Julie was not there, so he went out to his work-room and sprawled in an old easy chair. After a few moments he opened the envelope and drew out several sheets of lined paper which had been torn from a school exercise book and then clumsily trimmed. In some places the damp which had obliterated part of the address on the envelope had affected the paper, but the ink had held fast and although some patches were faint all, as far as he could see, was legible still.

He began to read.

My dearest Boy,

Spring has come early this year and the high passes are becoming dangerous for the post-runners because of treacherous snow conditions, so I hope this letter, and the parcel, reach you safely.

As you may imagine, this is a difficult letter to write, since you have not replied to any of the others. But after the death of your mother, you may feel differently – at least, I tell myself that this might be so. And for that reason, I am sending you, under separate cover, a manuscript containing all the facts about the race.

The light was beginning to go and Daniel rose to switch on the big overhead spot which he used when working at night. He looked towards the house, but Julie's light was not on yet. He sat down again and picked up the letter. The disquiet he had felt after emerging from the Foreign Office had returned more intensely. He knew that his grandfather was addressing his, Daniel's, father, long before he was born, yet the letter seemed to speak directly to him. It continued:

I imagine that your mother kept most of the details of the scandal from you, and perhaps you have not wanted to find out the truth for yourself. I can understand that. Your mother was very bitter at the time, especially when we divorced. She told me that as far as she was concerned I had ceased to exist. Perhaps you can realise what my feelings were at the time. Now I am no longer troubled by any of it, I am thankful to say.

I had kept a detailed diary from the moment I left England. It became a habit and I have done so ever since. Often the very act of writing has sustained me here in the Golden Valley. The manuscript I am sending you has been taken from the diaries. I have not embroidered it or turned it into a narrative because it is for your eyes only.

I have long since ceased to care what the rest of the world thinks of me, though it was not much fun at the time. The crucial question has always been that of the note. Hollande told the committee he did not see it. It is his word against mine – and if you have read the newspapers of the time you will know whose word the public accepted. I was not even given a hearing.

I sound bitter, but I'm not. The events are so long ago now they seem to have been in another life. But a war is coming and who knows what might happen. I want you to read the truth before it is too late.

Your loving father,
H. C. Wynter, Capt.

Daniel sat for a long time, letting his mind probe at this astonishing document. It was cold in his work-room, but he did not feel it. He got up, restlessly. What the hell was he supposed to make of it? His hands needed something to do while he thought.

He brought out one of the cupboard doors, measured it and found that it was an eighth of an inch too wide. He took down a box-plane and as he shaved off the wood with long, even sweeps, the room filled with the scent of pine.

It was a smell out of his childhood when he had stood at his uncle's bench and watched him use the same box-planes. He had been three when his parents had been killed in the B.O.A.C. Comet crash in the sea off Italy in 1954 and he had gone to live with his mother's sister in Suffolk. His Aunt Maggie must have been in her forties then, for she was a good fifteen years older than his mother, and his Uncle Bob was older than that. Their own children had already left home by the time they took Daniel in, and he had grown up in a world that had passed by. This was heightened by the fact that East Anglia itself was more old-fashioned than most other parts of Britain. His uncle had a small farm on the River Blyth just north of Aldeburgh. He remembered as a child being taken into Walberswick and Southwold and his memory was that they were like the seaside towns he saw later in post-card albums of the 1920s. He would recall the shop fronts in Halesworth with their old-style lettering and their dark blue blinds. He had been back as a grown man and found them little changed.

It had been a lonely childhood. He had gone to school in Norwich and in the holidays he had spent much of his time in an old skiff, sailing in Minsmere marshes or rowing up the river, feathery reeds on either side, pretending to be Robinson Crusoe or Jim Hawkins.

His uncle had died when he was in his teens, but his aunt had carried on farming for another half-dozen years. He was at university when he received her letter. She was going into hospital and she wanted to tell him about his parents and something of her side of the family. But she would do that, she said, in the next few days; in the meantime, she wanted him to know that the farm was being sold and that a share of the money would come to him.

She was never able to write her letter about the family.

He had travelled down from Edinburgh that night and when he reached the hospital in Lowestoft she was already unconscious. He was the only relative at her bedside. Her own children, his cousins, had long since left Britain. Her son had emigrated to Australia in the 1960s and her daughter was married to a school-teacher in Africa.

He didn't like to remember the death of his aunt. She was the first dying person he had ever seen. He liked, instead, to remember being taught how to use tools by his uncle, in a real workshop with lathes for turning chair legs and a steam cabinet for bending wood. He had inherited from this time his love of wood and construction. In another age, his uncle would have been a master cabinet-maker and Daniel his apprentice.

Julie opened the door and said, 'I saw the light. Do you want to be left alone?'

'No. Let's go in.'

In the warmth of the sitting-room, he told her about his visit to the Foreign Office and gave her the letter. 'Read it while I have a shower.'

When he returned she was sitting in much the same position and, he imagined, in much the same fascinated confusion as he had been when he finished it.

'What's it all about?' she said.

'God knows.'

'You say this was handed into the British Embassy in. . . ?'

'Islamabad.'

'Pakistan?'

'Now. When it was written there wasn't any Pakistan, it was all India.'

'But who handed it in?'

'According to Rowse, the Pakistan Postal Service.'

'How did they get it? I mean, it's nearly fifty years since it was written.'

'No idea.'

'What about the manuscript?'

'Rowse didn't mention that there was one. I'm going to give him a ring first thing tomorrow and ask about it.'

'It's astonishing!'

'Rowse says there have been previous cases like this of letters being lost for years and then delivered.'

She nodded. 'I've seen newspaper items. Half the time they're bills, or letters from someone's tailor saying they're ready for a fitting. But this. . . ! What race?'

'I've been thinking about that, too. I suppose it could have been an air race, they were pretty big in the thirties.'

'He talks about high mountain passes. Perhaps it was a race for one of the unconquered peaks. There were lots then.'

'Something must have happened. He talks about a tragedy, and clearing his name. Remember Whymper?'

'Who's Whymper?'

'He led the first successful assault on the Matterhorn. But a rope broke and several of the team were killed. There's always been a scandal about that. Perhaps something similar happened.'

'What exactly do you know about your grandfather?'

'Not a great deal. He was Army. He was said to have married one of the most beautiful women in England. My uncle and aunt hardly ever spoke about him. I used to ask them, but they seemed to know very little themselves. I remember thinking how romantic it sounded. Dying out there, I mean. At one time I tried to dig up a few facts about my father's family and traced them back to the Crimea. A General Coles Wynter on Raglan's staff. I suppose I was much more interested in my mother and father. It wasn't unnatural. The Comet crash was a cause célèbre at the time because of the metal fatigue problem and I read all the accounts of that.'

26

'Where *is* Kashgar?'

He went up to her room, searched among the open books, the unironed washing and the scattered papers and came back with her atlas. They looked up the index together, then found a relief map of Central Asia, the colours of which changed with the increasing height of the land from brown through dark brown to white. The white parts were the Himalayas and, farther west, the Pamirs and the Karakorums.

His finger found Kashgar, beyond the Karakorums. 'It's in Sinkiang.'

'Formerly Chinese Turkestan,' she read.

'He talks about mountain passes. He must mean the ones over the Karakorums.'

'Does the name Hollande mean anything to you?'

'Not a thing.'

'And he talks about wanting you to read the truth. And a race.'

The phrases hung in the air, tantalising and inexplicable. Then she said, 'What a sad letter.'

'I thought it sounded fairly formal.'

'Formal! It's a lonely man trying to be heard across time and space. Something terrible must have happened to cause him to live his life out in that remote place. He says he's written before and had no reply. Don't you see how sad that is? And now he's written again. And again he had no reply because the letter never got through.'

There were tears in her eyes. Julie was emotional. She didn't bottle up her feelings. When she was moved, she cried. When she was happy, her body seemed to expand and her happiness communicated itself to everyone around.

'When did your grandfather die?' she said.

'No idea. I think he just wasn't heard of for so long that he was assumed to have faded away. I imagine this place, the Golden Valley, was so remote. . . '

'Are you going to do anything about it?'

'My God, wouldn't you! There's a Major Desai at the Pakistan High Commission. Rowse said he might have some more details. I'll give him a ring.'

Julie left early the following morning for a script conference and Daniel was left alone. This was usually the worst time for him, with the long day yawning ahead. But today was different. He felt an excitement grow inside him: he had an interest, something to mull and fret over.

He began by going through both flats, seeking any books that might throw light on the background to the letter, but there was nothing. Then, when he judged that even diplomats might be at work, he telephoned the Pakistan High Commission. But Major Desai was on leave. Daniel left a message, giving brief details of his quest, then paced up and down the sitting-room as he wondered what to do next. What he needed were reference books or newspaper files.

Then he remembered that newspapers had libraries. He telephoned *The Times* and spoke to one of the librarians, but she told him that no facilities were available for members of the public to study the clippings files. However, she said, the Westminster Reference Library kept a *Times* index and microfilm of the newspaper itself.

He took the Tube to Leicester Square and found the Library tucked away in a narrow side street. It was not yet ten o'clock in the morning and the big reading-room was deserted.

He followed the librarian to a dark corner where there were stacks of red leather volumes. 'It starts in 1906.' The librarian ran his finger along the spines. 'Four volumes per year. If you find what you want, come to me. I'll get out the microfilm and you can look at it on the reading machine.'

Left standing in front of the stacks, Daniel did a mental calculation: 1906 to 1968 was sixty two years. Four volumes to the year made 248 volumes of the index alone. Christ, he thought, how did I get into this?

He decided to take a stab at ten years before the letter's date, and pulled out the four volumes for 1929. The first was January to March. He paged up 'H'. There were references to Holland the country: see Tulips, Polders, Rijksmuseum, Flooding . . . and so on. There were references to the Holland-Afrika Line, the Holland Tunnel, Holland blinds, but not to Hollande-with-an-e. He turned to Winter/Wynter. There were a great many references to Winter (Severity of; see Coal stocks; *A Winter's Tale*) but there was no Harry Coles Wynter.

The morning wore on and the library began to fill up. It was a long time since his university days, when he had spent hours in research, and he found his concentration wavering. Then, in May, 1937, he hit pay-dirt.

There, just below the entry 'Holland, Zuider-Zee Reclamation Scheme', was 'Hollande, General Sir Edward, operation on'. He felt a surge of excitement. He went back to the desk and asked for microfilm of the newspaper for the second quarter of 1937. Another librarian showed him how to work the reading machine. When he had learnt the controls he let the microfilm run forward until he came to 18 May, Page 8, Column 4. Down at the bottom was a small paragraph headed GENERAL HOLLANDE FOR OPERATION. The text read:

General Sir Edward Hollande, the 57-year-old explorer, entered the Royal Military Hospital in Knightsbridge today for what was described as 'a minor operation'. Sir Edward, who returned last month after completing a single-handed canoe journey from the source of the River Congo to the sea – the first white man ever to do so – said he was looking forward to an enforced rest as it would give him 'time to catch up with my reading'.

A week later, under the heading GEN. HOLLANDE LEAVES HOSPITAL, a second story read:

General Sir Edward Hollande, who has been in the Royal Military Hospital, Knightsbridge, undergoing a minor operation, left hospital today for Luscombe Park, the family seat in Hampshire. Sir Edward, whose battalion suffered sixty percent casualties in a courageous break-out from a pocket on the Western Front in

1916, said he was feeling 'fit as a fiddle' and that his doctors said he would make a complete recovery.

Daniel jotted down the salient points of the stories and fetched the two volumes of the Index for the last half of 1937. Evidently Sir Edward had completed his convalescence undisturbed by journalists from *The Times* and had not canoed down any more of the world's major rivers, for his name did not reappear. Then in 1938, there was another entry, for which Daniel requested the microfilm. This was longer: two columns on an inside page. It was headed: FAMOUS EXPLORER TO LEAD 'LOST CITY' SEARCH EXPEDITION IN AMAZONIA. It began:

> General Sir Edward Hollande, the explorer, has agreed to lead an expedition to try to discover a lost city in Amazonia. It was first mentioned in the diaries of Spanish conquistadors, but its existence has never been proved. Said to be between the Amazon and the Rio Negro. . . .

He skimmed down the columns. The remainder of the report dealt with the four-man team, the boats, the stores and the equipment. Then he came to a paragraph which quickened his interest:

> General Hollande's daughter, Victoria, was due to accompany the expedition, but has elected instead to climb in the Himalayas. General Hollande said today that if the lost city exists, 'We'll do our damndest to find it.'

But the expedition was caught in unprecedented floods, lost most of its gear and had had to be rescued by a search party organised by a Seventh Day Adventist Mission in Manaos. For the first time there was a photograph of Sir Edward Hollande. It was a head-and-shoulders and showed him in his Army uniform. The face was square, with heavy bags under the eyes, receding hair and a clipped military moustache. The eyes were stern, the mouth beneath the moustache a thin line.

Lunch-time came and went, and Daniel read on. By mid-afternoon his eyes were feeling sandy and he decided to leave. He was hungry and he already had several pages of notes.

*

Julie was asleep on the big double bed when he reached home. She lay on her back with her arms above her head. Wisps of blonde hair lay across her face. She looked like an albaster statue, but softer, human, lovely. As he went towards her, her eyes flickered, she gave a groan and turned on her side. 'What's the time?' she mumbled, her head half buried under a blanket.

'Six.'

'Morning or evening?'

'Evening. I've made you some coffee.'

She pushed herself up. She was wearing one of his unironed shirts.

'I missed you.' Her lips were still soft from sleep. 'The place was so dark and gloomy. Where were you?'

He found himself retreating. For the first time in their relationship he caught a hint of criticism in her voice. Like the equal-shares arrangement, they had also made it a condition of living together that part of their lives remained their own, that they went their separate ways without having to feel a sense of guilt.

'I was at the Westminster Library.'

'Whatever for?'

'Because that's where *The Times* index is, love.'

'Aha! Daniel the boy detective. And?'

'And a hell of a lot. Maybe.'

'Really?' She kicked off the blanket and was naked from the waist down. Daniel found her lack of inhibition exciting. Jo had always covered up. Even at night when they made love she had liked the light off.

He could see the light blonde down on her thighs and put his hand on her leg. She took it up, kissed it and replaced it on the blanket. 'Business before pleasure. Tell me.'

'Not until you get up. I'm going downstairs. I need a drink after my labours.'

She joined him in fifteen minutes, showered and changed, and he told her the story of his day.

'What lost city was Hollande looking for?' she said.

'God knows. Every South American country claims some lost city or other. Anyway, he never found it.'

'And then?'

'After the reports of the expedition there was quite a long break. Then in. . . ' He looked at the note-book. '. . . in 1939 he was given the Gold Medal by the Royal Geographical Society. Then war broke out and there were occasional references to him. Nothing much. He was something to do with transport and his big moment came when he was one of the planning staff moving men and materiél to the coast in the early stages of the D-Day invasion.'

'What about his daughter . . . what's her name? Victoria?'

'I'll get to her in a minute. Let me finish with the General first. He's the Hollande of the Hollande Trust.'

'That rings a bell. Something like the Peace Corps or Voluntary Service Overseas?'

'Young people could apply for grants to travel in the more remote parts of the globe. It was his way of promoting Britain in the hearts and minds of the Third World. For instance, if you wanted to go down the Zambesi by raft and were planning to count the number of hippos or crocodiles, you could apply to the Trust and if they thought you and your ambitions were worthwhile, and if your group was going to be an advertisement for Britain, you were helped financially.'

'Showing the flag.'

'Based on the sort of thing Hollande used to do himself, I think. The Great White Chief travelling through the Empty Quarter with a stock of iodine, laxatives, aspirin. . . '

'And everyone was supposed to love you and love Britain. Does the Trust still exist?'

'Don't know.' He glanced back at his notes. 'There's a blank for a few years, then suddenly he's attacked. A military historian at the Staff College in Camberley wrote a book soon after the war comparing the generals of World War II with those of World War I: people like Montgomery and Alexander and Eisenhower and Patton with Haig and Gort and Kitchener. General Hollande came in for a terrible caning. I told you there was a reference to a courageous action by his battalion on the Western Front in 1916. This book claimed it was *his* fault that his battalion was in an indefensible position from which they had to break out. That's why his losses were so heavy. According to the historian, it was one of the worst examples of generalship to be found in World

War I or any other war. He as good as called the old chap an irresponsible butcher. There was a terrific stink. Letters to *The Times* from other old generals, but none from Hollande himself.'

'Very dignified,' Julie said. 'Very British.'

'Then there's just silence. The General doesn't seem to have done much more, nor shown himself. He may have been ill, for all *The Times* index knew. The next thing is his death in 1955 and *The Times* gives him a long obituary. He certainly had a hell of a life. Born 1880. School, than Sandhurst . . . married the Hon. Daphne Gore-Hutchinson . . . one child, Victoria . . . Won Pekin–London Automobile race, 1910. . . '

'The race!' Julie said.

'*Right!*' He turned back to his notes: 'Major-General Royal Hampshire Fusiliers . . . action in Belgium . . . here's the bit about the action on the Western Front. They call it "controversial", that's nice, isn't it? Then after the war he really takes off. First man to cross the Empty Quarter by car . . . first man to cross Africa on the Equator by car . . . first man to fly single-handed from London to Singapore and back . . . led team which conquered three unclimbed peaks in the Darwin Range in Southern Chile . . . led British Scientific Expedition to Antarctica – knighted for that – then there's the lone journey down the Congo which I read to you, and the Gold Medal – and you know the rest.'

'Sounds exhausting.'

'I've only touched on the high spots. You'd wonder how he had time to get his wife pregnant.'

'Was there anything about the daughter?'

'A great deal. She's a carbon copy of her father. First woman to cross the Sahara from East to West. She did it in a Land Rover and when it broke down the Tuaregs pulled her along with camels. First woman to cross the Danakil. First woman to cross the Kalahari from north to south. Won International Gliding Championship . . . took up ballooning and won the Transalpine event in 1968.'

'Married?'

'Briefly. When she was nineteen. It only lasted a few months. She wasn't in one place long enough to sustain a marriage, I imagine. The only time she was stationary for any length of time was towards the end of General Hollande's life. He'd become a recluse by then and she looked after him. But the moment he died she was off again. Patagonia, Greenland, you name it.'

'No children, of course?'

'None.'

'So that's the Hollandes. What about your grandfather?'

'Not a word. Nothing. It's as though he never existed – at least during this period, which was all I had time to investigate.'

She got up and wandered around the room. 'That's annoying. You find out all about Hollande and nothing about the "scandal", nor the person who really counts.' She sat down again. 'Did you ring this Major Desai at the Pakistan High Commission?'

'He wasn't in. I left a message explaining what it was about.'

There was a pause and she said, 'Did you go to the agency?'

He frowned. 'What agency?'

'The one that head-hunts for jobs in the City. Weren't you going today?'

He'd forgotten.

'I postponed the interview,' he said. 'Anyway, I have a couple of appointments tomorrow. I had too much to do today.'

'Aren't you getting a bit too carried away by this letter?'

'For God's sake! It was written nearly fifty years ago and talks of scandal, a car-race from Pekin to London, a manuscript that's been lost, a General who turns out to be famous and controversial, a daughter who has obviously tried to follow her father's footsteps! If you don't see possibilities there, then you're. . . '

'Possibilities for what?'

'Off the top of my head, for articles, a book, perhaps even a T.V. documentary about the race. My God, in 1910, in primitive cars, the competitors, whoever they were, drove all the way from Pekin to London. What a journey! General Hollande won, but somehow my grandfather was involved and whatever the scandal was, it sounds as though it caused him to live out his days in one of the world's remotest, least-known areas. I want to know more about him. And about the Golden Valley.'

'Who's going to write the articles and make the documentary?'

'We are.'

'Darling, you – '

'You're a writer. I've had some experience of camera work in the Navy and at home.'

'You can't sell a home movie to television.'

'With a bit of instruction, I could do better than that. There are schools for teaching one how to use cameras.'

'But, Daniel. . . '

'Of course, we'd have to do a lot of research first.'

'Not me. I've got too much work.'

There was a nasty silence.

'Well, I haven't,' he said.

He parked his car near the Lancaster Gate Tube station and walked through a light drizzle towards Bathurst Street. He hardly felt the rain. He walked with a spring in his step that hadn't been there for months. He was wearing a light grey suit without a topcoat and as he walked past the lighted foyer of the Royal Lancaster Hotel a group waiting for taxis turned to look at him. Julie was waiting at their usual table in the window of Père Michel and he waved to her from the pavement. She smiled and raised her glass. 'Sorry I'm late,' he said. 'It's in a good cause.' He leaned across the table to kiss her, then poured himself a glass of wine. 'You're looking at one of the employed!'

'Tell me!'

'It was by chance. You know I had an interview with a merchant bank this morning? That was a wash-out, so was the afternoon one: stockbrokers who kept talking about equities and preferreds and asked me if I could read a balance sheet and I had to say, not with any confidence. When I left them I thought I'd go into the White Ensign Association – just to check if there was anything. An offer had come in literally ten minutes before.'

'What sort of job?'

'It's a market research company. I phoned and they told me to come along straight away.'

'Where is it?'

'Not the most salubrious area. Lambeth, to be exact. But,' he added hastily, 'they're moving into the West End.'

'Lambeth's not too bad.'

'The job's not actually in Lambeth at the moment. They have to take me on as a trainee. They do that with everyone. 'They've got a big office in Glasgow and that's where I'll be to start with.'

'Glasgow!'

'It won't be for more than six or nine months.'

'And then?'

'Then I become what's called a Team Leader.'

'A *what*?'

'A Team Leader. They have groups of people in various parts of the country called Teams and they go out on the streets and. . . '

'Daniel! A Team Leader. You?'

'All right, it is sort of American jargon, I agree, but. . . '

'Darling, you'd hate it!'

He looked at her in amazement. 'I thought you'd be pleased.'

'I would've been if you'd found something that was worth your talents. But not this, not for some crummy little market organisation that hasn't even got a West End address! These are the sort of people that do mail drops or stand about on draughty corners asking people how many times a day they brush their teeth. Is that your sort of thing?'

He felt his high begin to crumble.

'I'd rather you went to sea, rather you worked for the man with the bleep-bleep watch,' she said. 'If you hadn't had those two unpleasant interviews earlier you wouldn't have considered this job. What about the I'll-never-work-in-an-office Daniel I used to know?'

As he looked at her over his wine glass, he hated her for reminding him. But it was true. He had talked and talked in the early days of their relationship of the things he really wanted to do. It had crystallised into working with young people, having an adventure school in Wales or Scotland where he could teach them climbing and canoeing and sailing – but that needed capital.

He leant back and said, 'You've no idea what it's like to be unemployed, because you've never been unemployed.'

'I can't be unemployed,' she said. 'I employ myself. That's what you have to do. You must stop thinking in terms of working for other people and work for yourself.'

She was lecturing him, and his resentment increased. What should have been a festive dinner with the large double-bed looming pleasurably in both their minds became instead a hastily eaten meal with tension like a barrier between them.

She was silent during the drive home, but when they reached their front door she said, 'If I apologised, how would you react?'

'Favourably.'

'If I became your plaything, your sex object for the rest of the evening, how would you react then?'

'More favourably!'

The tension exaporated. Entwined, they had coffee on his sofa. Just before they went upstairs to bed he said, 'I forgot to tell you. I found Victoria Hollande's address.'

'Whose?'

'The General's daughter. The Hollande Trust still exists, all right. She lives in Hampshire, where there's also something called the Edward Hollande Collection.' He paused. 'I think I'll go and see her.'

'Are you really serious about this?' There was a cautious note in her voice.

'It could be the alternative to being a Team Leader. You told me I should be self-employed.' He tried to make it sound light-hearted, but the tension was back.

[5]

The traffic on the Portsmouth Road was usually light on a Saturday morning and Daniel and Julie were past Guildford by ten. They took the Hog's Back, then the Farnham bypass and were soon having to consult maps of secondary roads as they entered a world of copses and hangers and fields hidden by hawthorn hedges. The wind was from the south-west and grey clouds scudded across the sky. They passed villages seemingly cut off from the main stream of life, yet barely sixty miles from London.

'This is what it must have been like when Jane Austen lived in these parts,' Julie said. 'Imagine the effort needed to get to a town! Imagine what life in winter must have been like.'

'We're nearly there,' Daniel said as they passed through the village of Highclare, and soon they pulled up at two large brick gate-posts. On one was the sign LUSCOMBE PARK and on the other THE HOLLANDE TRUST. On a large white board by the side of the gate-posts another sign read THE EDWARD HOLLANDE COLLECTION, OPENING HOURS: MON-THURS. 10.30am to 4.30pm. ADMISSION: Adults £2, CHILDREN and O.A.P.s 50p.

The gate was open and they drove through. The house came into view almost immediately. It was a small Queen Anne manor; beautifully proportioned and set in parkland. Behind it was a complex of Victorian barns. The house was of old red brick, the barns of unknapped flint. The drive to the house was blocked by a chain with a NO ADMISSION notice and visitors were directed to the HOLLANDE COLLECTION in the barns.

Daniel stopped in front of the barns. Everything was silent and closed and seemed to be uninhabited, yet the place was so neat – even the gravel drive had been recently raked – that human hands could not be far away.

Signs guided visitors to the MAIN COLLECTION, the SHOP, the TEA ROOM and the TOILETS. At one time the barns must have housed old reapers and binders, mechanical hayrakes, even steam traction engines, but now they had been renovated and smartened up.

'I'll have a look round,' Daniel said.

He had hardly taken a few steps from the car when a Mercedes station wagon came round the side of the main barn and stopped. A man got out.

'Good morning,' Daniel called.

The man, in his early forties, did not reply as he crunched towards them. He was of medium height, but sinewy. His movements were catlike and he gave an impression of fibrous strength and toughness. His face was almost Slavic, with high cheekbones, his hair dark and, in dramatic contrast, his eyes were light blue.

When he reached Daniel he said, 'We're closed. Didn't you see the notice?'

His voice was educated, but with a trace of rustic Hampshire in the background. It was not so much hostile as chilly, dismissive.

'We haven't come to see the Collection,' Daniel said. 'We wanted to have a word with Miss Hollande.'

Julie joined them. The man's eyes moved towards her and Daniel saw her own widen slightly as a smile formed on her lips. The man did not return the smile, but looked at her intently for a few seconds before turning back to Daniel.

'Do you have an appointment?'

'No.'

'Then I'm afraid it won't be possible.'

'We've driven all the way from London.'

'It's important,' Julie said.

'If it's about the Collection, I'm in charge of that.'

'No. It's a private matter.'

'Miss Hollande doesn't receive visitors without an appointment.'

'I think she may receive me,' Daniel said. 'My name is Daniel Coles Wynter.'

After a moment's silence, as he studied them, the man said. 'Wait here, please. I'll see if she's in.'

He let himself in a side door of the house and disappeared.

'Come on,' Daniel said. 'I'm not going to be treated like some bloody serf.'

They strolled over and stood just outside the open door. He could hear voices coming from a room to the left: the rumble of the man's and then a woman's voice, clear, imperious: 'Did he give a name?'

'Wynter. Daniel Coles Wynter.'

'What!' The word cracked like a pistol. Daniel saw a blurred figure pass across a nearby window.

'Do you know him?'

'I'm too busy to see anyone. Tell him I'm not in.'

The man appeared at the doorway and looked surprised and annoyed to see them there. 'I'm afraid Miss Hollande isn't in. Why don't you make an appointment with her sec. . . ?'

'Of course she's in. D'you think we're deaf?' Daniel said.

'I must insist that she is *not* in.'

'Did you tell her we had come from London specially to see her?'

There was a pause, then he said, 'I'm sorry. I'm rather busy.' He closed the door.

Again Daniel had the impression of a figure near the window. He took Julie's arm. 'Come on.'

'You're not going to leave it like this!'

'Of course not.'

They returned to the car, and drove away, but once they went through the gates Daniel took a narrow wooded lane at the side of the estate and pulled up. They now had a view of the house from the rear.

'Did you hear her reaction?' Julie said. 'She knows exactly who you are, she doesn't want to see you?'

'Look!' said Daniel.

The Mercedes station wagon came down the drive, through the gates, and headed away from them.

'What are you going to do?'

'Beard her in her den.'

'You might not have to.'

He followed her glance. A woman had emerged from the house and was walking along one of the estate roads accompanied by a large black dog.

'D'you think that's her?' he said.

'There's only one way to find out.'

They climbed through a fence and hurried across a rough-cut lawn the size of an air-field, dotted with beech, elm and oak trees. The dog must have smelled them on the wind for it suddenly whirled round and raced towards them, barking. The woman stopped.

The dog paused in front of them, growling.

The woman came towards them. 'He won't hurt you.' It

was the same imperious voice Daniel had heard in the house. 'Not unless I tell him to,' she added.

She was small, about five foot two, and slender. She was dressed in well-cut cavalry twill trousers and a heavy woollen plaid shirt. There was a thin gold chain around her neck. Daniel knew she was in her mid-to-late sixties, but she looked younger. She had a frank, open face, a thin mouth and a squarish chin. She must once have been attractive, rather than pretty, and now had that slightly weather-beaten, handsome, outdoor look of women Daniel had seen around yachting marinas. She wore almost no make-up and her short hair was grey, the same colour as her eyes. The impression she gave was one of overall command; command of herself and her surroundings, of her dog, even of a couple of strangers. Her hands were small and square and well-kept. She held the dog's lead in her right hand and the only visible sign of her inner feelings was the way she tapped it in her left palm.

The dog, which was a Bouvier des Flandres the size of a small calf, had been eyeing Daniel with undisguised anticipation. Now the woman said, 'Down, Jacko,' and it lowered itself to the ground but kept its eyes fixed on Daniel's legs.

'Miss Hollande?' he said.

'Yes.'

'I wondered if we could have a few minutes of your time?'

'You're the young man who came to the house?'

'Yes.'

'I told Chris to tell you I wasn't in.'

'We heard you.'

'This is private property. Just because we open to the public on some days doesn't mean we encourage trespassers.'

'I'm sorry about that,' Daniel said, 'But we've come a long way just to be fobbed off.'

The tapping of the dog's lead quickened. 'I like to have my week-ends to myself.'

'You recognised my name . . .' Daniel began.

'Chris told me.'

'And even so, you wouldn't see me?'

'That was the precise reason.'

'We wanted your help,' Julie said.

41

'Help? My dear child, what possible help could I be to you?'

Daniel said, 'I received a letter the other day from my grandfather, Harry Coles Wynter.'

It was then he realised how supremely well she controlled herself. Apart from that inadvertent 'What!' which had cracked out when she had heard his name in the house, she had shown no emotion.

Now she said flatly: 'Your grandfather's dead. What do you mean, a letter from him?'

He told her briefly what had happened. She listened, frowning, then shook her head as if in disbelief.

'The point is,' he said, 'we don't really know what it's all about. We could find out, I suppose, if we had time, but we thought you could save us that. From what he says, we gather he feels he was unjustly treated in the Pekin–London race but. . .'

'There's nothing new about that! Anyway, what do you want from me?'

'Anything that might explain this.' He took a sheet of paper from his pocket.

'What's that?' she said suspiciously. At her change of tone, the dog growled.

'It's a copy of the letter.'

'I don't want to see it.'

'Why not?' Julie said. There were spots of colour on her cheeks and her ash-blonde hair was blowing in the breeze.

For a second, Daniel found himself comparing the two women. There was a tensile strength about Miss Hollande and her eyes were direct, her glance firm. She was confident and controlled. Physically, Julie was the opposite, but no less formidable. Tall, rangy, emotions all on the surface, eyes flashing, challenging. He thought that if they ever took an aggressive dislike to each other, he would hate to be in the middle.

'What possible harm could it do you?' Julie said.

'It's all in the past,' Miss Hollande said. 'The situation upset my father every time he thought about it, especially. . .' she hesitated '. . . especially during his last years when he was ill. He thought about it often. That someone he . . . well, never mind. It's decently buried and I think should be allowed to remain so.'

She turned and looked over her shoulder towards the gate.

Daniel said, 'Something happened during the race. What was it?'

'What difference can it make? Your grandfather's dead. My father's dead. No one cares any longer.'

'One is a dead hero and one's a dead . . . we don't know what. There's a possible injustice.'

'You know, my father never blamed your grandfather. Not in public, anyway. I've already made my attitude clear. Now I must ask you to leave.'

Daniel found himself frustrated and angry. 'I won't stop looking into it, you know. I'll go on trying to find out what really happened.'

She looked at him for a moment in silence, then said. 'I met your father once. You look very like him. I understand that all the Wynters were stubborn men. Please don't climb through the fence on your way out.'

They walked through the gates to the car and as they drove away, Daniel saw that she was still standing where they had left her.

As they came out onto the Alton by-pass, the Mercedes station wagon passed, going the other way. The man she had called Chris was at the wheel, but he didn't see them.

Julie said, 'Did you mean it, about going on?'

'Of course. Even more so. She made me angry. I keep wondering *why* she reacted like that. I mean, here's something that happened, as she says, a long time ago. All right, she thinks it's not a good idea digging up the past. But *why* not?'

When they reached the flat there was a message on the answering machine. A woman's voice said, 'I have a message for Commander Wynter. This is Major Desai's secretary at the High Commissioner's Office for Pakistan. Major Desai says he has some information for you. He suggests you come to the High Commission on Monday morning at eleven o'clock.'

'It's a bit of a lump.' Major Desai touched the package on the floor with the toe of his suede chukka boot.

43

They were in an empty office at the Pakistan High Commission in Lowndes Square. It was a small room with a desk in one corner on which were stacked four office chairs and a filing cabinet. In the middle of the floor was a small wooden crate with a tin lining from which the Major had taken the package they were now looking at. It was still partially wrapped in newspaper which had been torn and in some places had disintegrated so they could see what looked like a twisted block of grey papier mâché with ink marks on it.

Desai, a large man in his fifties, was dressed in a dark blue double-breasted blazer and grey flannels. His grey moustache was brushed into bristling sweeps along his upper lip. He pointed to a piece of the newspaper wrapping. 'Calcutta *Statesman* for November, 1938. Jolly romantic, isn't it?'

'When did it arrive?' Daniel asked.

'It's been here for weeks. Our chaps in communications had it. They hadn't a clue what action to take. Couldn't make out the address.'

'Looks like it was found in the bottom of the sea,' Julie said.

'Couldn't be further from the truth. Our chaps found it up in the mountains. The report I had said they were building a road up there, towards the border. Seems they dug out a skeleton and he had a couple of leather saddlebags with him. There were other letters of course but all of them ruined.'

'Do they have any idea what happened?'

'The skeleton probably belonged to a post-runner on the Kashgar road. This sort of thing has happened before, even in my time. They're attacked by bandits or bears or they die of cold. The wolves get at the body. But usually the post is lost. This chap was buried deep, they say.'

Daniel tried to visualise the man, his body, wolves, bandits, bears; but here in the heart of London on a sunny winter morning, with the plane trees casting long shadows and the brickwork of the nearby buildings glowing, it was hard to imagine the tragedy.

'You say your grandfather lived near Kashgar?' Desai said.

'Somewhere in the region. I'm not sure exactly where. Does the name Hollande with an 'e' mean anything to you?'

He shook his head. 'I know something of the area. I've climbed in the Karakorums. And we were there in the emergency, of course.'

'The emergency?'

'When the Chinese threatened to invade. I was building roads to bring up artillery. Hell of a job. Still a sensitive area, for that matter. Who owns which mountains. That sort of thing.'

'I thought the Chinese were being Little Lord Fauntleroys at the moment,' Julie said.

Desai showed perfect white teeth in a smile. 'That's just propaganda. You mark my words, if the Sino-Russian talks are successful they'll re-equip their Army with Russian hardware and then they'll be back putting pressure on our borders. Marvellous, isn't it?' He stood, looking broodingly at the lump of manuscript. 'The point is, how do we know this is yours?'

'If it came from the same place as the letter, it has to be,' Daniel said.

'The only way we're going to find out is to look,' Julie said. 'But how? The thing's solid.'

'Steam might work,' Daniel said.

Desai nodded. 'My secretary has a kettle. . . .'

But it was useless. The snow and the melt water and the years of damp had produced a paper pulp that either broke off in brittle chunks or turned into a kind of cellulose porridge. The room became dotted with small grey lumps on which not one word could be deciphered.

[6]

'You're pacing,' she said.

They were back in their sitting-room in Swiss Cottage. She was lying on the sofa, unusually quiet.

'If only there'd been something,' he said. 'Just a few words.'

'Darling, you're becoming obsessive.'

45

He didn't seem to hear her, but went to stare out of the window. 'I was as good as there.'

'And what were you going to find?' Her tone was cool, but he did not register it.

'God knows – but *something*.'

They were silent for a moment, then she said, 'What about Glasgow?'

'To hell with Glasgow. As you said, I'm not cut out to be a Team Leader.'

She sat up. 'Daniel, listen to me. . . '

'No. You listen to me. You want me to get a job. Okay, *I* want to get a job. But every time a possibility crops up which means me leaving the country or London, you try to put me off. You want it both ways.'

They were on delicate ground now. She went to him and touched his face. 'I've got used to you being here.'

'Like an old ring on your finger?'

'No. Not like an old ring. Darling. I'm in love with you.'

They had used the word after or before making love, but it had never carried the weight of this statement, not made in the heat of the moment.

Yet he felt a sudden apprehension and chose to turn the phrase. 'But?' he said.

'No buts.'

'Yes, there are.'

'All right. There is one. In all this, you're forgetting about me. I've been offered another series. If for some reason I wasn't here, I might lose it.'

'That reason being something like this business about my grandfather?'

'Exactly.'

'But what if it turned into something big?'

' "If" is a big word. Anyway, darling, be practical. If you were to go chasing after your grandfather's story, what would you use for money?'

'I've got a bit of capital left.'

'And when that's gone?'

'Sufficient unto the day. Anyway, at least I'll have tried something. It's a hell of a lot better than queueing for the dole.'

She put her arms around him and held him close for a moment. 'You're really serious, aren't you?'

'And if it comes unstuck and I lose the lot, you can keep me. You can buy me gold chains and Gucci loafers.'

She tried to match his mood. 'And a sports car. Isn't that what kept men always want?'

It came to him suddenly 'Cars!' he said explosively. 'The motoring press! It'll save me from that bloody Index!'

'I don't follow you.'

'There may have been motoring magazines in 1910. Why not? This must have been a big deal at the time. Pekin to London. I mean, a race like that would be tremendous even now. Otherwise I'm going to have to spend days and days in libraries looking for bits and pieces.'

At that moment, the telephone rang.

He picked it up and a voice said, 'May I speak to Commander Wynter?'

'Speaking.'

'This is Victoria Hollande.'

He would have recognised the firm, controlled voice without the identification. He placed his hand over the mouthpiece and told Julie. Her eyebrows shot up.

'I've rung up to apologise,' the voice said. 'I was extremely rude the other day. Please put it down to surprise.' He heard her laugh. 'Shock might be a better word. It was that name, coming out of the past. I wasn't prepared for it.'

'I should have telephoned you first,' Daniel said.

'No, the blame is mine.' He could sense in her tone the effort to be friendly. There was a pause and then she said, 'I was wondering if I could make up for it by asking you to come and have a drink with me. You and your . . . of course. . . '

He put his hand over the mouthpiece again and said, 'She's inviting us for a drink.' Julie's mouth turned down at the corners. 'Her name is Julie.'

'. . . and Julie, if she'd like to come.'

They made an appointment for the following week. He put the phone down and opened the palms of his hands in an unspoken question.

'What do you think she wants?' Julie said.

'She said, to apologise. But she could have apologised on the phone or written a note. I wonder what she's up to?'

The building lay on the wrong side of the tracks near Waterloo Station. It was narrow, built of grimy brick and only three storeys high. On the pediment was the faded lettering, AJAX HOUSE, 1902. It was the home of Ajax Publications, Ltd.

Daniel paused in the dingy foyer and looked at the list of magazines on the wallboard. It was prodigious: from *Teen Triangles* to *Nymphette* on the first floor, to *Easy Knitting* and *Shoe Shop Monthly* on the second, with *Motoring Universe* and its stable companions, *Cosy Caravan* and *Motorbike and Sidecar*, on the third. He went up a rickety staircase and came to an office on the third floor where a young receptionist with light green hair was making tea.

'My name's Wynter,' he said. 'I phoned.'

He was shown into a small room, the walls of which were covered in framed drawings of car engines. In one corner, at a draughtsman's table, under a powerful Anglepoise lamp, sat a small, gnomelike figure. He must have been in his seventies, Daniel thought, and he wore magnifying glasses. He was crouched over the inclined plane of the table, and did not look up.

'This is Mr. Clifford,' the receptionist said, and left.

'They're all out at the launching of the new Jag,' Mr. Clifford said. 'All booze and fags and bosoms. What can I do for you?'

Daniel's eyes had been scanning the walls. The engine drawings, all in section, were magnificent. They were done in pale blue and silver and the detail was meticulous down to the last nut and bolt. 'I was wondering if I could see your back files,' he said.

'What year?'

'1910. 1911. It says on the masthead of *Motoring Universe* that you were founded in 1908.'

'Fire. They went up in smoke in 1935. What do you want to look up?'

'I want to find about the Pekin to London race.'

The old man pushed the magnifying glasses up on his forehead. He looked at Daniel with interest.

'What was your name again?'

'Wynter. My grandfather drove in the race.'

'Wynter . . . Wynter. Yes. Abbott Special. And the other one. Bulldog-Saxon. Can't remember the driver's name, but he should never have won. Not against the Abbott.'

'Hollande.'

'Was it? Can't remember names so well now, but I never forget an engine. Not that I ever saw it. No one did after that. Abbott never made another. Went bust. Shot himself. But, my God, what an automobile!' He turned away from Daniel and looked out of the dirty window that overlooked the back of Waterloo Station. 'Forty horsepower . . . four speed . . . four double-block cylinders . . . L. T. magneto ignition . . . conical clutch . . . transmission by Cardan shaft . . . leaf spring suspension and axle-trees. . . .' It was as though he were reciting the Nicene Creed. Then he chuckled. 'Of course it only did about seven miles to the gallon. Not much good for today except as a collector's item. Goodness me! Worth a quarter of a million now, I suppose.'

'*What?*'

'Pounds. That's what a Yank would pay.'

'That seems a lot of. . . '

'Pirelli tyres . . . they would have been wider than usual. . . .'

'I wasn't really interested in the car,' Daniel said.

'Not interested in the car?' Mr. Clifford said in disbelief. 'What *are* you interested in, then?'

'Anything I can find out about the race or the two English drivers. Any of the drivers, for that matter.'

The old man pushed his glasses down over his eyes again and returned to his drawing. 'I've never been interested in *people*.'

'Well, who would know?'

'Now you're asking. You might try Archie Preece. Used to write for us at one time. I've got a feeling he wrote a book about it, or something.'

Daniel's heart leapt. 'Where would I find him?'

'God knows.'

Archibald Preece's name was in the Authors' and Writers' *Who's Who* which Daniel found in his local library. The entry had an address in Guildford, but no telephone number.

Julie was busy discussing her new series, a television adaptation of Wilkie Collins' *The Moonstone*, to follow up her success with *The Woman in White*, so he went to Guildford alone.

Preece's house was in the lower section of the town. He drove past several abandoned factories and old warehouses and reached a terrace of semi-detacheds built between the wars. They were finished in pebble-dash painted white and each had a bow window on the ground floor. A woman in her forties opened the door. She wore a headscarf and a flowered apron over her dress. She might once have been attractive, but there were hard lines of discontent around her mouth.

'I'd like to see Mr. Archibald Preece,' Daniel said.

'Father's working. He works every morning until twelve.'

Daniel checked his watch. It was ten-fifteen. 'I could come back, but I wonder if you'd just tell him that I'm here. My name is Wynter. Daniel Coles Wynter.'

She looked at him suspiciously. 'Is he supposed to know you? You're not from his publisher, are you? He said he'd have the book done by Friday. I think you should respect that. It's not fair to keep on at him. He's not a young man any more. He's seventy-six next birthday.'

'I'm not from his publisher.'

'Well, I'm sure I don't know. He doesn't like to be disturbed. Gets his temper up and then there's trouble when the boys come home from school.'

'If you could give him my name and let him make up his own mind. . . .'

'Come in, then.'

There were gumboots in the front porch, and fishing rods, old cricket bats and tennis racquets. He followed her to the dining-room at the rear of the house and was surprised by its contrast with the dreary street at the front. A well-kept garden ran down to the River Wey. There were still a few roses in the flower beds. Weeping willows grew at the water's edge and small boats were moored along the banks. A canal narrowboat was tied up at the bottom of the garden.

'Father's down in the boat,' the woman said. She opened the dining-room window, pulled the end of a piece of clothes-line several times. A brass bell on the narrowboat peeled out. One of the boat's windows slid open and a loud and angry voice shouted, 'What?'

She leant out of the window and called. 'There's a gentleman to see you, Dad. Says his name's Wynter.'

'If he's from the publishers, I told them Friday. I'm not a bloody computer.'

'Says he's not from the publishers.'

There was a pause. 'Oh, all right. Send him down.'

Daniel walked over the back lawn and climbed into the stern of the narrowboat. As he bent to enter the door of the saloon the voice said, 'Mind your head!' It came a fraction too late. His forehead met the top of the door-frame with a crack. He stood for a second, his eyes watering. There was a chuckle from the saloon. 'Happens every time,' the voice said.

He descended the last of the steps and found himself in a long, narrow room. The boat was about forty-five feet long and only six feet wide. Most of the space had been turned into one long saloon. The sides, up to the level of the oblong windows, were hidden by shelves of books. At the far end, seated at a cheap office desk and facing down the saloon's length, was Archibald Preece.

He was elderly, and looked like a tortoise. His skin was old and leathery and lined and his lower jaw had retreated. He wore on his head a large white Stetson hat and was crouched behind an ancient Underwood upright typewriter, as though he were about to pounce upon it. He was a large man who had shrunk, so that the essential Archie Preece seemed to have disappeared beneath the folds of loose skin, but his eyes were bright.

'Well, what can I do for you?'

'My name's Daniel Wynter,' Daniel said, and paused.

'Is that supposed to mean something? Betty said you weren't from the publishers.'

'I'm not. *Motoring Universe* gave me your name.'

'Good God, are they still going? Look, Mr . . . er . . . I've got a deadline to meet.'

'This won't take long,' Daniel said. 'Mr. Clifford at *Motoring*

Universe . . . you may remember him?' The Stetson moved negatively from side to side. 'He said you'd written a book that partly concerned my grandfather.'

'I've written nearly three hundred books.'

'This one was about motoring.'

'Motoring . . . sailing . . . dogs . . . cats . . . gardening . . . westerns . . . thrillers . . . flying . . . mining . . . treasure-hunting . . . Africa . . . Spain . . . Yugoslavia . . . ocean liners . . . you name it, I've written it.' It was said with pride. 'I'm a professional writer. Earned my bread and a lot more besides for damn nearly sixty years. Beat that.'

'This was about the Pekin to London motor race in 1910.'

Preece's hands, which had been slowly approaching the typewriter as though he wished to take it by surprise, stopped, and withdrew onto his lap.

'What did you say your name was?'

'Wynter with a "y". My grandfather drove in the race.'

'What's your interest?'

'I'd like to read about it. I want to know about the people, to try and find out what happened. I think there may have been an injustice done to my grandfather.'

'That's true enough.'

'I've been trying to get hold of your book, but neither the London Library nor the one at Beaulieu has a copy. The librarians hadn't even heard of it.'

Preece leant back in his chair, tilted the Stetson forward in the manner of a gun-fighter and laced his fingers behind his old head. He might look like a tortoise, Daniel thought, but his eyes were shrewd and full of life.

'That's understandable,' he said. 'It was never published.'

'I see.' Daniel didn't try to hide his disappointment.

'You a writer?' Preece said. 'Or a journalist?'

'No.'

'What do you want to do with the information then?'

'I'm not sure at the moment. Why?'

'Just wondering why somebody should show an interest after all this time. It mean, it's *interesting* all right. Bloody interesting. I just wondered why.'

Daniel hesitated, then pulled out a copy of his grandfather's letter. He watched Preece read it, and then he recounted how it had reached him.

Preece pushed his Stetson back in the manner of John Wayne. 'What about this manuscript? I suppose that's gone for good?'

'I'm afraid so.' Daniel told him about the manuscript.

Preece stared at him, then said, 'There's still a piece missing.'

'There are a whole lot of pieces missing.'

'No, I mean, missing between you and me. Say you found out the details. Are you going to say, that's it, thank you very much, and go home?'

Daniel told him about his ideas, about the possibility of a television investigation, articles for magazines, perhaps a book. A tight smile appeared on Preece's lips and the old man nodded.

'I thought so,' he said. 'Even after all these years, I could smell it. Competition. Well, you're right. It always was a bloody good story and with this letter, it's an even better one. My God, if I were twenty years younger and wasn't tied up with all this silly business. . . ' He waved at the book-shelves. 'Betty's husband left her, so she and the boys are dependent on me. . . .' He looked at Daniel for a moment in silence, then said, 'They say God works in peculiar ways. There's none more peculiar than this. Your grandfather was in that race – so was my dad.' He chuckled. 'Thought that would make you sit up. Never heard of Percy Preece?' Daniel shook his head. 'No, why should you? Percy Preece was the General's mechanic.'

'The General?'

'Hollande – only he wasn't a General then. The man who won the race.'

'Your father was Hollande's mechanic?'

'That's it. You don't think those early automobilists knew anything about a car engine, do you? They could hardly change a tyre. They all had mechanics who could strip a car and put it together again and also do most of the driving. And when they weren't driving, put up tents and cook meals and dig the car out of sand and talk to the natives about getting across the rivers. Oh, yes. In those old endurance

53

tests and races and crossings of this and crossings of that, they all had someone like my dad. Us and them. Manager and workers. Upper class and lower class. That's how it was in those days. He'd started working for Hollande before that. He was his chauffeur as well as his mechanic. And his valet for that matter. He used to look after Hollande's cars in the hill climbs and then when he was trying for the land-speed record on the Pendine Sands in Wales. Yes, he. . . '

'Did he leave anything?' Daniel interrupted. 'Any papers or diaries? Did he tell you anything that might help?'

'Not much. Don't forget, I was only a kid when he died. Anyway, by the time I grew old enough to be interested in things like that – you could say about eight or ten, well, that would have been about 1920, I was born in 1910 – there'd been a whole war between. I suppose it was old stuff to my father. I remember asking him about it a couple of times, but he was always too busy. Ran a car-hire firm in those days. Nice little business. In Battersea. We lived in one of those houses near the Albert Bridge. He had two or three cars. Big Daimler limousine for weddings and funerals and I think he had a Lanchester. Can't remember now. Minerva, was it? He used to drive a lot of the racing boys. Take them down to Brighton and Sandown. Well, anyway, he died in twenty-two and my mother sold the business. We were never poor. She could afford to send me to the Battersea Grammar School.' He paused, opened a drawer in his desk and pulled out a bottle and two glasses. 'I think this needs celebrating, don't you?'

'It's a bit early for me.'

'For me, too, but you've buggered my morning.' He poured two shot glasses. 'Rye. Always drink rye when I'm Luke Masterton.' He pointed to the rows of books on Daniel's left.

Daniel turned and saw they were all paperback Westerns with the name Luke Masterton on the spines. 'That's why I wear this.' Preece pointed to his hat. 'Gives me the feeling.' He removed it to show a bald and freckled pate, then he reached behind his chair and replaced it with a snap-brim trilby which he pulled down over one eye in the manner of Humphrey Bogart. 'And this is my Lance Hillman hat.' He

54

pointed to Daniel's right where a similar quantity of paper-backs bore the name Lance Hillman on their spines. They had titles like *Double-Cross in Chicago* and *Coffins Can't Talk*.' He smiled, a small boy's puckish, sickle-shaped grin. 'Keeps me off the street, and it turns an honest penny. Maintains this place, and Betty and the boys. One a month, I start in January with a Western, February crime, March Western, and so on. Every month a book. Every book two hundred pages.'

'You must have spent a lot of time in America.'

'Funny you should say that. One of the few places I've never been. That's my America.' He pointed to a T.V. set under which sat a video recorder. A shelf on one side of it contained a dozen or more tapes among which Daniel saw *Shane*, *High Noon*, *The Untouchables* and *Little Caesar*.

'If I want some dialogue and atmosphere, I put one of those on.' He raised his glass. 'Well, here's to crime.'

They drank and Daniel felt the fiery rye whisky slide down and explode in his stomach.

'Is there any way you can help me?' he said.

Preece pushed his trilby back in the manner of James Stewart and said, 'There is. But I think you and I had better come to an arrangement.'

'Financial?'

'Of course, financial. My father's motto was, nothing for nothing. Same with me, specially writing.'

'But you said you didn't write the book.'

'You didn't listen. I said I didn't publish it. Wrote a good deal of it, though.'

'What happened?'

'There you go again. Questions. Have you got an agent?'

'No, but Julie – a friend – has.'

'I've got an agent, too, but on something like this we can make our own arrangements, can't we?'

'It depends what you've got.'

' 'Course it does. And I can tell you right here and now, I haven't got everything. But I've got a lot to go on. I've got everything your grandad knew.' Preece was looking at him over the top of the glass and Daniel felt a shiver, a prickle of goose-flesh, move like a shadow over his skin.

'How do you mean?' he said.

Preece flicked the letter on his desk with his forefinger. 'He talks about diaries in that letter, right?'

'That's right.'

'I've seen them.'

'What!'

'He let me see them.'

'You met my grandfather?'

'Oh, yes. I *found* him. Well . . . I mean, he wasn't lost, really.'

'Where? When?'

'There you go again, old son. No more questions until we've had a chat. Pass your glass.'

Twenty percent,' Julie said above the noise of the shower. 'That's a hell of a lot.'

Daniel was lying on her bed, his head cradled in his hands. She turned the shower off and padded into the bedroom, her skin glistening with droplets of water. Her body was like an athlete's, he thought, but where there would have been bunched or stringy muscles, hers was only rounded, inviting flesh.

'Flesh,' he said. 'Lovely word.'

She was drying her hair and didn't hear. Her breasts were full but still tight and high and, for the first time, Daniel thought what a good mother she'd make. The wide hips, the full breasts: she was built to have children. He looked at his watch.

'I know what you're thinking.' She was looking at him through the tangled strands of blonde hair. 'And there isn't time.'

She dried herself and began looking in her drawers for underclothing. The bedroom, in deference to Daniel, who spent so much time there, was less untidy than her work-room, but 'less', as he had told her several times, was a comparative word.

'I think we could have got the figure down,' she said, pulling on a pair of bikini pants.

'He wanted thirty. Anyway, eighty percent of something is better than eighty percent of nothing.'

'I suppose so.' She put on her bra. 'Why wouldn't he let you take the material?'

'He says it's in a mess. He hasn't looked at it for years and it's not in any coherent form. Some of it is in narrative, some in notes. The diaries are separate. All in his own handwriting, I suppose, which is going to be something of a problem. He's going to photocopy the lot. You can't blame him for not letting the originals out of his possession. It's his protection against us.'

'You mean he doesn't trust us?' The word 'us' seemed to be in inverted commas.

'You and I know we're trustworthy. But how is he to know? Anyway, I didn't say that.'

'Do *you* trust *him*?'

'I think he's shrewd and has learned to look after number one. Told me all about himself. He started doing little bits and pieces of journalism as a kid. He'd see things in London on his way to school and sell a few paragraphs to the suburban press. Then when he left school he worked for the *Exchange Telegraph* and at the same time he was sending items to the national papers. Again little London paragraphs. His big break came when the magazine *Tit-Bits* asked him to do a series on little-known London; the sewers, the Fleet River, the Hackney Marshes, Highgate Cemetery. That sort of thing. It was published as a book and had quite a good Christmas sale. That launched him on his writing career. He wanted to be a travel writer, only he says that travel writers in the thirties had all gone to Oxford or Cambridge and were scholars or archaeologists. They were amateurs with private means. He was a professional without means. But he saved up enough to get him to China, because he'd become fascinated by the race.'

Julie had put on a dark blue, clinging dress and was blow-drying her blonde hair. 'No wonder, with his father in it. Do you think he knows?'

'What?'

'Whatever it is we don't. Whatever it is that your grand-father was writing to give his side of. I mean, there's some central incident, the crux of the whole story, that we don't know. Without it, everything else is meaningless.' She switched off the drier.

'He knows, all right. But he likes playing games. He's got a strange sense of humour. I cracked my head when I went into the boat and he thought that was pretty funny. Another thing, I think he's written so many plots he doesn't like his right hand to know what his left is doing. Anyway, we'll know tomorrow or, at the latest, the next day.'

She disappeared into a walk-in cupboard and emerged wearing a corduroy coat with a fur collar.

She said, 'What I don't understand is why he never published the book. I should have thought it was a natural.'

'He saw Harry Wynter in 1939. Got back just before war broke out. Then there was a shortage of paper. He says when he tried to sell the book after the war his publisher was interested at first, then later turned it down cold, without explanation.'

'Was Hollande still alive then?'

'Oh, yes. He went down to see the old man.'

'It's all very odd,' she said. 'How do I look?'

'Not bad. And me?'

'Not bad.'

'I thought I looked rather beautiful.'

'You're beautiful,' she said. 'Come on, we'll be late.'

[7]

Victoria Hollande's apartment was on the north side of Eaton Square. There were two bells and one, the ground floor, was marked HOLLANDE TRUST. 'She lives above the shop,' Julie said enviously. 'That's what you can do if you're a charity.'

'You sure?'

'No taxes if you're a charity, so you can have your offices in Eaton Square and live above them.'

He pressed the buzzer and spoke into a door telephone. The big door swung open. They were in the hall of a house rather than the foyer of an office. It was tiled in black and white marble and from its centre rose an ornate mahogany

58

staircase. Glass doors to the left and right were marked HOLLANDE TRUST.

Victoria Hollande came down the staircase to meet them. She was wearing a beautifully cut fawn trouser suit with a yellow silk blouse and a heavy gold chain around her neck. She greeted them crisply and with a smile that had been lacking at the first meeting. Daniel felt the cool, dry firmness of her square hand and thought that the word 'competent' fitted her well. He marvelled at the way she walked and moved. She looked no more than forty-five.

She put their coats in the porter's cubbyhole.

'This is the headquarters of the Trust,' she said. She opened a door, switched on the light and said, 'Interview room,' and then, indicating a formidable array of grey filing cabinets: 'Case studies.'

She gesticulated around the room. 'The General would hardly recognise it now. In the early days its function was to show the flag for England, but that's all changed now.' Daniel detected a note of regret in her tone. 'We sent people all over the world then. Young people with what the General used to call "fire in their bellies". Some of their achievements were outstanding.' She led them back into the hall and closed the door behind them. As they stood, waiting for her to lead the way to the stairs, she said, 'It was one of our young men who mapped all the waterways in the Beagle Channel. Another discovered a new plant species in the Namib Desert. Now our role is more an attempt to fulfill a social need: taking deprived young people and giving them a chance in life. You know about our scholarships?'

Julie shook her head.

'There were only two originally, but we give four now: two to Manchester University and two to Durham. Of course we try to place all our young people in jobs later. That's what the Trust is all about. Once someone comes to us – and we get them in many ways, from social workers, probation officers, young people who've gone wrong but seem to have the right stuff in them – once we get them, the Trust sees them through the difficult times. And we don't just leave them after that. Once they're ours, they're ours for life.'

'Sounds admirable,' Daniel said.

She turned to him and for the first time there was genuine warmth in her smile. 'Thank you. We're proud of what we've done.'

They went upstairs into a well-proportioned drawing-room. It was oblong, with long windows and ceiling mouldings. The overall colour scheme was beige, tan, terracotta – desert colours. There were wall-hangings from Central Asia, Abyssinian armour and wood carvings from the Okavango. The windows looked out on the leafless branches of plane trees in the square. The sound of traffic moving along the King's Road came softly through double-glazing.

'You remember Chris Parker, don't you?' Victoria said.

It was the man they had spoken to in Hampshire. He was dressed in a dark grey flannel suit, blue shirt and black knitted tie. His dark hair and light blue eyes made the colour scheme dramatic and Daniel made a silent bet with himself that Parker had dressed with that in mind. He watched Julie as she shook hands with him. Her smile, her whole manner was subtly different from normal. He could not define the change, but knew her well enough to be certain.

His eyes returned to the surroundings. There were framed blow-ups of photographs on the walls. One showed a climber hanging in space on an exposed rockface, another a group of people wearing parkas on a frozen landscape, a third was of a magnificent black woman with jutting breasts and a swollen, pregnant belly standing in front of a grass hut. There was a pile of loose photographs on a table. The one on top showed a sand-dune, orange in the evening light, with a Landrover leaving two deep wheel-tracks.

'Chris took those,' Victoria said.

'I made some dry martinis, but there's whisky, or anything else you prefer,' Parker said.

They chose martinis, and talked generalities for a while: the weather, new plays. Then Victoria said to Daniel, 'As I said on the phone, I owe you an apology. Hearing your grandfather's name after so many years was like an electric shock.'

Out of the corner of his eye, he saw Parker and Julie move to the side table on which the collection of photographs lay.

'How much do you know about your grandfather?' Victoria went on.

'Very little. When my parents were killed I was brought up by an aunt and uncle on my mother's side of the family. The only thing I really learnt as a child was that my grandfather had lived in India. I suppose that's Pakistan now.'

'Not really. Have you heard of Sahr?' He shook his head. 'Hunza?'

'Vaguely. It's somewhere up in the Himalayas, isn't it?'

'Not quite the Himalayas. North-west of that. Sahr is rather like Hunza. A small kingdom of its own. Five countries meet there. Twenty-thousand footers all around. Snow and ice. Some fertile valleys. A few villages. One or two monasteries. It's been conquered by half a dozen countries since Timur Leng held it in the fourteenth century. The British won it for a time in the nineteenth. Tibet has held it, so have the Afghans. The Russians had people in there when the Great Game was in full swing. I'm not sure who claims it now. It's probably under what the geographers call "Chinese Administration". On the maps, it's about as remote as you can get. Anyway, that's where he lived.'

'You climbed in the Himalayas in 1939, didn't you?' She raised her eyebrows. 'I found the reference in *The Times* Index,' he said.

'You *have* been busy.' There was a sudden chill in her tone. 'Chris.' She held up her glass. Parker gave them each another drink. 'And what else have you found?'

'We're only just starting,' Daniel said. 'There have been a lot of innuendoes in what we've read but not many facts. The problem is, I'm not sure what Harry Wynter was supposed to have done that all the fuss was about.'

'Oh, I can tell you that,' Victoria said. 'He tried to murder the General.'

A brief, shocked silence was broken by Chris Parker. 'You never told me that!' There was a hint of exasperation, combined with interest.

'You never asked,' Victoria said briskly.

Daniel recovered more slowly. He looked at her searchingly. The pupils of her eyes seemed to have widened, as though dilated with atropine.

61

If she had wanted to create an effect, he thought, she could hardly have done better. Yet, except for the strange widening of her pupils, her handsome, weather-lined face showed little expression.

'I can't believe it,' Julie said.

'I can understand that. It doesn't change things, though.'

'You have the details, of course, to back it up?' Daniel said.

'Enough. We'll probably never know them all.'

'If you accuse someone of attempted murder you should be certain.' The hostility the two women had felt towards each other in Hampshire was suddenly back.

'It was well known at the time,' Victoria said. 'It happened during the race. Each driver had his own route and fuel dumps of petrol, oil, spares, tyres, arranged months in advance. Your grandfather and the General had decided to take a southerly route through the Black Gobi and Chinese Turkestan because of flooding in Russia during the summer. Somewhere in the Gobi, Harry Wynter sabotaged the General's fuel dump. When my father reached it, the taps on the drums had been opened and the petrol had flowed into the sand. He and his mechanic nearly died.'

'You mean Preece?'

'More research? Yes, Percy Preece.'

'How do you know all this?' Julie said. 'How can you be certain Harry Wynter did it? Were they travelling together?'

'No. Their routes were parallel.'

'Well then?'

'Wheel tracks were seen. Tyre marks. Harry Wynter was driving an Abbott Special. The tyre-treads were distinctive.'

'But why would he have done such a thing?' Daniel said. 'What would be the point?'

'To win,' Victoria said.

'You try to murder two men just to win a race?'

Julie's disbelief seemed to touch Victoria: two bright red spots appeared on her cheeks.

'You'd understand if you knew the background,' she said. 'They'd been rivals since they were children.'

'That doesn't necessarily mean. . .'

'Let me finish. A first prize of ten thousand pounds had been offered by the International Race Committee in Paris, but the London *Daily News* had offered thirty thousand to the driver of the first British car home. There were only two British cars. A lot of people entered to begin with, but when the entrance fee was announced – nearly two thousand pounds – and other expenses, most of them pulled out. You'd have to multiply thirty thousand by a factor of, oh, about twenty, to understand today's value of the prize.'

'Going on for a million pounds,' Parker said.

'And Harry Wynter was broke. His estate was mortgaged to the last penny.' She paused, but no one spoke. 'I'm sorry, but you pressed me. The General reported the facts to the International Committee and to the Chinese Government, because it happened on Chinese territory.'

'Did the Chinese investigate?' Julie said.

'They were rather too busy by then. Sun Yat Sen was leading the first revolution.'

'What did Preece have to say?'

'He made a statement. The General didn't particularly want him to, but he couldn't stop him, of course. My father never accused Harry Wynter in public. It was against his honour as a gentleman. Especially since he and Harry had once been friends.'

'That's only one version,' Julie said. 'Your father's and this man Preece's. It's that version that Harry Wynter wanted to correct. That's why he wrote the letter, and sent the manuscript to his son.'

'You don't think Harry hadn't tried to clear his name before, do you? My God, it was his obsession for years. He even wrote to the General about it.' There was anger in her voice. 'No, I'm sorry, but there it is. You can see now why I didn't want to get involved in what you're doing. Why I didn't want to read your grandfather's letter. I'd read letters from him not once, but a dozen times. I knew exactly what he wrote about. I didn't want to get involved because I didn't want the Trust involved.'

'But isn't that what the Trust is for?' Daniel said. 'Isn't it supposed to bring up young people to believe in truth and justice?'

She turned on him. 'What does your generation know about truth, justice or honour? The words are meaningless to anyone

63

under fifty. Well, they were not meaningless to the General and they aren't meaningless to me.'

'If that's so, I should have thought. . . '

'Leave it!' Parker said.

'What?'

'I agree with Miss Hollande.'

'Are you an expert?'

'No more than you are.'

'How do you know all about this, anyway?'

'Miss Hollande told me some of it a few days ago.'

'After we had come to Hampshire?'

'Yes. It was natural in the circumstances.'

Parker was cool, but Daniel realised there was a barometer indicating his real feelings: his Hampshire accent, normally carefully masked by the cardinal vowel chart, had become noticeably stronger.

Daniel spoke directly to Victoria. 'When we came here this evening we didn't know what my grandfather had been accused of. Now we know. He says he was innocent. It makes the story even better.'

'That's all you're really interested in, isn't it?' she said. 'The story. You don't care about your grandfather, or my father's memory, for that matter.'

'You're right,' he said. 'I'm not going to fake some sentimental interest in a man I never knew and had barely heard of until recently. But it could make a book or a T.V. documentary. Archibald Preece thinks it's an even better story now than the one he wrote.'

'You've seen Archie Preece? I didn't know he was still alive.'

'Very much so. He was writing a book about the race, but he couldn't get it published. He has copies of Harry Wynter's diaries.'

'I know. But you'll never publish them.'

'Why not?'

'They're libellous. They were then and they are now.'

'You can't libel the dead,' Julie said.

Ignoring her, Victoria concentrated her powerful personality directly on Daniel. 'I'm asking you, for the sake of the Trust, for the young people who are in its care at the moment,

64

and for young people who have yet to benefit from it, to stop turning this into a commercial circus. It's squalid and muck-raking and money-grabbing.'

Julie stepped forward. Daniel saw the brightness of anger in her eyes and moved quickly between the two women. He said, 'I'm afraid I can't give a guarantee. I don't know what we'll do with any material we find. That's my business. Harry Wynter was *my* grandfather.'

They were half way down the stairs when Victoria came onto the landing above and said, 'Commander Wynter, may I have a private word with you?'

'No, I don't think so. Julie is part of me.'

'Well . . .' She hesitated. 'If you feel that way . . . what I was going to say is this: digging into the past often reveals unwelcome ghosts. There may be things in your grandfather's past that are more distasteful than you can imagine.'

Daniel stopped on the staircase and looked up at her. 'I think you'll have to explain yourself.'

'Harry Wynter was a. . . ' She paused again, choosing her words with care. 'An urning.'

'A what?'

'An urning. If you don't know what it means, look it up.' She went back into the drawing-room and closed the door behind her.

He turned to Julie, questioningly, but she shook her head. 'Someone who makes urns? God knows. I've never heard the word before.'

Half an hour later they were in her room with the huge M-Z volume of the Shorter Oxford English Dictionary open on her desk. She ran her finger down the column. 'Here we are: "uriniferous . . . urino . . . urinous . . . urn . . . urning. . . ?" '

He craned forward. The entry read; 'Urning (urnig) 1890. [Ger. (Ulrichs). Cf URANISM.] A homosexual person.'

'So?'

'So what was she getting all fussed for? Why *urning*? Why not just gay, or queer, or simply homosexual?'

'She didn't want to say the words,' Daniel said. 'Not in front of you, anyway. That's why she wanted a private moment with me.'

'No one's embarrassed about things like that nowadays.'

'She is. You could see the way she used words like honour and justice. They do mean more to her generation than to us. And they wouldn't use other words that we take as a matter of course.'

'Perhaps she finds the idea of homosexuality distasteful rather than embarrassing.'

'What do you think about her relationship with Chris Parker?'

'He's more like her son than her lover. Anyway, with his looks he wouldn't have to bed a woman old enough to be his mother.'

'You find him attractive?'

'Of course. He's remarkably good looking. By the way, did you mean what you told her on the stairs?'

'What?' He knew precisely what she meant. 'Remind me.'

'Like hell.' She turned back to the dictionary and said, 'What about this homosexuality thing? It'll be hard to pin that down. In those days it was hardly spoken about.'

'Archibald Preece may know. I'm going to pick up the stuff he has tomorrow.'

'I'm coming with you.'

But she had a script meeting the following day, so it was a further twenty-four hours before they went to Guildford. It was a cold, miserable day with sleet squalls coming out of the north-east and the row of semi-detached houses looked mean and depressing.

Preece's daughter answered the door. She was dressed as before, in an apron, but her eyes were vague and her fingers picked constantly at a piece of loose skin on her thumb.

'Oh. It's you,' she said.

'Julie, this is Mrs. . . ?'

'Mrs. Stone.'

'I phoned your father yesterday to say I'd be coming down.'

'You can't see him. He's been taken sick. He's at the hospital.'

'I'm sorry to hear that. . . .'

'He's had a slight stroke.' With sudden anger she said, 'He'd be all right if he was left alone. He's seventy-six next birthday and never left alone. If it's not the publishers, then it's you people on about this other thing.'

'What other thing?' Daniel wondered if Preece had discussed the diary with her.

'Those papers about grand-dad. That's what caused it. I said to the doctor, I said, they never leave him alone. There was that woman yesterday. Badgering. I said to her, I'm sorry, but you'll just have to go.'

'What woman?'

'I can't recall the name. Small. In her fifties. And you could smell the money. Dad seemed to know her.'

'What did she want?' Daniel said.

'I took her down to the boat. All I know, she was cross when she left, and I found Dad down there looking awful. Chalk wasn't in it. So I brought him back and gave him a whisky and milk. He seemed all right. He got the loft-ladder down and went into the attic and spent an hour or so looking for something. I could hear him moving boxes and suitcases about. And then he brought a whole lot of stuff down to his room. Maybe that's what caused it.' She stopped and again she stood for a long moment inspecting her thumb. Suddenly she went on. 'And I've got the boys coming home and they'll be wanting their dinner. I don't know. . . ' She began to cry quietly. 'He's always looked after us. Always been there.'

'You said it was only a slight stroke,' Daniel said. 'And he looked a pretty tough old gentleman to me.'

Her eyes brightened. 'Yes, he *is* tough. I've always said that. He said it, too. Used to joke about it. Stringy, but tough, he said.'

'Mrs. Stone, do you know why we're here?'

'It's about those papers.'

They followed her into the house and up the stairs to the small front room which had been occupied by Archibald Preece and Luke Masterton and Lance Hillman. Unlike the narrowboat, it had no style. It was simply a bedroom with cheap prewar furniture and a pink candlewick spread on the bed. Under the windows there was a cardboard box and several expanding files.

'Those are the papers,' she said. 'He was going to sort them, but he never had the chance, see?'

'He said I could take them to London, to look at them,' Daniel said.

'I don't care.' She looked about vaguely. 'So *there* they are.' She bent and retrieved a pair of slippers from beneath the foot of the bed. 'We were looking for them when they came to take him.' She inspected them. 'Fancy going to hospital without your slippers.'

BOOK TWO

The Diary

They were in Daniel's chilly bedroom. The bed had been pushed against the wall and they were using the entire floor-space to lay out the papers from Preece's boxes and files. Julie had at first suggested they do this in her work-room, but Daniel had blenched at the thought of working in such chaos.

It was a measure of Archibald Preece's professionalism that the mass of paper had been split into two readily understand-able and assimilable categories. In the box file was the copy of Wynter's *Diary* of the Pekin–London Automobile Race of 1910. This, to their relief, had been typed out by Preece from the copy he had made in his own handwriting of Wynter's material. The pages were yellow with age and some were brittle and the typewriter ribbon was of the old light blue variety. But they were there, numbered and legible.

In the expanding file, Preece had started to build up his index. There were single sheets and notes on bits of paper and these they assumed he would have slotted into his own narrative once he began to write it. He had already begun this interpolation, as they soon discovered, when they started the *Diary*. Wherever he had details of an event and could expand Wynter's *Diary*, Preece tended to place his own additional material in it, marking both the page and the space into which it would eventually go. Much of this material came from interviews as well as newspaper cuttings. There were cross-references to the index file, all of which had to be checked.

Also in the cardboard box were a series of photographs, now brown with age.

It took Julie and Daniel several days to sort out the mass

of paper. In a way they were doing what they had attempted in the Pakistan High Commission, only now there were no lumps of cellulose porridge, here they were dealing with the legible written word.

When they had finished, they went up to Julie's bedroom and lay on her bed, reading aloud to each other.

DIARY OF THE PEKIN-LONDON RACE. *May–October, 1910. by Harry Coles Wynter, Capt. (Handwritten copy taken by A. Preece, 1939.)*

10 April: Well here we are on the high seas at last. And not before time. Tilbury and Gravesend are ghastly places. Is that publishable? My publishers – my intended publishers, that is – told me to jot down everything, no matter how insignificant. It could be edited later. You never knew, they said, what you might need. Out of my porthole I can see a sea-gull. It is a dull morning with a strong north-easter and the sea is rough.

I haven't found my sea-legs yet. Saw Eddie Hollande at breakfast and he, of course, was supremely fit, or so he told me. Said he'd had a run round the ship at seven. Told him I was feeling somewhat queasy, which seemed to please him. He said I should drink olive oil. That's what he did and it settled the stomach. I could see he felt he was one up already. But I'm not going to worry about that sort of thing now. It's just Eddie. Perhaps he thinks I'm the same. It's a point of view. I'll try to keep my real energy for the race, that's what counts. Funny to think of the Abbott and the Bulldog-Saxon tucked up in their packing cases down in Hold No. 4.

Yesterday we went down to Tilbury early, George Abbott, two of his mechanics, Eric Burten and myself, and saw the Abbott aboard. Preece and the people from the Bulldog-Saxon Co., had already loaded their automobile and were down in the hold making adjustments. Hollande only came aboard when the Press arrived about noon and we had the champagne party in the First Class Verandah Lounge. Abbott drank too much and I thought he was going to be sick. He's a marvellous automobile designer but I think he's on the edge of a breakdown. He told me that if I win everything will be all right for him, but if not . . . Well, I'm going to win, so never mind the if not. Anyone who knows anything about automobiles knows that Abbott has designed something quite outstanding. The Bulldog looks like an omnibus compared with it. God knows what it's going to do in the Gobi. It's even heavier than the Abbott.

NOTE: [This was an interpolation by Preece.]

Both Hollande and Wynter had chosen the route through the Black Gobi. The French and Italian competitors were going through Mongolia and Siberia. All kinds of reasons advanced for this choice. The two British competitors said it was because of flooding in Russia; the Italians and the French said theirs was the more travelled route and that their fuel problems would be lessened. The facts were: Wynter had been approached by the then biggest tea importers in the world (the China and the Oriental Tea Co., Ltd., of Fenchurch Street, London) to see if a lorry route was possible through the Gobi so that they could bring tea to Europe overland and not have to rely on the long sea voyage. Hollande was travelling that route because he would never have wanted to be too far from Wynter. The Italian, Dutch, German and French drivers, who were taking the Siberian route, were in the pay of butter companies in Denmark, Norway, England and Germany, who were fighting for the diary produce of Western Siberia and looking for truck overland routes that would link with the Trans-Siberian Railway. The point about petrol is spurious. Not more than six or seven cities in Eastern Russia had ever seen a motor car. Petrol at that time was used exclusively in the dry-cleaning trade in those parts.

April 12: Off the coast of Portugal. Weather warmer. Saw two whales. The *Orient Star* is quite a decent ship, full of tea-planters and their wives, some of them new. Then there are the I.C.S. people, the more senior ones travelling first-class. One or two carry briefcases to show how busy they are. Both Hollande and I are at the Captain's table; celebrities, I suppose.

Weather has calmed down considerably since we came out of Biscay but poor Burten doesn't seem to have found his sea-legs yet. He has been very sick and I visit him two or three times a day. He can't keep anything down.

NOTE: Start of problem. Hollande and Wynter travelling first class, of course. But Wynter had put Burten into second class. My father, Percy Preece, was in steerage, over the propellors.

73

Dad resented Burten's superior position. This, coupled with the daily visits by Wynter, was to give rise to rumours about the two men. (See later notes.)

This seems good place to sketch Burten.

Eric Arthur Burten, twenty-six at time of race. Came from Highclare in Hampshire. (See Photo No. 12.)

Julie and Daniel studied the old, sepia photograph. It showed a young man with a boyish, open face and light-coloured hair cut short back and sides. He was wearing a collarless shirt, braces, knickerbockers, stockings and heavy shoes. There was something appealing about him, perhaps in the clear way he looked at the camera, with a curious kind of innocence. He was leaning against the Abbott Special. In the background, slightly blurred, was the shape of a pagoda roof.

Burten a good example of the New Man whom Shaw portrayed in his character, Straker, the chauffeur in *Man and Superman*, who says: 'Very nice sort of place Oxford, I should think, for people who like that sort of place. They teach you to be a gentleman there. In the Polytechnic they teach you to be an engineer.' This hit off Burten and Wynter to a T. Burten had, in fact, gone to the Polytechnic in London before joining the Athena Motor Manufacturing Co. of Croydon. From there he had gone to the Abbott works in Acton to help build the Special. He and Harry Wynter had known each other from childhood. Burten's father had been a keeper on the Wynter estate. The boys had played together as children, gone bird-nesting together, had shot rabbits in the lanes with rook rifles. Then, as usual in these relationships, they had split up in their teens when Harry Wynter had gone to Sandhurst and Burten to the Polytechnic on a Church scholarship.

EXTRACT FROM FIRST INTERVIEW WITH IRIS BURTEN, *78 (Eric's mother)* and DORIS PINK, *56 (nee Burten, Eric's sister). Interview took place at Pear Tree Cottage, Highclare, Hampshire, on 17 November, 1941.*

Mrs. Burten had inhabited the cottage since she married: two up, two down, with thatched roof. Picturesque from outside but dreadful interior. Floor of hard-packed earth. Only heating anti-quated range on which she did all cooking. Smelled strongly of drains and old frying. Mrs. Burten, thin, small, warts on hands, some facial hair. Doesn't resemble good-looking son.

Doris Pink, rolypoly, face like her name, kept on apologising for her mother. Seems the old lady thought at first we were talking about her other son, Claude, who had died of Spanish influenza in 1918, having survived the war.

Doris did most of talking. Covered much of ground already in papers about childhood friends, etc. Mrs. Burten kept repeating, 'He was a good boy. Knew more about pheasants than his dad.'

'It's not Claude, it's Eric he's on about. Not Claude, mother.'

When I put it to them that there were rumours, etc., always had been, Mrs. Burten said, 'What rumours?'

Mrs. Pink said it was time for her mother's rest and she took her upstairs. When she came down she said, 'I know what you want. You can't write that. It's dirt.'

I said I wasn't going to write dirt but the rumours were there. I wanted to deny them if possible, but had to know.

'There was never any of that.'

'What about bi-sexuality?'

'What?'

'Could he have liked men *and* girls?'

'I don't know what you mean, men and girls. That's real filth, that is. Don't you go asking mother. She wouldn't understand. I don't think I do myself. You mean there really are people like that?'

I said, yes, there were.

I pressed her and she said there may have been the usual boys' stuff. She said she had found her brother and Harry together in the lavatory of the big house once – she had been a parlour-maid there, as had her mother before her – but she thought this was natural. 'All boys get up to it. I've had five of me own and I could tell you things that'd make you sweat.'

She said that the estate had been a happy place until Harry Wynter had brought his wife there. When pressed she couldn't think of details, except that the new Mrs. Wynter wanted to run things 'her way', which upset many of the staff. The old lady, Harry's mother, was by this time almost bed-ridden with arthritis and simply handed over.

April 16. I'll never be able to keep this diary going every day. What am I to put down? Got up. Had breakfast. Drank a cup of beef tea at eleven. Lunch at one. Slept. Read the ship's newspaper. Is that the sort of thing publishers want? I've never been much good at writing. The Med. is looking very good and we should be in Naples in a day or two.

Burten's getting on now. Says he's begun to eat, which is excellent news. Poor chap lost about half a stone in the first few days. Jolly worrying, that, since there are only the two of us. It's rather a dull ship. People have started forming cliques already. There's a bridge clique and the chess clique and the deck-games clique. Then they all sit round together at the dance after dinner. The I.C.S. people talk about pegs and tiffin. We've got a long voyage ahead of us and if you pick wrong 'uns for company, you're saddled with them. Eddie Hollande seems to feel that way, too, but he's a cold fish to start with. I asked him to have a gin before lunch with me yesterday and he said he didn't drink in the daytime.

Don't know whether to try and avoid him or not. We do get together . . . why not, we've known each other all our lives? Yet there's something stiff and formal about him. I suppose there always has been. People look at us and you can see them thinking: those two are rivals, they're going to race against each other. Creates an artificial atmosphere.

The main thing is there's nothing to do. Can't get at the Abbott because she's locked away in Hold No. 4 in her own packing case. Burten spends a lot of the day designing extra fuel tanks for her. He doesn't think the one she's fitted with now will be adequate for the Black Gobi, especially if something untoward happens.

I go down to chat to him even though he's better now, or I send for him to come up and see me. I've always liked him and I know he wants to talk about carburettors and filters and universal joints. It's a good thing I'm not like Hollande. He doesn't understand the first thing about engineering. Leaves everything to Preece. Burten and I couldn't functiom that way. We both know about the mechanical side, but I'm not in his class.

He's always trying to improve things. He loves technology for its own sake. Once I couldn't find him, then I saw a pair of boots sticking out under the Abbott and when I bent down to look there he was, lying on his back, arms folded, not doing anything, just staring up at the bottom of the engine. I think it relaxed him. You get a feeling that he's superior to the machinery and that he knows it. He knows he can put it right if it goes wrong, but he's always thinking ahead a bit trying to improve it. Preece is nothing like him. He's small and dark and his skin is pitted with tiny black craters. It's almost as though he'd been cast in a foundry himself. I'm not saying he's not a good mechanic, but I don't think he's a patch on Burten. Burten's like the conductor of an orchestra, Preece is a euphonium in a brass band.

I know Burten goes down to steerage to talk to Preece. He's always got on well with him, but there's something sharp between the two of them now. I'm not sure what it is. Maybe it's because their masters are rivals, but I know Preece hasn't welcomed Burten. I don't think it makes much difference to him, he'd probably prefer to stay in his cabin with his drawings and his draughtsman's paper and his books on the internal combustion engine. I'm just the opposite. I'm like a racehorse at the start, except the crowds haven't arrived yet and there's a long time to wait before the off.

It's at night that I miss Mary. In the day, too, of course, but at night most of all. I'd never do for a monk. They say celibacy causes eczema. I'll have to watch my skin. I keep on thinking of the last time I saw her at Highclare. I said she shouldn't come to Tilbury. I wanted to say goodbye to her at home. I don't think she wanted to come, anyway. I'm glad she didn't. Abbott was embarrassing after he'd drunk too much. And all that business with the streamers and the bands as the tugs pulled us out into the Thames is said to be very affecting. The fact is, you can't really see anyone and there's always a crowd at the rail, shouting and waving, and half the people worse for drink. I think it was better the way it was.

I keep thinking of that last day. I always hate leaving Mary; always have; always will. We took the dogs for a walk. It was chilly for April and we were wrapped up. We walked to the top of Beacon Hill and looked down on Luscombe Park. Funny to think that Eddie was there. Funny to think that our estates march and the two of us are going ten thousand miles to race against each other and eventually hope to end up back in the same place just a few miles apart. To think that Mary nearly married him!

EXTRACTS FROM SECOND INTERVIEW, IRIS BURTEN, DORIS PINK AND

Old Mrs. Burten in big basket chair wrapped in blankets. Valerie pretty, fluffy bottle-blonde about twenty-one, nursing baby. Day very cold. We all sat close to range, but even so I was frozen. Don't see how Mrs. Burten has lived this long in this place. Chest very loose. Had been drinking tonic wine and was tipsy. Put to them questions about Mary Wynter they had not answered last interview (17/11/41). Then, Doris had said she couldn't remember what changes when Harry Wynter brought his wife back to the estate after marriage. Pressed her on this.

Mrs. Pink: 'It's a long time ago.'

Mrs. Burten: 'You never did have a memory. What about them keys?'

Mrs. Pink: 'Keys? What keys?'

Mrs. Burten: 'The cupboard keys. She took them.'

Mrs. Pink: 'Oh, yes. Before she came we never locked nothing. All the linen cupboards and the food cupboards and the store cupboards, all them cupboards were never locked 'cause no one took nothing. Well, not much, anyways. A little bit of food now and then. Well, I'd taken a piece of pie, game pie it was, been in the larder three days. Not more than a slice left. Why throw it out?'

Mrs. Burten: 'We never threw nothing out. Not what you could eat, anyways. In them days you didn't throw things out, not like today. Nowadays you throw everything away. Why, I've seen rubbish bins. . . '

Mrs. Pink: 'All right, mother. Anyways, she give me a telling off and from that time she carried the keys. We even had to ask her if we wanted a bit of silver polish. Didn't make for happiness.'

Mrs. Burten: 'And what about old Mrs. Wynter? She put 'er in a home. Gawd's truth. On the Isle of Wight. Think of that. They'll never do that to me. I tell you right now. I've got a shot-gun. It was me husband's. First person who comes to put me in a home, I'll shoot. And that's fair warning.'

Valerie: 'No one's going to put you in a home, gran.'

Mrs. Burten: 'Upstairs. Over me bed. Two cartridges. Been in there all the time.'

Mrs. Pink: 'Now, mother. (To me) There ain't any cartridges in the gun. Haven't been for years. But we don't let on.'

(I asked about rumours that Hollande had been engaged to Mary Wynter before marriage to Harry.)

Mrs. Burten: 'Not engaged. I don't think it was proper, with

78

a ring and all. But it was understood, if you know what I mean. In them days people did that. They had an understanding. I had an understanding with Mr. Burten. Five years. Then two years engaged. People don't wait these days: All they care about. . .'

Mrs. Pink: 'Mother, I think you should have your rest now.'

Mrs. Burten: 'I don't want a rest. I rest all the time. Never see nobody. But then when he – Mr. Wynter – won the Sword of Honour and then all them car races and records, she breaks off with Mr. Hollande and marries Mr. Wynter. Her family was from these parts. Father was an Archdeacon in Winchester. At the Cathedral. They all knew each other. Balls and picnics. London parties. Nowadays they don't have no more balls. It's all jazz and nightclubs and them Andrews Sisters. Why, when we had a picnic we used. . .'

Mrs. Pink: 'You're dribbling, mother. And you've had enough tonic wine. You'll be at the brandy next.'

Mrs. Burten: 'Brandy? You don't let me 'ave no brandy.'

(I asked her what Mrs. Wynter had been like.)

Mrs. Burten: 'Dressed like a duchess, she did. Didn't want nobody finishing up a bit of pie, yet she spends money like water. Oh no, nothing too good for 'er. Doris, you fetch that photo. Show the gentleman.'

Mrs. Pink: 'Where is it?'

Mrs. Burten: 'In the box in the bedroom.'

(Mrs. Pink went upstairs.)

Mrs. Burten: 'Pass me that medicine, Val.'

(Val gave her the bottle of tonic wine which Mrs. Pink had placed on table out of her reach.)

Valerie: 'Don't you say I give it you, gran.'

Mrs. Burten: 'They don't allow me nothing these days. Always just say, "There's a war on." '

(Asked her about Eric. Did he like girls?)

Mrs. Burten: 'Engines. He liked engines. Give 'im a piece of machinery and he was happy as a lark. Right from the time he was a baby. Anything with oil or grease on it. Turn his hand to anything. He was a good boy. Funny to think of 'im lying out there in China.'

Mrs. Pink: (Shouting from upstairs): 'I can't find it.'

Mrs. Burten: 'In the box, by the window. You tell her, Val, I can't shout. (To me) Engines, petrol engines . . . cars . . . that was Eric. Cars. Crazy about them. Didn't think of nothing else. We called them automobiles in them days. Dirty smelly things.

Always making dust. But Eric loved them. No . . . Harry was the one for girls.'

(Mrs. Pink returned.)

Mrs. Pink: 'Is that the one?'

Mrs. Burten: 'Show the gentleman.'

(Photograph was six by eight, mounted on heavy cardboard with words, 'Glanville Studios, Winchester' on the bottom. Showed young woman in her twenties standing in front of a scrap-screen with hands loosely folded on fiddle-backed chair. Thin, fine-boned face, almost pre-Raphaelite.)

Mrs. Burten: 'Never wanted another child after the little boy. Never had one.'

Mrs. Pink: 'That's true. Never married again.'

Valerie: 'Weren't she beautiful!'

Mrs. Pink: 'D'you think so? I wouldn't have said *beautiful*.'

Mrs. Burten: ' "Course she was. Known for it. But hard as nails.'

April 22: Some diarist! Haven't written a word for days and now find I've forgotten to put in the London *Daily News* man. It's really only because of their prize for the first Briton home that I'm in the race, and I overlook him. The reason was, he's been sick too. The grippe, apparently. Must have got it just before he came aboard, and it laid him low. Anyway, he made his appearance after we left Naples and wanted an interview with Eddie and myself. He's a decent enough chap. About thirty-five, I'd say, smooth and plump. Sweats all the time and niffs a bit. Looks like an overgrown baby and wears the same white cotton drill suit all the time. He's got shrewd eyes, though. You don't work for a newspaper like the London *Daily News* if you're a fool. It's not the sort of paper I like to read, but you've got to admire its professionalism. His name is Maurice Ives, and he takes his own pictures.

He interviewed us in the First Class library after it had closed. Purser only too glad to give permission. We talked about the race and the other competitors. He asked about us: the usual sort of stuff about our rivalry. I thought Eddie would freeze him. He usually does chaps like Ives. Stares down his nose at them until they go away. But not this time. I was amazed. On his best behaviour. Courteous. Took everything very seriously. It was only when Ives touched on the fact that I had held the Land Speed Record for a time that the look I know so well came over his face. Don't know how to describe it, really. Sort of blank, empty. Ives must have sensed he was on delicate ground because he passed onto something else and then took us up to the deck to pose for pictures.

Again David and Julie studied a photograph. Hollande and Wynter standing at the rail of the ship. Wynter, on the right, was the taller of the two. His hair was loose and was being caught by the wind. He had a pipe clenched in his teeth and was smiling. He had dark hair, his face was narrow and the cheek-bones were high. He had a long, straight nose. Altogether he looked an engaging and amusing character, full of life. Hollande was different. He was shorter, squarer, more powerfully built. His dark hair was parted in the middle and brushed carefully to both sides of his head. He must have been using Macassar oil or pomade for his head shone and none of the hairs had been blown out of place. Where Wynter wore an open-necked shirt, Hollande wore jacket and bow tie. He stared at the camera, a serious, ponderous-looking man.

Attached to the back of the picture was a cutting from the London *Daily News*. It was a reproduction of the same picture. Much of the detail had been lost by the block-makers. It was headed 'The Rivals', and underneath was a deep caption that read: 'From our Special Correspondent. Aden. Britain's two most famous automobilists on the *Orient Star* in the Red Sea. Capt. Harry Wynter and Capt. Edward Hollande, long-standing rivals in automobile racing, are seen together on the voyage out to China, where they will compete with each other and automobilists from Europe in the Pekin to London race. The London *Daily News* has offered a prize to the first Briton home. So one of the above could prove to be the winner of £30,000 – but he will have to finish the race within three months and in the automobile in which he started.'

NOTE: London *Daily News* had put up prize money because French motor industry was getting big lead. *LDN* was flag-waving paper up to late twenties, offering big prizes for flying, climbing, sailing, motoring, etc., until it collapsed under weight of its own patriotism in 1930.

May 9: Thank God, the really hot weather is behind us. The Red Sea is a dreadful place. We had air-scoops out on every porthole but the air we scooped seemed to come from a furnace. The public rooms were boiling, even though the fans were going all the time. Pimms and gin slings were the order of the day. Burten's cabin is on the starboard side; the hottest side. The poor fellow couldn't sleep, so during the worst of the weather I had him up with me since I have a stateroom with a sofa. Anyone with money and experience travels port out and starboard home.

But now we're in piping weather. Still warm, of course, in the Indian Ocean, and still in the tropics, but not that dragon's breath that dried one's tobacco to sand. I don't look forward to the Black Gobi at all. Still, we should be well out of it before the really hot weather starts. Touch wood.

Burten's still worried about fuel. He thinks if we miss a dump it could mean the end of the race for us, and I think he's right. There'll be enough fuel in the dumps all right. It's just a matter of getting to them. Fuel and water are going to be the big problems in the Gobi. Once we get past that we're in more settled country. Although even in the Gobi itself there are nomads. Last reports I heard were that tribesmen on the border of southern Mongolia had come into the Gobi and were marauding. Just our luck. Although I can't think what a nomad would want with an automobile – or with petrol, for that matter.

When I'm not working on the new fuel tank design with Burten, I go over our carnets and specification papers. They're six inches thick! Wonder what the Chinese Customs will make of it all?

I entered the deck games for a bit of fun. At least, that was the plan. But of course Hollande has now put his name down too, so I've had to take things seriously. He beat me easily enough in the bucket quoits and then I won at the new game of ping-pong. This afternoon we played a mixed doubles at deck tennis. I was partnered by LS. Eddie's lady was a lean and hungry widow from Ooty who played like a Dervish. It should just have been good fun, but it wasn't. I think it started with a disputed decision: was the ring in or out of the court? That sort of thing. There was a bit of an argument.

Eddie thought it was out, I thought it was in. A few spectators had collected and that made things more tense. We beat them in the end by the odd point or two.

Then Eddie lost his temper. No one else would have noticed, but I've known him long enough. He loses it in an odd way. Coldly. He doesn't go red in the face and stamp his feet, but something betrays him. He loses control of himself. This time he threw the ring at me. People who play this game ashore usually have a rubber ring. At sea it's a heavy ring made of twisted rope and smelling of Stockholm tar. It hit me just above the bridge of the nose. He was very profuse in his apologies of course. Said he thought I was ready and all that. Ready for what? We'd just finished. It's taken the skin off and it bled a bit, but LS did a nursing job on it in my cabin. Nothing serious, but she was very indignant. She thinks he did it on purpose. I played it down. One doesn't want things to get out of hand. Already there's too much talk of rivalry, and Ives, even though he's in Second, might easily get to hear.

Later I remembered something that had happened years ago when we were at prep school. I think it was the first time Eddie and I clashed. We couldn't have been more than eleven or twelve. We were running the quarter and he and I had left the rest of the field behind. There wasn't more than a couple of feet in it and as I crossed the line first, he spiked me. Said he was sorry, and all that. A friend of mine who was watching said it had been deliberate. But I never knew. It took a long time to heal because he'd damaged a tendon. Of course, it might have been an accident. Who knows? And does it matter? The point is that Eddie doesn't like to lose. I don't, either.

NOTE: Fuel business needs comment. It became vital later on in Gobi.

Two big oil companies were involved in the race: the Nobel Company, which held mineral concessions all over the Russian Empire and owned the Baku oilfields. And the Asiatic Petroleum Company, which was much smaller. Hollande was dealing with Nobel, Wynter with Asiatic. But the organisation which had the responsibility for guaranteeing the fuel supply during the race, was the Russo-Chinese Bank, because it had a network of officials in all the major towns on the route, at least until the drivers reached Europe.

The main problem, as Burten had foreseen, was the provision of oil, petrol and spare parts. He and Wynter had designed extra tanks. My father had discussed this with Burten on board, but Hollande pooh-poohed the idea. The Abbott could carry eighty-four gallons of petrol and thirty-five gallons of oil. Theoretically, if the Abbott could do seven miles to the gallon this would give it a range of about 600 miles. The fuel dumps were up to 450 miles apart. But this was only on paper, for in deep sand the Abbott would do less than seven and the Bulldog-Saxon, a heavier car, would be even worse off.

Note first mention of letters LS in Diary. Took me some time to discover what they stood for. Because of war the Star Line had moved records from Cockspur Street to a depository in Eltham. After several applications, I managed to see passenger list for Orient Star's voyage to Shanghai April/May, 1910. Several names with the initials LS but was soon able to reduce this to one since others were male and Harry Wynter had been playing mixed doubles. LS stood for Lucy Somerville. Copies of ship's newspaper also on file and all first-class passengers got a few lines. She was wife of official in Shanghai and Oriental Banking Co. and was returning to Shanghai. Managed to track her down through Chartered Bank of Hong Kong which took over Shanghai and Oriental Banking Co. in thirties. She was in charge of Leicester Square canteen which served hot meals, tea and coffee to soldiers in uniform twenty-four hours a day. Her husband had died in 1937. She lived on his pension in flat in Eccleston Square. Canteen was in disused cinema between Leicester Square and Gerrard St. Queues of servicemen in street outside waiting to get in. Dingy sort of place, but very busy. Made myself known to her but she said I'd have to wait. Sat at one end of long trestle table on a bench until nearly midnight. Then I only got to speak to her because of an air raid. Soldiers left to shelter in Leicester Square tube. Mrs. Somerville said she was too tired to go. We sat in empty cinema hearing bombs drop on City and Fleet Street. She was then in her early sixties. Rather stout. Faded light brown hair. Light blue eyes. Possible to see she must have been attractive once. She was about thirty when she was a passenger in *Orient Star*.

EXTRACT FROM INTERVIEW WITH MRS. LUCY SOMERVILLE. *12 March, 1942.*

'I'd taken Jeremy, who was nine then, from Shanghai to stay

with his grandparents in Hove. He was going to his preparatory school. The return voyage was the first time I'd been entirely free of any responsibility since I'd been married. Wonderful feeling.

'I'd heard of Harry Wynter, of course. A lot of people had, you know, because of the Land Speed record. But that was all. Just what I read in the newspaper. I wasn't really even very interested in automobiles. My husband used to mention the record. I mean, we saw all the newspapers and magazines we wanted to at the Club in Shanghai. Of course, a ship is a small place. You soon get to know who's who, especially if they're sitting at the Captain's table. I was at the Purser's. So I was flattered when Harry Wynter asked me to be his partner.

'We'd noticed each other. There were dances after dinner every night and I'd danced with him once or twice. He was very good. Light. Held you firmly. And we'd said good morning on deck. That sort of thing. Anyway, he asked me to partner him in the deck tennis. The match was the first time I'd spoken to General Hollande – not that he was a general then. We all knew who he was, too. People talked about the race and their rivalry. Rather exciting, really, to have them aboard.

'They were very different. Harry Wynter was taller. I can't remember his face very clearly, but he had a nice straight nose. A good looking man as well as attractive, if you know what I mean. A charmer. Hollande? Shorter, stockier, powerful looking. I suppose some women would have found him attractive. There was something closed about him, though, almost as if there was a notice on his back which said KEEP OUT. I remember in that game you mentioned Harry was hit on the nose, quite a hard blow with the ring. It bled a bit. I had some peroxide and I went to his stateroom to clean it up. There was a young man there, his mechanic. Can't remember his name. He was working on some papers and he left when we came in.'

(Just then a bomb went off very close by. Discovered later it was in Trafalgar Square. Asked Mrs. S. if she wanted to go to shelter. She refused.)

'We saw quite a lot of each other after that. Dances. Tombola. Horse-racing. The usual games they have on board. The ship's sweep. He was fun to be with.'

(I asked her if she was aware of the allegations about Wynter and Burten.)

'There was some talk in the Club later. I thought it was

nonsense. Why? You would have had to know Harry Wynter. It was just silly, that's all.'

(I asked her about the relationship between Wynter and Hollande.)

'Well, there was the business about the deck-tennis game. I'm not sure they saw too much of each other. It's not difficult to understand why. There was tension. I mean, they were going on this adventure – call it what you like – and no one knew what would happen. There'd be danger. They might be killed. And I had a feeling there were money problems. Harry didn't talk much about it but I sensed that all was not as it should be. On the other hand, everyone knew how wealthy Hollande was. I think that was a problem. I think it was either just before or just after Singapore that Hollande gave his big cocktail party. He'd won a few pounds on the day's run but that was nothing to what it must have cost him. He invited the whole of the First Class. Served nothing but Bollinger. Pots of Beluga. That kind of thing. Harry could never have done that. I think the race meant a lot to him. I mean, the money part. I remember saying something about if he won and he turned on me and said, not if, when. I had the feeling he couldn't afford to lose.'

(Pressed her on Burten.)

'I don't know what happened before or later, but I can tell you that there wasn't anything going on between them on the ship that I knew of. And I would have known, because we saw quite a lot of each other.'

May 14: I'm sorry now that Eddie Hollande and I chose the same ship. I think it would have been better all round if we hadn't seen each other until we got to China. Apart from all the other considerations, I mean the natural tension and the fact that people expect us to be rivals, there has always been a characteristic of Eddie's that has put my back up. He's the perfect prefect. Head boy. He wears a self-righteous expression all the time. Holier than thou. I'm not saying he's not a good organiser – he is – he used to organise me, or try to, when I was a lad. Sometimes I'd let him in small ways, just to make life easier.

I remember at school and at Sandhurst, whenever we were playing games and went to the showers afterwards, Eddie would always take two towels: one to stand on. He'd have his shower and then put one towel down on the concrete floor and stand on it to dry himself with the other. At Sandhurst they laughed at him but that didn't seem to bother him. As I got to know him I realised why he did it: he didn't like to touch things that others had touched, especially in environments like shower rooms and communal bathrooms.

He was always very neat. Still is, for that matter. I remember seeing his locker for the first time. Everything was folded neatly, everything in its place. Mine looked like the threepenny stall at a rummage sale.

Most of the time he made no comment on my habits, there was just a look of faint contempt on his face. But sometimes he couldn't resist saying something. He used to wash the laces of his rugger boots, for instance, then put whiting on them. Mine were filthy. He said to me one day, 'You know, Wynter, you let the whole side down dressing like that.' I told him to mind his own business. He was dropped soon after that, so it didn't matter. He wasn't much good at rugger. Dogged is the best description. He played lock. No flair. I was captain then. I think he always held it against me that he was dropped, but I had nothing to do with the team selection.

What I object to is his taking this attitude into adult life. He doesn't approve of me. All right, that's his privilege. But when he starts on my behaviour I feel like throwing him overboard . . . which is what almost happened last night. I was with LS in the Verandah Lounge after dinner, smoking a quiet cigar, when he came up and asked if he could have a word with me. We went and stood a little apart at the rail. It was a warm, calm evening in the China Sea and there were better people to stand at ships' rails with than Eddie. I asked him what the problem was and he said that people were beginning to talk. At first I thought he meant about me and LS, but he explained it was about Burten. He said some of the other passengers were annoyed that Burten was spending so much time in First Class. It wasn't done to have one's mechanic up in First. He said he felt the same way himself, and wondered why he was even travelling Second Class, especially as Preece was in Steerage.

I told him we weren't at school now and he wasn't a prefect

any longer, but if he really felt bad about it he should cut along and see the Captain, otherwise leave me in peace.

LS was only about ten yards away and she must have heard because I heard her laugh. He must have heard her too. His face suddenly dropped into that expressionless mould which I knew from prep school days. Thought he was going to say something, but he didn't, just walked away.

LS was amused when I told her. She says Shanghai is full of people like Hollande. In some way he reminded her of her husband – and wasn't it a good thing *he* wasn't there?

NOTE: Make point that at their prep school it had looked as though Hollande was the boy of destiny. He'd been a monitor, then head boy. Had played in the teams, been captain of cricket. But he'd begun to slide at Sandhurst. Wynter used the word 'dogged' to describe him in the *Diary* and this seems right. It was as if he didn't have a natural talent for anything in particular but often got there by perseverence and hard work.

May 29: A lot has happened since I last wrote. First, I'm not in the *Orient Star* any longer, but aboard a German coaster, the *S.S. Woermann*. So is Eric Burten, so are the Abbott Special and the Bulldog-Saxon, and Percy Preece. But no Hollande. We're landing the motors at Tientsin and then taking them to Pekin on the railway and I was told the *Orient Star* couldn't berth at Tientsin because the water is too shallow at the mouth of the Peh-ho River. We didn't go up to Shanghai itself, but when we anchored off Woosung, the motors in their crates were lifted out of Hold No. 4, transhipped to lighters and then reloaded into this ship.

My plan had been to do what Eddie Hollande has done, go up-river from Shanghai and then take the Hankow Railway to Pekin; much faster that way and much more comfortable. But I haven't been able to leave Burten. Hollande will have Ives for company, which he won't like.

Thought Burten had recovered from his seasickness at the beginning of the voyage, but now I wonder. In fact, I wonder whether it wasn't seasickness plus something else. He's never really got back to the Burten I knew in England, full of enthusiasm and optimism. Not that he's been lying about, we've done a great deal of work together redesigning the

88

Abbott's body. It's just that he's not a hundred percent fit, not even eighty percent. So when we transhipped the motors I decided to go with him. Didn't even put a toe ashore in Shanghai.

LS and I had stayed up to watch the dawn. We passed the Saddle Islands in the mist and the lightship off Nanhui and then came into the great mouth of the Yangtze itself. We stood up in the bows and I admit I could feel a tight knot in my stomach. I kept on saying to myself: 'This is China, this is where it'll begin.' Up to now it's been a holiday. But from the moment we get the Abbott ashore things will change. So much depends on the outcome that I daren't even think of losing. And here's Burten not up to snuff.

I noticed that the closer we got to land, the less I seemed to recognise LS. In those few hours between dawn and disembarkation she changed into someone different. By the time I said good-bye to her she had her hat on and was more intent on counting her pieces of baggage than saying good-bye. I think she was relieved that I wasn't going ashore.

Apparently we're going to be the last to arrive in Pekin. There were two ships through a week ago, the Messageries Maritimes *Dieppe* and the Norddeutscherlloyd's liner *Bismarck*. There are more starters than we'd thought. We knew about the French and the Italians, but now there are also German and Dutch. I'm not worried, the Abbott is the best there is; I put up the Land Speed record in an Abbott. Hollande, particularly, doesn't like the French.

This coaster isn't bad, I suppose, as coasters go, but after First Class on the *Orient Star* it leaves something to be desired. Black bread, sauerkraut, wurst, wurst, wurst – and when it isn't sausages, then it's pork, pork, pork. Burten's longing for tea and roast beef and, if the truth were known, so am I. He's not happy, but doesn't complain.

We've also got Percy Preece on board. There is only one class here, so we all muck in together. Burten and I share a cabin, Preece is with a Chinese gentleman travelling to Tientsin. I think Preece feels it's infra dig, but it should be the other way round. The Chinese gentleman is a judge. Anyway, Preece complains a lot. He doesn't like the food either, but where Burten says nothing, Preece is voluble.

Can't find anything decent to say about the ship or the Germans or the Chinese. He's also got rather nasty habits. Smokes a lot – Woodbines – and when we're in the saloon he uses the saucer of his cup as an ashtray then drops the butt into the cold remains of his coffee.

Burten is worse off in the coaster. The weather's relatively calm but being a small vessel the movement is greater. I'm hoping his seasickness doesn't catch up with him again. It'll weaken him and that's what I'm afraid of.

It was sad parting from LS. This struck me later when I was already aboard the *Woermann*. Now I can hardly remember her face. It always seems to rise in my imagination with Mary's features. It is she I'm missing, not LS.

NOTE: When I saw Captain Wynter in Kashgar in 1939 he warned me that the diaries contained unpleasant references to my father, and apologised for them, but said he hadn't changed them because that's how he felt at the time. He was right about one thing: my father did smoke Woodbines. My memory of him is having the butt, sometimes not even alight, stuck in the corner of his mouth. He had a slight yellow streak on his upper lip from the smoke. I can't ever remember him putting his cigarettes out in saucers or teacups, but my mother may have put a stop to that.

Point about Hollande's reaction to the newspaperman Ives is interesting. Hollande always very good with the press. He seemed to know how to handle reporters and always managed to get a good press, even when some of the things he did were disastrous, like the South American 'Lost City' expedition.

June 10: Well, we've arrived! Pekin at last! Not quite accurate: we got here two days ago. I should have written then, I should have been writing every day. I keep telling myself that I'll write in the evening or after breakfast, or any time that isn't now. I'd rather drive a thousand miles than write a page.

Everything went smoothly until Pekin. We got the motors ashore at Tientsin and, apart from some sea-damp which had penetrated the cases and affected the ignition, they were both as good as gold. Burten and I helped Preece get the Bulldog out of its crate and running, and he helped us.

There's a British colony at Tientsin and they gave us a

rousing welcome and we ran the motors up and down the streets – well, you'd hardly call them streets, alleys more like it – frightening the bullock drivers and being sworn at by the rickshaw coolies. Curious thing is that although the locals had never seen a motor until the other drivers came through they don't seem terribly interested. When I drove through the Balkans last year villagers used to collect and wait for the motor to arrive. Here the Chinese look away as though pretending we're not there.

Lots of rumours were flying around Tientsin. I heard that the other drivers had been arrested, that the motors had been impounded and, most incredible of all, that the race was off. It was only when we reached Pekin that we found that things were better in some ways and worse in others. I'd better try and give a picture of where we are and what's happening right now, and not put this diary off to be written tomorrow.

We – all the drivers and their mechanics – are encamped outside the city gate. We're not allowed in – at least, not in our motors – and those are the direct orders of Na-Tung, the General Commandant of the Pekin Gendarmerie. He has issued an edict: if we want to come through the gate we come on foot. We've all agreed that that is nonsense. I say all, we haven't seen Eddie Hollande yet because there have been flash floods along the Hankow railway and part of an embankment collapsed onto the line. I'm informed by the British Minister here that they are being brought along by cart and camel. Hollande won't like that. In the meantime, we could do with a bit of rain here. Every day a wind comes up, blowing dust and more dust until we feel it in our eyes and up our noses. We try and keep the motors covered. The dust gets in everywhere and we don't want to start off with carburettor trouble – that's if we start at all. The rumours that the race will have to be abandoned are strengthening every hour.

NOTE: Insert here chunk historical background. In 1910 China was on the verge of change and the revolution, which was to put Sun Yat-sen in power, was only eighteen months away. The Empress Dowager was dead, the new Emperor was only two years old and the Regent, Prince Ch'un, was trying to drag China back into the great days of the Manchus. But the Boxer Rebellion

91

had taken place ten years earlier and China had been defeated by the foreign barbarians. In Pekin itself ten western countries, including those who had drivers in the race, kept garrisons of soldiers. Power lay with the conquerors and not with the Chinese, even though the Grand Council of the Celestial Empire, the Wai Wu Pu, still issued edicts. Na-Tung, whom Wynter calls the General Commandant of the Pekin Gendarmerie, was also Grand Secretary of State, Manchu President of the Grand Council, and Acting President of the Department of the Interior, a very powerful figure indeed. It was learned later that his objections to the race were twofold: he suspected that what were called the 'oil chariots' – there was no word for motor in the Chinese language, just as there wasn't for steam engines, which were called 'fire chariots' – were a way of bringing weapons into the Forbidden City; the other reason was that drivers would have to leave Pekin by the north-western route through a gap in the Great Wall. This was the direction from which most major attacks on Pekin had occurred. It was a sensitive, strategic part of the country.

For these reasons the Chinese began a series of delaying tactics and the man caught in the middle was the British Minister, E. V. Henshilwood. According to reports in *De Telegraaf* of Amsterdam and *Corriere della Serra* of Milan, Mr. Henshilwood had been affronted by having to organise the rally in the first place. He felt it beneath the dignity of his office, but organise it he had.

The Chinese now used a familiar weapon: they tangled everything up in a web of bureaucracy. Since the automobilists were foreigners, they were the responsibility of the Foreign Ministry. But since Na-Tung had specifically accused them in the Council of being enemy spies, they were also the concern of the War Minstry. Then there were the routes to be driven. Dutch, German, French and Italian drivers were taking the northern route through Mongolia to Lake Baikal, following an ancient caravan route. The two British competitors were crossing the Black Gobi to Urumchi on the old Silk Route. Therefore they were also the responsibility of the Ministry of Posts and Communications. The whole endeavour needed the approval of the Imperial Grand Council.

Within minutes of their arrival the competitors were fast in this web of *firmans* and edicts, applications, proposals, counterproposals, forms to gain permissions and forms to gain forms to gain permissions. Each country had a Legation in Pekin and each country's minister ran from one department to the next, trying to overcome the delaying tactics – while the people who counted, the drivers, camped in tents outside the city gates.

In the meantime, rumours began to circulate that the motors were armed and that once entry was effected they would fire indiscriminately on the inhabitants. These rumours were believed to such an extend that the *North China Herald and Supreme Court and Consular Gazette* carried a story stating that banners had been placed in several quarters of the city bearing the legend: 'The chi-cho (oil chariot) must not pass.'

June 15: One moment we hear we're going to be allowed into the city, the next we aren't. We can go in without the motors, but all of us have agreed to stand firm: either we drive in or we don't go in at all. We are in tents lent us by the Legations, with all that implies about food, water and bodily functions. And talking of bodily functions, we're all suffering from a strange affliction brought on by the dust in the air. This is dried human manure blowing off the nearby fields. Many of us have coughs and inflamed eyes. We protest twice and sometimes three times a day, each nationality taking it in turns, but we don't get anywhere. Henshilwood, the British Minister, is not a bad fellow, but he's not very effective. He's let it be known that he considers the whole thing to be childish. You can see it by his manner. He's tall, round-shouldered, with a heavy moustache and thin, greying hair. Bookish sort of chap. I know he wishes he'd never had to organise the race, or what the French call the *raid*, in the first place. He has a point, I suppose. He has to continue here and live with the Chinese once we go.

June 20: A new edict from the Grand Council: the motors are to be allowed into the City! Henshilwood came down to let us know this decision. We had grouped ourselves in a small crowd between the tents and he climbed up onto the running board of the Abbott to make the announcement. We were about to cheer when he told us the condition: we would not be allowed to *drive* the motors under their own power; each would have to be pulled by two mules. This was ludicrous! It seems that the Grand Council, as well as delaying us, also wants to humiliate us.

We held a vote then and there and agreed to stand firm. But an hour later we saw two mules being led out of the City towards us and harnessed to the French motor, a Panhard-Levassor. We stood and watched the French being pulled into the City. I know we all felt bitter, but managed to contain our feelings, except for one of the Italian mechanics, who spat at the French as they passed. In the midst of all this, Hollande arrived.

He'd had a hell of a time, I heard later. The floods had cut the railway line and he'd had to come on by camel. He had pushed on ahead of his fellow-passengers, including Ives, and was now hot, tired and dusty, and in a filthy mood. After I'd explained what had occurred he went off to search for Henshilwood. I went with him because I could see he was on the verge of rage and I didn't want anything untoward happening. We found Henshilwood with a group of Chinese officials near the gate. Eddie brought him back to the camp. I was almost going to say, dragged him back. He took him by the elbow and there wasn't much Henshilwood could do.

He told Henshilwood to get into the Bulldog-Saxon and told Preece to start it. Henshilwood began to protest but Eddie said, who ran China, the Christians or the Chinese savages? Eddie got up into the driver's seat and told Preece to get into the back. In a cloud of smoke he started off towards the Gate of Heavenly Peace. The officials were standing nearby and Chinese soldiers were guarding the opening. Hollande simply opened the throttle and charged them. Everyone fled.

Hollande drove several times up and down the Imperial road as though to show who was who and what was what. The Germans cheered like mad and got their own motor started, then the Italians and the Dutchmen, and I shouted to Burten to start up the Abbott and we formed a kind of convoy and drove into the City as though we had a perfect right. Which we did. We found out later that there was no power that the Chinese possessed under the Boxer Treaty to keep us out. The Western foreigners cheered us. Eddie led the convoy in his Bulldog, then came the Germans in the Protos, the Dutch in the Spijker, the Italians in the Brixia-Zust, and Burten and myself in the Abbott. We passed the French, still being drawn along by the mules. We all looked dead ahead. No one jeered. We didn't have to.

It was wonderful to be in the motor again. We all went joy-riding round the Forbidden City for what remained of the day, and then moved into our hotels and had a decent meal and a bottle of wine and slept between sheets for the first time for what has seemed ages.

July 2: Still no news of whether we are going to start this race or not. The Dutch and Germans are talking of pulling out. It seems that whenever Henshilwood, or the other ministers overcome one objection, the Grand Council immediately puts forward another. They – the Chinese – now say that they cannot let us go into the hinterland because they cannot protect us! We say, in reply, that (a) they cannot stop us under the Treaty and (b) it's our business if we want to take the chance. They reply by saying that we are guests in their country and therefore their responsibility. And there's nothing even Hollande can do now, although he's done enough as it is. We were all carried away by the drive into Pekin and the air of Hail the Conquering Hero. The trouble is, the Chinese don't hail conquering heroes, they resent them. Now they resent us even more than they did. The French, on the other hand, have been given a pat on the back for allowing their motor to be drawn by mules and put into accommodation in the Forbidden City, a great treat. The Grand Council – according to Henshilwood – doesn't like the French any better than any other group, they only do this as a kind of slap on the wrist to us.

Hollande spends all his time in the Legation reading six-week-old copies of *The Times* and badgering Henshilwood. The poor man's life is made a misery.

If it wasn't for the frustration of not knowing if we've come all this way for nothing, I might be enjoying myself. Pekin is fascinating. A lot of it must be what London was like in the eighteenth century: narrow, filthy streets on the one hand, spacious gardens and magnificent temples on the other. Immense riches and abject poverty go side by side and you can see the two in close proximity at Kierulfs, the only Western store allowed in Pekin. Carriages draw up at the doors all afternoon and evening and beautiful young women like enamelled figurines hobble in on their mutilated feet, guarded by fat eunuchs, while outside, if a horse defecates, two or three manure-sellers fight for the steaming droppings and carry them off for sale. You'd never think that the Manchu dynasty is said to be crumbling. Princes still stroll about the streets followed by their concubines and singing girls. Some even have eunuchs walking in front to drive the hoi polloi out of the way. And that applies to everyone, Westerners and coolies alike. So we tend to keep to the Legation Quarter, which has had a wall built around it since the Chinese armies besieged it in the Boxer Rebellion. There we are received with some respect. Outside it, even the rickshaw coolies look down their noses at us.

Pekin is an odd place. It reminds me of one of those box mazes. At the centre is the Forbidden City with its palaces and pagodas. Round it is the Imperial City with its Government offices. It, too, is surrounded by a wall. Beyond the wall lies the Tartar City, with the Chinese City like a growth on its southern ramparts.

The Abbott is parked at the rear of the hotel and Burten and I have stripped the bodywork. It now has two spare fuel tanks, a wooden chest to hold tools and spare parts, and we have removed the rear seat because there will only be the two of us and we want to save weight. From the upstairs of the hotel we can look towards the Western Hills. These are going to be our first great obstacle. How will we get through them? *Will* we get through them? Will we even be allowed to try? We don't know. As yet we don't even have permission to carry out a survey there.

NOTE: It became clear after a while that the delaying tactics employed by the Chinese were meant to keep the motorists there until the rains set in. The Chinese hoped they would then pack up and go away.

The new fuel tanks on the Abbott meant that it could probably carry more petrol and oil than any other motor in the race. The dumps had been set up months before by camel train and of course no one was certain what might have happened to them. In a rally of this kind, the drivers had to take a great deal on trust.

Think a map here might help.

July 10: Rain. It's been raining now for five days. The alleys are like muddy canals. We've had rain before, but this seems set in. Nothing more calculated to reduce one's spirits especially after what happened yesterday.

We all – that is, the drivers – met in the boardroom of the Russo-Chinese Bank to listen to Henshilwood. It seems that the Chinese are now saying that it's too late in the year to start and that if we leave the motors in Pekin we could begin again next year! Don't they realise what could happen to the carefully-prepared plans over a year? There is not even a garage in Pekin where we could store the cars and where there could be some maintenance done. And who would stay to look after them? The whole situation is hopeless. These people live in another century with their carts and their palanquins and rickshaws, their princes and concubines and lords of this and lords of that and celestial this and celestial that. If we leave now, we leave for good and the race is over, finished. But the Chinese would only say, good, splendid, the sooner you leave, the better! We've told Henshilwood to keep on pressing them.

The rain, of course, will make motoring much more difficult, especially for the first part. It looks as though we shall all be together until Kalgan, which is past Nankow, then Hollande and I turn west.

Everyone is now talking about the Nankow Gorge and the road from Pekin to Kalgan. It isn't much more than fifty or sixty miles, but it's said to be mountainous and precipitous most of the way. If we fail on the first few miles we are going to look rather silly after having come all this way and waited all this time.

July 12: Another meeting in the Bank. Hollande was very rude to Henshilwood. He stood up and said he intended to leave Pekin by motor whether he, Henshilwood, or Na-Tung gave permission or not. Then he simply walked out. This seemed to stiffen everyone.

When I got back to the hotel I found Burten in bed running a slight fever. By this morning, it was gone. I don't like this up and down. If he'd got ill and recovered, I'd have been happier, but it seems to have been neither one thing nor the other. I'm going to ask a doctor at the Swedish Legation to look at him.

August 3: Hollande and I have started our final preparations. We were told not to leave the city – this applies to all the drivers – but we got horses from the Legation and simply rode out along the route we propose to take. No one tried to stop us. I think Hollande's tactics seem the best: do what you want to do and to hell with anyone else.

We cut bamboo poles the width of our cars and rode up into the hills to measure the width of the gorges. The cliff paths cut into them are terrifying. There are places where rocks jut out and Hollande, who has now organised a work-party of coolies, has ordered them to be widened.

August 17: Hollande has broken an agreement and acted like a cad. When we were surveying the Nankow Gorge and the mountain tracks on the road to Kalgan it became increasingly obvious that the motors will not be able to get through on their wheels. There are some parts that are so difficult – where the road simply disappears – that they will have to be carried. We talked about this and decided we would organise gangs of porters from one of the many contracting companies in Pekin. We were going to arrange this through Henshil-wood. But then Hollande acted on his own. He has made a private agreement with the haulage firm to put on as many men as they need and he will pay them four thousand francs to get his motor through the mountains.

It's an enormous price, almost exactly what we paid to ship the motors from England to China, and the firm is demanding that the rest of us match it if we want to use their coolies.

There is consternation among some of the others. The Italians are all right. Their motor is owned by Prince Cortese, who has half-a-dozen estates in Italy and who can match anything that Hollande pays. The same goes for Count de Reske of France. But the Dutch Spijker is a works entry and I'd heard that the company was in difficulties before we left. The German entry is shared between two enthusiasts from Berlin. I think they've spent most of their money getting here. The same applies to me.

(*P.M.*) This afternoon one of the Germans, with his Dutch colleague, came to me and asked if I could do anything to persuade Hollande to withdraw his offer and allow agents who know the value of such things to bargain with other haulage firms. I refused.

The news is all over the place now and the *North China Herald* is dubbing the rally 'the rich man's race'. The Dutch Minister has approached Hollande, but he is imperturbable. Says there is nothing in the rules which states that you cannot pay porters a decent wage. He was then asked why he didn't lighten the car – it weighs more than two tons – by taking off some of the body-work as others of us have done (he even has a huge picnic hamper and silverware). If he stripped the Bulldog he'd need fewer porters. He said as he understood the rules he was to drive the race in the motor which he had brought. He was not going to modify it for reasons of cost.

I went to see Henshilwood and told him that if we weren't careful the race was going to become a farce. He said he didn't see what he could do about it. Wished the whole damn thing had never happened.

The Press have the story, of course. Apart from Ives, there are several other journalists in Pekin, some of them resident correspondents and some who have come from Shanghai.

The Swedish doctor cannot find anything wrong with Burten. Says he should drink milk. Since the Chinese don't go in for dairy produce this doesn't help much.

NOTE: This financial crisis nearly wrecked the race, but it was saved by the Press itself. Once the stories appeared in their home countries, money was cabled to the Russo-Chinese Bank for the competitors.

The race meant everything to Wynter. His estate was mortgaged beyond any credible value. No one knew this at the time and everyone assumed him to be as well off as Hollande. Granted that four thousand francs was an unexpectedly heavy charge, no one in England considered it might be difficult for him. He does not disclose any of this in his *Diary*. It is a cool, understated document typical of the Edwardian male, and belies the panic he must have felt and which he admitted to me when I spoke to him in Kashgar. He told me he was about to go to the Bank to see if he could borrow, when Burten came forward. He had brought some savings with him which would cover the costs. After that, Wynter hardly spoke to Hollande.

September 4: I am writing this by the light of a storm lantern somewhere in the Western Hills. Burten is asleep. I am so tired I can hardly hold the pencil. But at least we are on our way at last. Somewhere not far off Hollande is also encamped and, I think, the others, although late yesterday I saw the Panhard by the side of the track with what looked like a broken half shaft.

'Track' is almost too good a word. It is one thing to have surveyed it on horseback and on foot, quite another trying to drive a motor along its surface. I have driven in the Balkans and Turkey but nothing I have yet encountered has been as bad as this. I feel sorry for the Abbott, it has taken such a battering and shaking already, yet we are not more than thirty-odd miles from the start.

I must go back a few days. As with all such events, nothing dramatic happened to change our situation. The Chinese, I think, must have been as exhausted with us as we were with them and decided that if we wished to die in the Gobi or in Southern Mongolia, that was up to us.

We were ready – had been ready for weeks. The rains had stopped and within twenty-four hours, passports being issued, we decided to leave. There was a garden party at seven o'clock in the morning in the grounds of the French Legation.

When it came time to leave at nine o'clock sharp the band played each country's anthem in turn, starting with the Dutch hymn *Wilhelmus van Nassouwe* and ending with *La Marseillaise*.

The band then led us out of the Legation grounds and up the Rue Marco Polo where peole were letting off fireworks, probably because they were so pleased to see us go. Soon, led by the Spijker, we approached the high, fortified wall of Pekin and left the city by the Gate of Virtue Triumphant. Almost at once we had to go down into our lowest gear for the road became a cart-track with the ruts and holes made worse by the recent rains.

We kept together for a while but then the motors began to string out. Some stopped for readjustments, others pushed on. I'm glad to say that the Abbott performed magnificently.

It needed to. What has nearly undone us right at the start is a river called the Cha Ho. When we had surveyed the route it had seemed possible to ford it, or at least have the motors carried across. But once we reached it we saw that there was nothing for it but to attempt to cross it on its own bridges. These are nearly a thousand years old and are built of blocks of marble six feet long and three feet wide. Over the centuries subsidence and massive neglect has caused the blocks to move away from each other, some to fall out completely. If this wasn't enough, the road to the bridges on either bank has vanished completely, eroded by the years, leaving the bridges standing up like monuments about twleve feet above the road.

This is where the coolie teams we've hired came into their own. They built platforms of earth in gigantic steps and levered each motor up until it reached the top of the bridge proper. We then half-carried and half-pushed, until we reached the other side, where similar platforms had been built. There each motor was lowered from one to another.

There were two such bridges and it took the whole day to negotiate them. At first I had calculated it would take us three or four days to get out of the mountains, through the Great Wall and up onto the Mongolian plateau. Now I think it will take at least double that time.

After the bridges Burten, who was driving, let the Abbott have its head over a short flat plain, then began the climb to the Nakow Gorge, where we are now encamped. The coolies have gone to spend the night in a village about three miles away.

(*Later*). A curious thing has happened. I was in the midst of writing this diary when I heard a noise outside the tent. I thought it might be a robber. I had my revolver handy so I opened the flap and held up a lantern and called out, 'What do you want?' – as though a Chinaman would understand what on earth I was saying! But it was Percy Preece. I knew that he and Hollande were not too far away, at least I'd seen their fire and the Bulldog-Saxon by the trackside. Now Preece told me that Hollande had left him. There's a railway line that runs between Pekin and Kalgan and passes about a mile from us. Preece said that when they had stopped for the day Hollande told him to pitch camp but that he, Hollande, was going back in the train to spend the night in the hotel in Pekin and would see him the following morning. As he spoke I could see Preece looked out of sorts. He's a gnomish, dark little man, who looks more like a tin-miner than a mechanic and when he'd finished telling me about Hollande he said he wondered if it would be all right if he spent the night near us. I realised that he was in a blue funk. Not that I blamed him. These mountains with their wild gorges and precipices remind me of some of the tangled glens of Scotland. There is a feeling of ancient gods and the supernatural, a strangeness that both Burten and I felt. (Burten slept through all this, by the way.) Preece had brought a pup tent along and pitched it next to ours. I gave him a stiff whisky – part of our medicinal supply – and he went off into the darkness to his own tent, much happier than when he'd arrived. It's typical of Hollande that he should have left Preece on his own while he spent a comfortable night. Apparently there is a train back about eight in the morning and he proposes to arrive on that.

September 5: A day of grinding struggle. Spent most of it with my heart in my mouth. We haven't come more than a few miles but, thank God, we're both still in one piece and so is the Abbott. The Nankow Gorge is a fearsome place. There, towering above one, is the dark mass of the mountains, the light sky above, and then a slit in the top of the mountain rather like a knife-cut, through which we had to find a way.

We were now about thirty miles from Pekin and we had to go up the gorge on what seemed to be the bed of a spate torrent. Fortunately, it was dry.

The foreman of our team of coolies – there were twenty of them – passed stout ropes around the brackets holding the springs. The team of coolies was split into two and they began to pull us up the gorge. Burten steered the Abbott as best he could. He was unable to sit because the bumps were so great he would have been flung out. Instead he stood for hour after hour, his knees bent to take the shock, while I ran on ahead trying to direct some of the coolies to get the bigger boulders out of the way or fill the deeper holes with stones.

Late in the afternoon we came to Nankow. Poor Burten's back was badly strained and we were glad to find an inn with a courtyard where we could park the Abbott. At that point I suppose we must have been lying in third place, although in a rally like this such positioning is meaningless. Just to finish a day with the motor still functioning is in itself a triumph. Hollande and Preece came in with the Bulldog at sunset.

We hadn't seen Preece in the morning, for when we woke he had already packed up his tent and gone back to his motor and they had remained behind us all day. Now they came into the yard of the inn, dusty and tired and worn, as we were ourselves.

I had some linament in the medical kit and I went to Burten's room to rub his back. The strain was at the base of his spine and we can't afford to have him in only partial working order. I had just started when Hollande came in without knocking and in a towering temper. This was a different kind of rage from the ones I knew so well. He started off by shouting, 'What the hell do you think you're playing at?' I didn't know what he meant but I wasn't going to have a row with him in front of Burten so I told him to go to my room, where I joined him in a few minutes.

It transpired that he was angry about Preece. Apparently, because Preece had left the Bulldog-Saxon, there had been some pilfering and various items had been stolen, including his picnic basket, the one containing his silverware. He was beside himself. I asked him what it had to do with me and he said I'd no right to allow Preece to remain and camp with us, that these people had no sense of responsibility and it was up to fellows like ourselves to see that they kept straight. I said that without 'these people' like Preece and Burten, with their skills, none of us would be here. Then he said, 'You're always sticking up for Burten.'

After a bit more he left and I went back to finish massaging Burten. I was told later that Hollande had gone off to Pekin on the train again.

I'm writing this now by the light of a wax taper. It's only nine o'clock but I'm dead beat. Missing Mary very much.

They gave us a greasy stew for supper. Goat, I think. We'll have to get used to it. We've decided that we can't take the tinned food. it's too heavy. We're going to buy our supplies locally: flour, dried apricots, that sort of thing, sustaining, but light. Also we shall have to get something against the cold. Last night it was bitter in the tent and tonight it's cold even in the room. Winter comes early in these parts and we're prepared only for hot weather travel.

September 8: We've been stuck in Nankow for the past two days, and it's Hollande's fault. We're all here now, all the motors and their crews, and every one of us could cheerfully murder him. The reason is that he brought the police back from Pekin.

Burten and I were in the market when they all arrived by train. We'd been buying our food supplies and we had also each bought a *poshteen*, the knee-length sheepskin coat of Central Asia. Smelly garments, a bit like cuddling up to an old wether, but they'll keep us beautifully warm. Also bought some fur caps.

The first we knew of what happened was when we were stopped by police in the market and told to bring our coolies to the courtyard of the magistrate's *yamen*. And this is where they've been for the past two days while they are questioned. They say, of course, that they didn't touch anything. Perhaps they're telling the truth. Any passer-by could have done the pilfering. I feel sorry for Preece. This is the sort of thing Hollande will brood about. He never forgives and forgets.

The French are particularly incensed about Hollande's behaviour because they have been brought back nearly forty miles. They say that they must have a complete day's start on everyone else when we get going again. Hollande is impervious to the anger he has aroused. He clearly believes he is in the right and the regaining of the picnic basket and the apprehension of the thief or thieves is much more important than the discommoding of the French, or anyone else, for that matter. One good thing, it's allowed time for Burten's back to get better. I rub it two or three times a day. We both smell strongly of linament.

EXTRACT FROM A LETTER FROM JACOBUS VAN DER MEER (*co-driver of the Spijker*), *Spuysstraat forty-one, Amsterdam, 10/6/48.*

'Yes, I remember very well the incident of Nankow. One of the English drivers, Captain Hollande, brought the police because of something stolen from his motor. I cannot now remember what. We must wait for three days while the police ask questions. For us, it was good. The Spijker has a broken wheel from the

104

Nankow Gorge and we must mend it by cutting and fitting new spokes. But the French are angry.

'You ask if I remember Captain Wynter. Yes, I do. I must say, he was different from Captain Hollande. More friendly with us. He and his mechanic are always together, they are very friendly. We called his mechanic 'pretty boy'.

'It is sad what happened to them.'

EXTRACT FROM INTERVIEW WITH GENERAL SIR EDWARD HOLLANDE, *Luscombe Park, Hampshire, 3/9/1950.*

Met by Victoria Hollande at Alton Station and driven to Luscombe Park. Hadn't seen her for many years. She came with her father once to our house. She dressed in trousers and leather flying-jacket. Attractive woman. Strong hands.

House stands in beautiful landscape of oaks, elms and beeches just off Fareham road; large, built of grey stone, tower at one end; looked Scottish.

Warning from V.H. that her father – always calls him 'the General' – not keen to see me, only doing so out of sentiment. Why didn't I write something about the Hollande Trust, which was important, occupying all their time? Told her I had always been interested in the race since my father had been part of it. V.H. sat in on interview.

We talked in conservatory filled with yellow and red begonias. General had been separating corms before I came. We sat in basket chairs. General was looking old. Dressed in grey herringbone tweed, Tattersal check shirt, regimental tie, polished brogues. Did I know what day it was? I'd forgotten it was anniversary of outbreak of World War II and he seemed rather put out. Big watery eyes, bags under them, slight tremor of the hands. Smokes heavily. Silver cigarette case. Taps cigarette each time on case, wets paper carefully with tongue, then lights with old-fashioned flip-top lighter. Grey moustache, grey hair, everything about him grey. Asked why I was writing book. Repeated what I'd said to V.H. Then he said of my father, 'Fine mechanic. Best I ever had.'

Asked him particularly about Nankow incident. Said he didn't know what I was talking about. Reminded him of picnic hamper and silverware. 'Oh, yes, I remember that,' he said. 'The hamper had belonged to my father. It was an extremely beautiful one. I think it had originally come from Garrards. Preece left the car strictly against my orders and of course . . . well, what can you expect in a country like that?'

105

Asked him if he remembered having a row with Captain Wynter about it.

'Row? I don't have rows.'

'Discussion then.'

'No, I don't.'

Asked him if he remembered going into Burten's room.

'The mechanic's?'

'Yes, sir.'

'I don't make a practice of going into servants' rooms.'

Said Captain Wynter was there rubbing Burten's back with linament.

'Was he now?'

'Was there . . . some sort of . . . relationship between the two of them?

'I don't know.'

V.H.: 'The General has never for one moment suggested. . .

The General (breaking in): 'You say you saw Wynter in thirty-nine. What was he like?'

'Thin, but fit enough.'

'I used to be much fitter. That's before I took these up. Filthy things, cigarettes.'

He had changed the subject skilfully and each time I came back to it he talked about something else. V.H. was becoming irritated. When I started talking about the central incident in the desert, the one concerning the fuel, the General excused himself. I thought he was going to the toilet, but he didn't come back.

V.H. annoyed. 'I told you he wouldn't talk about that.' Then: 'You seem very sure of the details. It's years ago that you saw Harry Wynter.'

'They're in the *Diaries*.'

'Diaries? What diaries?'

I explained. She hadn't known there were diaries. The arrangement was that I was supposed to stay for lunch. Now this was changed. She made an excuse about the General being tired. We hardly spoke in the car going back to the station.

This is the only interview I had with Hollande or his daughter. Tried three times more but was refused each time.

LETTER FROM ERIC BURTEN TO HIS MOTHER, MRS. IVY BURTEN. *Dated Nankow. 8 September, 1910.*

(Burton had written several letters to his family from Pekin, now lost. This one was kept as a memorial to him because by the time it arrived in England he was already missing.)

Dear Mum,

Well, we are on our way at last and we have stopped for a night or two at this place called Nankow. It is not too far from Pekin and has taken us longer than we thought to get there. Terrible road. You can't hardly call it a road at all. Do you remember that time we went on holiday to Wales, up in the mountains, when Dad took us for a walk and we got lost? You remember that track there with the stone slabs and potholes and how you turned your ankle, well, that was like Pall Mall compared with this one. I can honestly say I never seen anything like it. I was afraid for the motor with all the banging and crashing over boulders and into holes as deep as your knee. But she's made really well. A few creaks and a broken spring which I have replaced and nothing worse seems to have happened. Thankgod-almighty, as Claude used to say.

I'm worried about the tyre-covers, though. We are supposed to get at least two thousand miles out of a set, but not on these tracks. Sharp stones cut them and then when we get onto the tracks round the precipices they rub against the boulders. I've had to throw two away already, the trouble is we got these ones with special treads for the desert. You don't blow them up as hard as the others, they are softer with a special criss-cross pattern which is supposed to go better through sand. They're thinner than the other tyre-covers. I am sure they will work well in the desert if that is what the experts say, but they don't work well on these rocks.

Doris will remember when I hurt my back playing leap-frog down on the sand at Wittering, well it got sore again bringing the Abbott over the mountains, but Captain Wynter has been rubbing it with linament and we both smell a bit like horses.

He has been very good to me. He is just decent. Not like Captain Hollande. He treats Percy Preece like he is a piece of machinery. There is a big row now about something being stolen from Captain Hollande's car. It is a silly row but Captain Wynter is also involved. I will tell you when I get home.

Tell Doris she would hate the food here. We are leaving behind all the tins, or at least a lot of them, to save weight and are eating the food of the land. My stomach doesn't like it at all.

I must write to Mr. Abbott and tell him about how the car is doing. Not sure of the gear ratios, though. I suppose we need two boxes, low ratios for the mountains and higher ones for the desert. That is if the surface is hard. They say it is a mixture, soft, then hard, sounds wonderful compared with these mountains. We have still got days of this kind of driving and then we reach the Great Wall. I am looking forward to that because I heard of it at school.

Tell Claude I will be back when the pheasant season starts (I hope) and we will have a day or two in the woods.

Love to everyone

Your loving son,

Eric.

INTERVIEW WITH MAURICE IVES, *Winter, 1948. (Can't remember date.)*
We met in the Bell in St. Bride's Lane off Fleet Street. Had been expecting plump sweaty man as described in *Diary*. Instead he was thin. Skin hanging on him. So was his suit. Rather rumpled. Suppose he was about sixty. Wearing a Press Club tie. Seems to have fallen on hard times. Told me he was working on the picture desk at Associated Press writing captions. Very cagey. Drank as many gins as I'd buy.

Said he was going to write a book about the race himself. Didn't believe it. Fleet Street people are like that. I've known them since I was a kid. Started talking about percentages. I said no. He said he had a lot of cuttings. I said I'd seen them all. I said I'd give him five quid. I told him I wanted to know about the Nankow incident. He said he'd been there. He and the other correspondents came up by train when they heard of the hold-up.

M.I.: 'I cabled the story but they spiked it in London. We were a bang-the-drum-for-Britain paper. Don't suppose they wanted a story about how the two representatives of the Island Race fell out at the start. I thought they were wrong. These two had been rivals all their lives. Hollande had nearly killed himself trying to take away the Land Speed Record from Wynter. The back wheels of the cars were chain-driven in those days. In one attempt on the Pendine Sands the bloody chain broke and sliced through the side of the car. Another inch and Hollande would have had his head taken off.

'He was a bastard, a right shit. All this guff about what a good general he was and what a bloody hero and explorer and everything. All balls. You've worked in Fleet Street, you know how it goes. The Press decides to make something of someone for some bloody reason or other and this time they chose Hollande. I mean, you've seen it a dozen times. The bloody papers just lie on their backs waiting for people to fuck them. Don't ask me how it happens but it does. Of course, he knew how to handle the

Press. Very civil, good manners, etc., etc. . . . . But underneath he was a right shit. . . .

'This business about the picnic basket. Christ, can you imagine a bloody race being held up for three days while this cunt gets the police to investigate?

'Then he has this row with Wynter. Nothing really, except he blames him. Can't remember why now but it wasn't his fault at all.'

Asked him about Wynter's relationship with Burten.

'I knew we'd get round to that, old sport. You want a hell of a lot for a fiver.'

Said I'd make it a tenner.

M.I. had a curious way of drinking. He'd set up the gin-and-tonic on the bar. Wouldn't sip it like a normal drinker. Just leave it there while we talked. Then he'd pick it up and drain the whole thing in one gulp and be ready for another. Must have bought him six or seven gins in couple of hours.

M.I.: 'Nobody ever knew. Not for sure anyway. I mean, how the hell can you be sure of a thing like that unless you catch them in flagrante delicto? But there were rumours, all right. I think some of the other drivers thought there was a little how's your father. They used to call Burten "beauty" – something like that. I talked to your father once in Pekin. We got a bit drunk one night on rice wine. He said he thought there was something going on. Kept on saying, "Well, why wasn't he travelling down with me? Why put him in Second if there was nothing?"'

'I was in Second Class and it's true that Wynter was often down our way and Burten was up in First Class just as often. Slept up there too, I was told. He said it was the heat. But you can *say* anything, can't you? I heard Hollande didn't like that and some of the other passengers were talking. There were also rumours that Wynter was having some woman on board. If he was, then maybe he was bi-sexual.

'But you ask about Nankow. It was the homosexual thing that caused the row then. Hollande caught Wynter in Burten's room, so they said. In those days it was pretty terrible even talking about something like that. Not like now: it's all rum, bum and a gramophone since the war.'

Asked him what he thought eventually happened.

'There's only two people who know, one's Hollande and the other's Wynter. The other two who did know are both dead. Your father and Burten. And they're the *only* people. Everything else is speculation. But no one can deny Wynter was at Hollande's

fuel dump. They saw his tyre marks. It's just that . . . well . . .
listen, I'll tell you something. It was us who made Hollande the
hero figure. The London *Daily News*. When the whole thing was
coming out I was called in to see the proprietor, Lord Lexton.
Never saw him before in my life. He said to me: "Ives, tell me
everything you know. Were they having it off?" And I told him
what I've just told you. That there were rumours. He thanked
me and said I could go. They paid Hollande the prize money
and from that moment the policy of the London *Daily News* was
to believe Hollande, to make him a hero. That was why during
the First War when he fucked up that attack in France and got
half his men killed, we said it was heroic. Everything he did,
right up until the paper collapsed, it was Hollande this and
Hollande that and Rule Britannia. And just the opposite for
Wynter. They put the boot in whenever they could.

'When he came back to try and clear his name they put me
on him. There was talk of court cases and injunctions and libel
and God knows what and I was supposed to get whatever dirt
there was. And I'll tell you something else: there wasn't any. No
dirt at all. The thing was, I believed him. All he wanted was to
clear his name and get back his wife and his kid.

'I know newspapermen aren't supposed to be sentimentalists
but I felt sorry for that poor bastard. And you know the thing
that really stuck in my gullet and still sticks when I think of it is
Hollande. He never said anything but he was able to make you
believe that by *not* saying anything he was being honourable
about this rotter Wynter.

'Of course your grandfather made a statement, more than one
if I remember. Right at the beginning. But the General never
said a thing. Never confirmed, never denied, just let us believe
what he wanted us to believe, which was that Wynter had tried
to scupper him.

'Did I ever go back? No, never. There was some talk of an
expedition but the revolution broke out in China soon after the
race and, anyway, the First War broke out, too, and Hollande
became a hero and by the time Wynter got back his regiment
didn't want him and his wife didn't want him and he was in debt
up to his eyeballs. After the divorce, the estate was sold to clear
up what he owed. The thing was, he'd inherited the debts with
the estate.

'No, it was a shambles, really. Funny how you can never tell.
I mean, I envied him, you know. There he was, young, famous,
aristocratic, rich – or at least we'd thought so – held the Land

Speed Record, Sword of Honour at Sandhurst, beautiful wife, child, land. Anybody would have swapped with him. And then the whole bloody thing collapsed.'

September 15: We're onto the high plateau at last! Out of the mountains and the rivers and the rocks and away from the others – which is even better. I know why people like deserts now. It's because everything is clean; cauterised by wind and sun. Not that this is the true Gobi yet. What pleases me most of all is to be away from Hollande. I mustn't brood. I've only got one object and aim in my life: to beat Eddie Hollande. I don't care about the rest. I don't care if it takes me two years to get back. I don't care if I have to carry the Abbott on my shoulders as long as I get back before him. So . . . now to my professional duties. . . .

We were held in Nankow for three days before being allowed to continue. Of course nothing was resolved. Nothing was found. We went on to Kalgan and there we split, the Continentals going up through Outer Mongolia on the way to Siberia; Hollande and I turning west towards Urumchi. His route lies fifty miles south of mine. On the flat plain we could see each other for a long time as we ran on parallel courses. And then finally, thank God, he disappeared.

We're on grassy steppe-land making for Pai-ling Miao. From Suiyuan it is ninety-six miles. Bad going up a stony valley with finally a steep ascent to the top of the first pass fifteen miles from Kweihua. Then a short steep descent followed by a long pull up another stony valley and onto the Mongolian plateau. From here on the track was good steppe road except for a few sandy and muddy patches.

At mile twenty-seven there was a village where there were Chinese soldiers. They greeted us suspiciously but we showed them our papers and passports and they let us through.

At mile forty-five we reached Chao-ho, a stream which required careful crossing. There was a walled fort above it and on rising ground beyond that a large monastery. At Pai-ling Miao there is one of the biggest monasteries in Mongolia. Nearby is a Chinese bazaar where we bought food supplies. Getting very cold at night now.

October 1: The Black Gobi. Days and days pass without me

writing a word, but I don't think it matters now. The race is probably lost. We've had trouble with the Abbott and with ourselves and we've lost our way a dozen times.

This is a terrible place. Flat, with tussocks of dry brown grass. Everything is barren and desolate. Occasionally in the far distance we see a small group of wild asses, nearer at hand lizards scutter among the coloured pebbles of which the surface is composed. Some stones are green, others yellow or blue, but the overall colour is that of a lightly-browned biscuit.

It seems to be the end of the world. Sometimes the surface is hard, sometimes it is deep sand. Whenever we have a following wind – and one comes up every afternoon – the Abbott boils. The carburettor becomes choked and we have spent hours taking it to pieces and cleaning it. We have had rain, which caused the desert surface to become like glue, we have had frosts at night so severe that we have had to light a fire in the mornings under the Abbott to unfreeze the cooling water before we could start her, otherwise we would have cracked the cylinder block. Yet at noon we fry in the sun.

Occasionally we come to a well. On my map they are marked with names like One Cup Well and Cartwheel Springs, the Well of the Seven Corners, Wild Horse Well. They sounded romantic in the ship's cabin when Eric and I read them out to each other, but now they are simply holes in the ground and I no longer know which is which, for I no longer know exactly where we are.

I worry all the time now, which is unlike me. Water is short, so is petrol, tyre-covers are worn and our next fuel dump is nearly two hundred miles away.

We have seen almost no one. A week ago we met a Tungan camel caravan carrying brick tea to Hami. Later we came on a group of Mongol lamas returning from an alms-collecting expedition to Khumbu Monastery near the Koko Nor. One of the lamas could speak a little English and he warned us of the Kazak bandits. He said there were several groups roaming the Black Gobi now. Lonely travellers made easy pickings.

In each case these people looked at the Abbott in total incomprehension. They touched it and one of the monks licked it. But it was so far beyond their world that when we sat down to eat they turned their backs on it.

My biggest worry is Eric. He's sick. He's wasting away before my eyes. God knows what I can do to help him. Is it something that has lain inside him ever since the ship?

Or is it caused by our diet? We left most of the tinned stuff behind when we decided to live like the locals. This means our diet has been *tsampa* – the most common food of the land – a ground barley meal which they eat like porridge mixed with butter tea or their beer or milk from camels or mares if they have any. Even with water. We pulled wild rhubarb on the slopes near Pai-ling Miao and boiled it. Perhaps that started it. But we were desperate for something fresh. For the rest, when we reach a nomad encampment or one of the tiny encampments round the wells we eat dishes of rice or stews of strange-looking meat. Sometimes we manage to get pilaus of chicken and mutton with rice; sometimes Turki bread. Eric says his trouble is the strange food and he just has an upset stomach. I hope and pray there is a doctor in Hami, but I doubt it. Perhaps in Urumchi.

October 9: We stopped for two days at the fuel dump past Pai-Ling Miao so that Eric could rest. Now he eats mainly soup. We have a quantity of Maggi in packets. It is dried and we have to add water. Perhaps the water is the problem. Much of it is bitter, like Glauber's Salts, but it is too dangerous to wait for a sweet well. We have tablets which are said to purify water – had to leave the proper contraption behind – and I don't think they do much good. If the water is affecting Eric, there is no help for it. I, on the other hand, seem as fit as anything.

October 15: Had great problems at the Etsin Gol oasis. It's huge. Great sand dunes covered by tamarisk and poplars and sparse reedy grass. A group of Torgut Mongols live here. It's about 200 miles long and up to fifty broad and we arrived at the worst time. It's an inland river that ends in large lakes. If we'd come through in the middle of summer it would have been an easy passage because the peasants of Kansu take the water out in irrigation canals, and if we came through in winter the ice would have been so thick we could have driven across. As it was, we struggled through a soup of sand and water before being finally dragged through by the Torgut Mongols. Strange place. Poplars and willows growing up out of the one trunk. The whole thing drained Eric of strength.

I was going to say that every day is the same, but no day is the same. The best we have achieved is between eighty and one hundred miles. Some days we do less than ten.

My thoughts are always on Eric. He never complains and yet I know he is feeling dreadful. He takes his share of the driving and of house-keeping. We have only one meal a day and that is in the late afternoon. We collect the tamarisk for fuel, make a fire, boil up tea, eat *tsampa* or Turki bread or whatever we have been able to obtain. He makes his soup. We are so exhausted that we roll up in our *poshteens* and our blankets and go to sleep. In the mornings we have tea and dry bread, or perhaps some boiled rice.

We could be completely alone in the world. Somewhere to the south of us is Eddie Hollande. Away to the north are the other drivers. Is it all meaningless now? I tell myself that we have no chance because of the time we have wasted, and yet they can't be having it easy either. The thing to do is to plug on. Yet how can I plug on with Eric in his present state of health? I wish I knew more about medicine. I have a small book on how to treat the more obvious illnesses and I have looked up dysentery. It says this usually occurs during the late summer and early autumn. 'Whatever may be its cause, it is certainly favoured by exposure to cold, by sudden changes in temperature, by excesses in eating and drinking and by indulgence in unripe fruits. The first requisite in treatment of dysentery is rest. The patient should be kept perfectly quiet, flat on his back. . . .' How? It is better not to read these things. I apparently should be dosing him with thirty drops of laudanum, some ipecac and camphor made up in syrup of orange peel to disguise the taste. Where am I to find these? The worse it gets, according to the book, the more severe the pains are in the bowels. And then there's prostration. On the other hand it doesn't *have* to be dysentery. Maybe it *is* just the food.

October 21: (Or it may be 22. I think I've lost a day.) Searching for the fuel dump between the Etsin Gol and Hami. Country flat. Dump should be visible. Arrangements made, when setting up both Hollande's and my dumps, were to place twenty-foot stayed poles with red flags on top. These would serve two functions: first we'd see them from a long distance, secondly they would appear – we hoped – like religious symbols to any passing nomad and that for this reason they might be left alone. They were to be sited just off the main track and not near a well so the chances of caravans passing them and pilfering or smashing them up in some way would be lessened.

We've searched and searched, criss-crossing our tracks, coming to rising ground and using the binoculars until our eyes watered and become sore, but not a sign. We still have some fuel left in the emergency tanks. Thank God Eric had the foresight to realise we would need them. We use a dip-stick three and four times a day. His estimate is that we may have seventy miles left, maybe a bit more if the surface is hard, but you can never tell in this damned place; it can change in a few yards.

Early today two things happened which have frightened me. The first is that Eric fainted. He had gone out to fetch tamarisk to make a blaze to thaw out the Abbott and as he came back he clutched at his stomach and fell. After a few moments he seemed to recover but he was shaky for a while. The second was that while searching the countryside with our binoculars for the flags that would show us where the dump was, I saw four horsemen. They were only faint dots and, unless they had binoculars too, I don't think they would have seen us, although inevitably they will see our dust. I don't know what Kazaks look like but the lama told me they were horsemen. I got out the revolver, cleaned and loaded it. It is the only weapon we have.

Heavy sand. Bogged down again. Decided to stop about mid-afternoon. We've come fifteen miles today but in what direction? I know more or less, but if you don't know precisely where you started from, not even a compass is much use. We decided not to make a fire in case the horsemen were Kazaks and saw the smoke.

The day has been grey and very cold. My Celsius thermometer read minus fifteen degrees at sunset.

NOTE: Expand here on Kazaks. Come into Chinese Turkestan through Tien Shan mountains when times are hard and raid in desert. Small, tough, nomadic. Huge flocks of horses and sheep. Practically born on horseback. Cossacks named after them.

October 24: The last few days have been terrible. Eventually we were forced to make a fire for the following morning the temperature had dropped to minus twenty-two Celsius and we could not start the Abbott. So we went out to gather tamarisk and built a small fire under the block. One has to be very careful with so much petroleum spirit and oil about. We try and keep the flames down as low as we can, sometimes throwing on a little sand, trying to let only the warmth reach the engine. But this means smoke and we were taking down the tent when we saw the horsemen come to the top of a ridge about a mile away. One of them had a telescope, for I saw the sun winking on the lens. We looked at them through the binoculars, they looked at us through the telescope, passing it from hand to hand.

There were four of them dressed in heavy *poshteens* with round Turki hats on, like upturned pie dishes. Each carried a rifle slung over his shoulder and wore a bandolier of cartridges. On their legs they wore sheepskin chaps. They sat on their small, shaggy ponies, quite composed. Our direct route would have taken us through sand about 400 yards away from them so instead, once we had the tent struck and the camp packed up, we walked a little way from the Abbott, searching for a harder surface. We found one going south.

The Abbott was capable of thirty to forty miles an hour along hardpan and even these tough ponies could not keep up that pace for very long. I asked Eric to drive and sat with the revolver on my lap.

The Kazaks watched us as we swung away from them and then trotted down the slope towards us as if they had all the time in the world. It was an alarming drive for there were rocks and old stumps and we bounced and crashed and bucketed about and all the time I was fearful we would suddenly hit sand and come to a complete stop.

Soon we lost them, but I knew that on this clear day they would see our dust for miles, and this proved to be true. We kept going for an hour and then stopped. I climbed a hillock where there were the old broken walls of a fort or a mausoleum. The wind had got up and I sheltered behind a tumble down wall as I swept the countryside with the glasses. It did not take them more than half an hour to come into view. The ponies were cantering, heads held low. They seemed very small under the bulk of their riders, but there was a remorselessness about their movement that ate up the miles. They seemed not to tire.

Got the Abbott going again and sped off along the hardpan as fast as we could go. We stopped three more times before noon and each time after fifteen minutes or half an hour I would pick out in the distance the bobbing shapes of the Kazaks.

Perhaps we should have just got on without stopping but we were being driven farther and farther from our true direction and in any case we were leaving tracks behind us like railway lines. I had to be sure they had given up before we could swing north-west again.

By early afternoon the wind had become a gale and the whole surface of the desert seemed to be moving. I had been warned of *burans* in Pekin but they were said to come mainly in spring and early summer. Great pillars of dust came swirling across the desert towards us like tornadoes and the air grew thick and dark. I knew then that if we could keep going we would have a chance, for they certainly could not.

We drove blind, praying and hoping that we would not hit a rock and have the whole of the bottom of the Abbott carried away. I have never admired Eric more. He must have been feeling terrible and yet he took his turn at the wheel as though he was on a Sunday hill climb.

Our speed had dropped, of course. We were not doing more than ten or fifteen miles an hour. But each mile took us farther and farther away from the Kazaks and now they could not track us. The wind was obliterating our signs as fast as we made them.

We went on as long as we could until night came, making the dark even darker. Wind made it impossible to put up the tent and we lay in our *poshteens* on the sheltered side of the Abbott. During the night the wind dropped but in the morning it was almost as dark as it had been because in the still air the dust was suspended. Slowly it came down and settled like the dust in a room after the fireplace has been cleaned.

At first I thought Eric was dead. Couldn't move, he was so weak. The effort of the day before had almost finished him. I felt terribly panicky. Wasn't sure where we were and wasn't sure what to do about him.

After the wind it was slightly warmer and the Abbott wasn't frozen but it made no difference because I still could not start her without Eric to work the spark and mixture levers. I gave him a drink of water and wiped his face and gradually he came to.

As the air cleared, the desert became visible once more and the sun beat down. I got him into the shade of the Abbott. When I heard a curious tonk . . . tonking noise, I thought for a moment it might be the Kazaks, but when I turned a sheep was staring at me from the top of a tussocky ridge. I had not noticed it, but we were surrounded by patches of coarse grass where last year's rains must have fallen. Each time the sheep moved its head the bell at its neck let out this curious sound. I knew that where there was a bell-wether there had to be people. I walked up towards the sheep. On the far side of the ridge were thirty or forty more sheep. But the more important thing was that there was a shepherd. He was a big man in a long sheepskin cloak and a fur hat. He wore a heavy beard and carried a long staff so that there was something Biblical about him. He came towards me, staring as though I had come from some other planet – which in his terms, of course, I had. Then he must have seen the Abbott, for he gave a slight start and went on past me and stood staring at it. He touched it, wiping away the dust from a patch on the body and then he touched the wheels. On the far side, in the shade, he bent down and looked at Eric. When he straightened up, he spoke. It was a strange, guttural noise. The sounds were not unfamiliar and after a few moments I realised he was speaking a broken form of English and had asked me who we were. I told him.

I could hardly make out his face because of the heavy beard and moustache and the fur cap which was pulled well down.

But his eyes were grey, which was unusual. Then he introduced himself as Colonel Alexandrov, once of the Imperial Russian Artillery.

I answered his questions briefly and he did not seem unduly surprised. He had heard about the race when the fuel was being placed in the desert. He knew about motors because he had seen them in Berlin, and helped me start the Abbott.

We drove to his encampment a few miles away. It consisted of a single yurt which he called an *ak-ois* in the Kirghiz style, so he said. He had a Kirghiz wife and two small children. She was young, nineteen or twenty, and pretty but shy. They made us welcome, giving me *kumiss*, their fermented mares' milk. They gave Eric fresh goat's milk which seemed to do him good.

Col. Alexandrov's story was a strange one but, he said, not unique, there were others like him in Chinese Turkestan. In 1905 his regiment had mutinied and he, with several other officers, had been arrested and sent into exile. He had been exiled to a remote village near Semipalatinsk and after a year of his sentence had escaped south through Dzhungaria to the Tien Shan where he had met his wife's family on the summer pastures. There were several other Russian exiles, he said, farther south in the Tsaidam, also living as nomads with their flocks. He himself had no wish to return to Russia, although he was fascinated by the Abbott and several times left the *ak-ois* to look at it, and once asked me to raise the bonnet so he could see the engine. He touched it with his fingers as though re-familiarising himself with a technology and way of life that he had lost, and missed.

The *ak-ois* itself is covered in thick felt over a wooden framework. It must be about twenty feet in diameter and very comfortable. There is a skylight at the top for smoke to escape; it is closed up at night against the cold. In the centre is a fireplace surrounded by carpets and bright-coloured padded quilts and bolsters which we use at night. There are several painted boxes in which they keep their treasures, the keys of which are tied to the ends of Madame Alexandrov's pigtails. It is warm and luxurious after what we have endured, but it is full of fleas.

We have spent three days in the *ak-ois*, allowing Eric to

regain some of his strength. On the second day the Colonel called me aside and said he had gone out into the desert following Eric's tracks and found where he had stooled. He said there was blood. Now we are sure it is dysentery.

There is nothing any of us can do nor, according to Alexandrov, is there a doctor in Urumchi. There was one, a Russian, until a year ago, but he died of alcoholism. He says there is one in Kashgar, attached to the China Inland Mission, but that is an enormous distance. I make it between seven and eight hundred miles on my map, and we would have to cross part of the Takla Makan desert. I discussed this with Alexandrov, and our dangerous lack of fuel. But he says our fuel dump is about thirty miles farther south. He was grazing his animals there when the reconnaissance party came through witht their camels and created it. Apparently the flags have worked. They are thought here to be Buddhist symbols like those on the prayer wheels in Tibet and he doubts whether anyone has touched them. He himself thought they had something to do with the Chinese Army. He has given me precise directions how to reach the dump.

I am writing this late at night. The others are all asleep. One of the children has a rasping cough. I think of my own son and my dear wife. At the moment I would give everything to have the love and family warmth which this lonely man possesses.

October 27: Left the Alexandrovs early this morning, making for Kashgar. There is nothing else we can do. Although Eric is slightly improved after our rest he has confessed to me that he has been passing blood now for several weeks. If we can get some medicine in Kashgar which will cure him, perhaps he can come on. Perhaps there might even be someone there who would come with me. I am loath to give up. So much depends on this race.

It has been slow going all day and we are almost at the end of our fuel. If Alexandrov is wrong things will be very black indeed.

October 28: Found the fuel dump at noon. Saw the flags from a great distance but when we got here discovered it was not our dump, but Hollande's. We must have been further south than we thought. Decided to camp here for the rest of the day. The Nobel Company have done him proud. It is an enormous dump. Drum after drum of petrol, oil, water, far more than he could ever use. I doubt that our dump at Pailing Miao was even half the size. Great relief because he cannot use it all.

October 30: Freezing wind came up in the night, blowing sand against our tent and making it difficult to sleep. We took extra drums of petrol, water and tins of oil. I made Eric as comfortable as I could, then I left a note for Hollande telling him what I had done. We left about eleven.

I have decided to rush it. If I do that I'll keep my energy up and my nerves wound tight. Anyway, speed is essential now for Eric. Thank God we have a clean, hard surface and we are going well.

NOTE: The *Diary* of the race ended there. Burten died approximately a week later. By then they were badly off-course. Wynter is convinced that his compass was faulty and had been from the start. See later interview with him. See also my father's statement.

That was everything in the file. There was no interview with Wynter nor any statement by Percy Preece.

[2]

A cold mist lay over the River Wey as Daniel came off the main road at Guildford and drove through the lower town to Archibald Preece's house. All the way from London he had lived in the world of the *Diary*, seeing vividly his grandfather and Eric Burten as they made that final dash across the desert. The last section had gripped him completely. He felt drawn to the man who had struggled on against huge odds, and drawn to Burten, too, the New Man who had died so far from home.

By the time the *Diary* came to an end, Daniel had already made up his mind he was going to follow his grandfather's trail. What arrangements he could make to finance the trip, or how he would recoup the cost, would have to be considered later. He simply knew that for his own peace of mind he must know the truth.

'Oh, it's you,' Mrs. Stone said as she opened the door.

'I phoned the hospital.'

'He said you'd be down. He's expecting you.'

A voice from upstairs called, 'Is that Mr. Wynter?' Daniel was surprised at its strength.

Mrs. Stone pointed the way to her father's room. Preece was sitting up in bed wearing his Stetson and writing with a fountain pen on a pad of lined paper held on a clip-board. Around his shoulders he was wearing a pink knitted bed-jacket which Daniel assumed he had borrowed from his daughter. There were several files next to the bed.

'Indigestion,' he said, giving a chuckle. 'E.C.G.s and G.E.C.s and computers and doctors and nurses and God knows what and it wasn't a stroke at all. Said I should stay in bed for a few days, that's all.'

'I'm glad it wasn't anything more serious.'

'Sit down, sit down. Said I had a heart like a thirty-year-old. Anyway . . . I know what you've come about.'

'The *Narrative* and your father's statement.'

'Right. But you've been naughty.'

'How's that?'

'I said I'd have the material photocopied but you took the original.'

'I've kept it safely.'

'That's not the point. Ah . . . never mind. You thought I was going to kick the bucket so you took what you could while you could. I don't blame you.'

He indicated the files on the floor. 'That's what you're after. But you'll have to read it here.'

'I'll take it into town and have it photocopied if you like,' Daniel said.

'That's what *she* said.'

'You mean Victoria Hollande?'

Preece suddenly put his hand on his heart. 'There it goes,' he said with a smile. 'Irregular beating. Wind. That's what causes it.' He paused. 'Yes. Victoria. Haven't seen her for years, then there she was, down at the boat. Wanted the *Diaries*, even offered to pay me.'

'The early *Diaries*? The ones that I've got?'

Preece nodded.

'What about the later ones? He said in his letter that he'd always kept diaries.'

'She kept on asking me about them. Told her he'd never mentioned them when I interviewed him. Then she got angry and said I was helping to try and smear the General's reputation. And I got angry. She threatened legal action. Tough as old boots, she is. Got in quite a state. So did I. Then my ticker began to go pocketa-queep as Thurber says in that story of his. Anyway . . . she didn't get anything from me. There's a photocopying place in the Tunsgate. When you've done that, come back and we can talk.'

It was nearly seven o'clock by the time Daniel was crossing the Thames into London. The mist had thickened and the air was dank and cold. The lights were on in his flat when he reached Swiss Cottage. As he locked the car and walked along Richmond Crescent he had a feeling, for the first time in years, of coming home. Not back to his flat or to his possessions, but home itself. He visualised Julie, having come in an hour or so before, going round switching on lights and closing curtains, turning up heating, getting out a tray of drinks, showering. He visualised her body, beaded with moisture, and immediately his mind made a quick game-plan for the evening: a drink, then Szechuan spare-ribs at one of the Chinese restaurants along the Finchley Road, where he would fill her in on the day with Preece, and then back to spend a long evening together in the double bed.

He let himself into his flat and was about to call her when he heard laughter. There was Julie's laugh, low and gurgling, and another, a man's voice. He went into his sitting-room. Julie was curled up on the sofa, her legs beneath her, wearing his favourite blouse of aquamarine silk with nothing underneath it. In one of the easy chairs – his own chair – was Chris Parker. He rose as Daniel entered.

Julie said, 'We thought you'd never get here.'

There was an empty bottle of white wine on the coffee-table.

'I'm afraid I've outstayed my welcome,' Parker said. He drained his glass.

'Don't go on my account,' Daniel said.

Julie cocked her head to look at him, her brow furrowing. 'How did it go?'

'He was too ill to talk.'

'Is that Preece?' Parker said.

'Yes.'

'Don't go,' Julie said.

'I must.' Parker turned to Daniel. 'I came in to extend the olive branch. Victoria asked me to. She is very ashamed of herself. Asked me to convey her apologies.'

He was wearing colours which set off his hair and eyes. His clothes were expensive: a dark blue roll-neck sweater which Daniel guessed was cashmere, a honey-coloured leather jacket and elephant-grey corduroys.

'She wants you to come down to lunch in the country on Saturday,' Parker said. 'She won't take no for an answer.'

'I said we'd love to go,' Julie said.

'Did you?' His voice was cold.

'I don't blame you for feeling irritated – that's if you do feel irritated,' Parker said. 'It's not like her to be rude, although she's a very strong woman, as you've probably guessed by now. I mean, in the last years she simply took over from the General and she's been running things ever since. You can't do that unless you have a powerful personality. Sometimes she overdoes it.'

'We understand,' Julie said.

'You'll come then? Say twelve-thirty. And I'll show you the Collection.' He moved towards the door, then turned to Daniel. 'By the way, are you still determined to go to that place where your grandfather lived?'

'Maybe,' Daniel said.

There was an embarrassed little silence, then Parker said, 'I must be off.'

Julie went to the door with him. 'See you Saturday,' she said.

When she had closed the door she turned to Daniel. 'You were bloody rude.'

'Must have been the sudden shock . . . coming home and finding you entertaining a man in my flat.'

'Would you rather I'd entertained him in my bedroom?'

He went to the fridge and saw a bottle of white wine. 'Since when have we been able to afford expensive Rhine wines?'

'Chris brought it.'

'That was very sweet of him.'

'Do stop being sarcastic. He came on behalf of Victoria to say how sorry she was and to invite us to lunch and –'

'And to find out our plans.'

'Right. And he might be able to help. There's nothing very sinister in that. Now tell me about Preece.'

'He's back home. He had indigestion. Wind. That's all.'

'Why make a mystery of it then?'

'Because I don't trust Parker or Victoria Hollande. If they think Preece is still in hospital they'll leave him alone. I have a feeling he could be bought. I don't want them getting in on the act.'

'What's happening to you? You're suspicious of Chris, Victoria, and now you don't trust Preece.'

He sprawled in his chair. 'I had plans for this evening. I thought we'd go out and eat spare-ribs and I'd tell you all about the day and when we came back. . . .'

She came up behind him and put her arms round his neck, letting her chin rest on the top of his head. 'That's good thinking.'

They went to the Shanghai Pavilion and Daniel took his folder of notes. While they were eating their spare-ribs Julie said, 'But how did Preece get there and see your grandfather? There weren't any trains in 1939, were there?'

'You mean from Pekin? No, I don't think there were. But he said it wasn't all that difficult. He flew in from Gilgit, on the Indian side. He found an Australian who ran sight-seeing trips into the mountains and hired him. There was a primitive airfield in Kashgar. He said there were several of these sight-seeing planes operating in and around the Himalayas.'

They finished their spare-ribs and rinsed their fingers in a bowl of lemon water, then he handed her some papers from his file.

'Chronologically, Percy Preece's statement comes first,' he said. 'It's by the reporter Ives, on the London *Daily News*.'

The headlines were startling:

COMPETITORS ALMOST DIE
IN DESERT DRAMA

FAMOUS AUTOMOBILIST ACCUSED
OF CHEATING

MYSTERY OF PEKIN–LONDON RACE
REVEALED

Then came the story:

Mr. Percy Preece, the mechanic of the winning team in the recent Pekin–London automobile race today accused a fellow-competitor of cheating. He said that Captain Harry Coles Wynter, driver of the second British entry in the race, had attempted to sabotage a fuel dump in the desert which almost caused his death and that of his co-driver and employer, Captain Edward Hollande.

Mr. Preece made his sensational statement at a luncheon given by the British Motor Racing Committee at the Savoy Hotel to celebrate a British victory in the race.

It is clear that Mr. Preece made the statement without Captain Hollande's knowledge or consent. He had just received his silver trophy from the Committee's chairman, Sir George Dalrymple, when he took out a prepared speech and read it to the guests.

He said that eighteen days after leaving Nankow they had run into a great sandstorm, but because they were extremely low on water – the motor had been using more than expected and they had had to use their drinking supplies – they had pushed on.

They had found visibility almost impossible and had struck a sharp rock which had cut the tyre-cover on their offside front wheel. They would not be able to get another cover until they arrived at the second fuel dump between Nankow and Urumchi.

Mr. Preece said that so far Captain Hollande's navigation had been almost perfect and, because he estimated that the dump could not be more than a few miles away, he left Mr. Preece with the Bulldog-Saxon and headed on by himself, on foot.

He had expected to be gone about twelve or fourteen hours, but was away more than two days. During this time Mr. Preece was frightened by a group of horsemen who kept a distance from the motor, but who looked as though they might attack at any moment. Mr. Preece fired several shots over their heads with a revolver Captain Hollande had left him.

On the second day Captain Hollande returned with a new tyre-cover and they were able to reach the fuel dump some hours later.

In his statement, Mr. Preece went on to say that when they reached the dump they discovered that someone had been there and opened the taps at the bottom of the petrol drums, thereby allowing the fuel to escape into the sand. He said there was a smell of petrol in the air for some hundreds of yards around the dump.

At first he and Captain Hollande had put this down to the horsemen – later discovered to be Kazak tribesmen – but then Mr. Preece said he had discovered a tyre-mark in the shelter of the dump which had not been erased by the constant wind that was blowing.

He said he recognised the marks of the tyre-cover immediately as belonging to the Abbott Special. He therefore concluded that Captain Wynter had been to the dump and he accused him of opening the taps so that Captain Hollande would be disabled and put out of the race.

When Mr. Preece finished, Captain Hollande said he disassociated himself from the statement. He said he had known Captain Wynter most of his life and had always thought him an honourable man. He could not believe he had tried to sabotage his, Captain Hollande's, chances of completing the race. He had made his own official statement to the International Race Committee in Paris and to the Pekin Government and would add nothing more. To questions from press representatives he said he had no comment.

Your correspondent understands that Captain Wynter is now somewhere near the town of Kashgar in Chinese Turkestan, where he is said to be seriously ill. Eric Burten, his mechanic, is understood to have died in the desert.

Questioned at his home later, Mr. Preece said he had nothing further to add to his statement, other than that they had found enough petrol in the bottoms of the drums to enable them to come within thirty miles of Urumchi. Captain Hollande had walked into the town by himself and brought back fuel by camel. Mr. Preece said they were fortunate that several of the fuel drums had been lying at angles so that all the petrol had not drained away. He felt that without this piece of luck they would almost certainly have died.

They sat staring at each other when Julie had finished reading.

'Do you believe it?' Julie said.

'Percy Preece may have *thought* that's what happened, but what about the note my grandfather left?'

'Maybe it blew away. There was a gale blowing, if you remember.'

'You're being devil's advocate. Don't. I believe my grandfather. An honourable man, Hollande called him. Talk about damning by faint praise! See what he's doing? He's letting Percy Preece make all the running. Then he just says he doesn't agree – and that's that. No statement, no explanation; too proud to get embroiled in controversy. If he'd come right out and said he thought Harry Wynter had done it, there would have been something for my grandfather to get his teeth into when he came back. But Hollande says he *doesn't* believe it was Harry. So we think *he's* the honourable man. But the fact that he says nothing – because that's what it amounts to – is accusation enough. Then on top of that is the homosexual thing. We have the classic scandal of the time: cheating, unnatural sex and cowardice.'

'Cowardice?'

'He cut and ran, didn't he? When he found out what was being said about him, he went back to his mountains and stayed there. What he should have done was stay in England and take his beating like a little man: resigned from his clubs, bravely faced the loss of wife, child, estates, friends. People would have *seen* him being punished and been satisfied.'

They returned to the flat, made some coffee and read the Archibald Preece *Narrative* – Daniel for the second time that day.

[3]

THE PREECE NARRATIVE

I met Captain Harry Coles Wynter in Kashgar in 1939, nearly thirty years after the Pekin–London race. It took me several days to locate him because of the complexity of the city and the lack of help given by the British Consulate.

Kashgar is, in fact, two cities: the Mohammedan Old City, and the mainly Chinese New City, about seven miles away. Both are surrounded by crenellated mud walls with moats beneath them, though what would happen if they filled the moats with water I do not know since it would certainly melt the mud bricks and bring down the walls.

I started my search at the British Consulate. It is like a large bungalow with a wide veranda, built on a bluff, quite near to the cliff-edge, outside the walls of the Old City. I saw first one of the Indian *munshis* who, when I told him my business, passed me on to the Vice-Consul.

The Vice-Consul, named Marlow, was playing tennis with a member of the Russian Legation. He made me wait for nearly two hours and then did not seem pleased that my aim was to see Captain Wynter. I got the impression that, to the British Consulate, he was persona non grata. He told me they did not know where he was – which I later found out was a lie – and that he spent alternate periods in his valley and in the city. He directed me to a Russian merchant who lived in the New City, with whom Wynter was said to be friendly. It took me nearly a day to track him down. He was old and rather dirty and lived in a large Chinese *yamen*. He said he did business with Wynter and occasionally played chess with him. He was rather drunk but directed me to an address in the Old City. There were no cars to be hired in Kashgar but

I had managed to rent a horse-drawn vehicle of Russian origin and so I returned to the Old City and entered it by one of the great iron gates. Soon I had to give up my transport because the streets, if you could call them that, are narrow and dirty and all are muddy from the water slopped over from the pails of the water-carriers. The alleys were lined with small dark shops and in some parts covered over with reed matting to give shade, which made the place even darker.

The alleys were infested by beggars, many of whose faces and limbs had been eaten away by leprosy. Others had great goitres hanging down their chests. The town was filled with people, some on foot, some riding donkeys, and there were strings of camels carrying bales of cotton.

Near the market square where the chief mosque stood I was directed down yet another alley. It was a hot day and the whole place smelled of rotting fruit and open drains. The house I came to was made of mud bricks. Its wall, facing the alley, was devoid of windows but through an open doorway I could see a courtyard reminiscent of the casbah in Tangier. It was shaded by a vine and a roofing of reeds and against one of the walls there was a fig tree.

I was taken to a room on the first floor by a young man with a wispy moustache, one of Wynter's servants. I supposed. He was about nineteen or twenty and I noticed him particularly for he had a pale skin and blue eyes. He was handsome in a wild way, there was nothing soft about him.

Wynter was seated at the window of a plain bare room, tapping away at an old Remington. He was then in his fifties, tall and thin, very fit-looking. He gave the impression of being as tough as a whip and his skin was burnt brown by the suns of Central Asia. He wore a long white shirt over white baggy trousers on top of which was a long apricot-coloured coat of fine cotton. On his feet he wore leather slippers and around his waist a wide embroidered belt fastened with a large silver buckle.

He greeted me civilly enough until he discovered that I was Percy Preece's son. I could see then that he fought an inward battle with himself. He adamantly refused to talk about the race or his life. I had expected this and I told him that it was precisely because I did not believe the rumours started by my father's statement that I had come. He expressed cynicism at this. He said it was the kind of thing journalists always said. But I told him that I did not work for any newspaper, that I had written several books – in fact, I had one with me and showed it to him – but the thing that swung matters in my favour was the fact that I told him quite honestly that to reach him had cost me nearly every penny I had.

That, plus the fact that one would hardly be human if one did not wish to have something sympathetic written about one, tipped the balance, though it was not until forty-eight hours later that he agreed to talk to me.

I spent nearly two weeks going to his house every day. First he gave me the *Diaries* of the race which I copied out into notebooks as I sat in the courtyard. While I was doing this we became less formal and I took several meals with him. I was struck by his total assimilation into the life around him. He dressed always in the local style and our food had nothing of the West in it except for one item, marmalade. He said he had great difficulty in obtaining decent marmalade. I promised him that when I returned to England I would send him a case of the stuff. That seemed to open doors that might otherwise have been closed to me.

He was a withdrawn man, not in any sense neurotic. I never had the feeling that he was bitter, although there must have been great bitterness in him at one time. It was as though he found his own company sufficient, which was not surprising, since he had spent so many years in the mountains. Although, of course, he was never alone. Apart from the young man who had shown me in on our first meeting, and whose name I learned was Ketek, there were several other man in the house with broad Mongolian features, some of them also with pale skins and blue eyes. They were dressed like Wynter, except that several carried revolvers or knives in their belts. They were a good looking group and, like Ketek, gave an impression of pride and dignity allied to a wildness hard to define. They watched me with suspicion and I was never left alone with Wynter. One of the men, usually Ketek, would not be too far off. He did not bother to hide his presence, but allowed me to see that he was keeping an eye on me. They spoke no English but, I was told, a form of Turki which Wynter spoke fluently.

I think he enjoyed talking to someone from England, although he said he would never return now. We spoke about Germany and the possibility of war. He was concerned about what might happen in China. He felt sure the Japanese would take the opportunity of expanding out of Manchuria. He could also foresee the possibility of an attack by Russia. Kashgar was heavily under Russian influence and Urumchi, he said, was even more so. He saw little hope for the future, especially as he thought China herself was planning to invade Tibet. It was a time of great uncertainty and he was making preparations to withdraw entirely from Kashgar to his valley if things got bad.

When I had finished copying out the *Diaries* of the race I asked him to tell me what had occurred next. There was, I said, a gap in our knowledge and anything he told me might help to rehabilitate his reputation. He laughed at that and told me there was only one person now whose opinion he cared about, and that was his son.

I asked him if he did not mind the fact that General Hollande had never given details of the alleged incident. He said he had minded at one time, but no longer cared.

I pressed him on the matter of the race and what had happened later, I said that the *Diary* had ended at the start of their dash towards Kashgar. Eric Burten had been terribly ill. In England we knew that Burten had died but the details were scant.

He asked me to return on the following day once he had given the matter some thought. I did, and he agreed to tell me his story. He had with him a leather-bound book the size of a ledger which he consulted from time to time. This is his account of what occurred in the desert, as I took it down.

Burten, he said, had grown weaker and there was no question of him doing any driving. Wynter knew that it was dangerous to do all the driving himself, that if he grew too tired and had a lapse in concentration he could bog the car down or hit some obstacle. He knew, too, from his map that there were areas of quicksand. But there was no alternative. He made Burten as comfortable as possible in the rear of the Abbott, surrounded by petrol, oil and water. He drove in spells of three to four hours, then took a break. He would try to get Burten to drink a little soup, but even this became impossible after a while. Whenever he stopped for a short rest he kept the engine running, but he could not drive at night and each morning had to light a fire underneath the engine and get Burten to help him start the car.

Burten just faded away. There was no moment of drama, no rattling in the throat – not that Wynter heard, anyway. Burten's spirit simply passed from his body. He had been alive when they started one morning and he was dead when Wynter stopped for a break. Wynter thought then that they must have been about a hundred and eighty miles from Kashgar but his compass had collapsed completely so he would never know exactly where it was: somewhere out in the Takla Makan, that was the most accurate he could be.

He sat with the body for several hours before he could convince himself that life had passed and it was only when Burten stiffened up that he took a spade from the car and dug a grave. He buried Burten and erected a cairn of stones over the grave to stop the desert foxes from digging up the body. Then he continued his journey.

In the distance he could see a range of snow-capped mountains. These were not marked on his map, or at least, not in the area he thought he might be, but he decided to drive westwards, keeping parallel with them. Later he knew he was a great deal farther south than he had ever intended. He hoped that by going west he would cut the road between Kashgar and Urumchi. He thought there might be fuel at a town called Kara Shahr. In this way he could keep going, perhaps even find someone in Urumchi to act as co-driver so that he could continue the race.

A day after burying Burten he ran into soft sand. He had desert mats but they proved useless. He spent the remainder of the day trying to dig the car out. He searched the desert for stones and small rocks which he packed into the holes made by the wheels. But all he succeeded in doing was to move the car from one area of soft sand to the next. As he got it out of one hole, it sank into another.

He knew by the following day that he could not get it out unaided; he needed animals to drag it to harder ground.

Part of the guidelines laid down by the International Race Committee warned competitors to remain with their vehicles if they became stranded. Wynter stayed near the Abbott for three days. He collected as much tamarisk as he could and kept a fire lit day and night. Soon firewood became increasingly difficult to find and he had to go farther and farther from the car. He began to worry about getting lost. Also, the effort was causing him to deplete the stock of water more rapidly than he had planned. On the fourth or fifth day – he was no longer sure – he realised that he, too, was becoming ill and discovered that he had passed a little blood.

He knew that if he stayed where he was he would die, and so he made a parcel of what food and water he could carry and set off, still moving in what he thought was a westerly direction. Winter was approaching fast and now the sky was overcast. He did not even have the sun to guide him.

He would always remember the bitter cold, the desperate exhaustion of his debilitated body, the struggle each afternoon to collect enough tamarisk to keep a fire going throughout the night.

He grew too weak finally to gather the firewood and had it not been for the *poshteen* coat he had bought in Nankow he would have died of the cold.

Soon he could only walk for half an hour at a stretch and then would have to rest for an hour or more. One morning he woke to find the water in his can frozen solid. The sky was slate-grey and the wind was from the north. He had never been to Siberia but there was a taste and smell about the wind that seemed to tell him where it had come from.

He was so stiff that he found he could not get up. He had seen Burten in a similar condition and was frightened. He managed to roll over onto his stomach and was raising himself onto his knees when he saw on the sky-line the four horsemen he had seen many days before.

They sat their small ponies and watched him as they had done before. He had left his revolver in the Abbott because it was too heavy to carry. But had he had it with him he would probably not have tried to use it; there were four to one and they had rifles.

He watched them for a few minutes. He was struck even in his extremis by the stillness with which they sat their ponies. It was as though they were waiting for him to die. He began to wonder if they were figments of his imagination; if they were Dürer's Four Horsemen, and which one was Disease and which was Death?

After what seemed like an age they came down the slope towards him. He tried to crawl away. He remembered starting, then he lost consciousness, for the next thing he knew was that it was dusk and he was lying near the blazing embers of a fire.

The men were crouched on the far side, still looking at him and talking softly among themselves. Behind them the ponies stood, heads down against the bitter wind.

His impression was of their poverty. Everything about the men spoke of wretchedness. Their garments were threadbare and they looked weary and hopeless.

When they saw that he had regained consciousness one man came over to him. Wynter thought that he was going to cut his throat but instead he brought a leather sack and indicated that Wynter should drink. It was mare's milk, rank and thick and acid, but he took several mouthfuls before becoming unconscious again. The next time he woke he found himself on horseback. He was tied onto the saddle of one of the ponies, his arms around its neck. Its owner walked at its side.

He had no idea how long they marched. Day followed night in a jumbled cycle. He could remember the horrible discomfort of the horse, the pain in his stomach, the need to empty his already empty bowels, the desert encampments, the bitter cold of the wind.

At this point Captain Wynter broke off, saying he had things to do, and he suggested I return the following day. I was unwilling to leave his account there, for I had a head full of questions, but there was nothing for it. I was staying at a primitive hotel in the Old City and spent the remainder of the day writing up my notes. When I went back the following day, I found the house locked and barred. I hammered on the door and called but no one came. A small crowd collected and one man who spoke a little English said that Wynter had gone. They laughed among themselves as though a good trick had been played on me.

There seemed no point in going back to the British Consulate so I hired again a droshky-like vehicle and went to the New City to the house of the Russian merchant. I had paid little attention to him when we had met briefly before, now he seemed to be expecting me. I was shown into the main room of his *yamen*. He was lying back on a bolster, a heavy corpulent man wearing a Chinese robe of dark red silk with blue facings, on the front of which were food stains. He wore a long grey beard in the style of the Russian Orthodox priesthood and a small round velvet Turkish smoking cap on his head. Altogether he made an unprepossessing figure. He insisted that I take a meal with him.

The house was furnished in the Chinese style and I found myself in a large room, one end of which was a *kang*, a raised platform built of brick under which a fire is made in winter to heat the house. We took the meal on the *kang* seated at a low table. There were ancient eggs which had been buried in lime and which were the consistency of gorgonzola, there was sucking pig and poultry, seaweed, lotus seeds, strange fungi. All was chopped up in the Chinese style and I would have found some of the unfamiliar dishes quite palatable had it not been for the fact that he used his own chopsticks to place delicacies in my rice bowl. This turned my stomach.

His name was Prasolov. He said he had been a Count in Russia but had fled southwards after his regiment of White Russians had been wiped out in the Civil War. I did not know whether to believe him or not. All Russians in the West now call themselves aristocrats. He had come first to Urumchi and then to Kashgar where he had set up in business. From the style of his house, its magnificent wall-hangings and fine carpets from Bokhara and Samarkand, he had obviously done well for himself.

He had known Harry Wynter for twenty years. And all that time Wynter had been something of a mystery man. One day he would appear in Kashgar with a group of his wild-looking mountain men, the next he was gone. No one knew exactly where his valley was, although several people had tried to find it. In the beginning, they had tried to follow him. That was why he had taken to moving unexpectedly – as I had experienced the day before.

I pressed Prasolov to tell me all he could. I wanted to know who the people of the valley were and why they had saved Wynter instead of cutting his throat as he had expected.

'Eat, eat,' he said, taking a piece of duck and placing it before me. 'Later talk.'

We drank rice wine with the meal and soon both of us were sweating freely for it was a hot day. When we had finished we smoked Russian cigarettes and the room filled with the smell of Sobranie.

'Did he not tell you who his people were?'

'I understood them to be Kazaks,' I said. 'That's how he described them in the *Diary*.'

'Not Kazaks, Kalmucks.'

He then told me a strange story which I later checked and enlarged on at the School of Central Asian Studies in London. The story of the Kalmuck Horde is one of the great dramas of Central Asian history. They came originally from the Gobi and the steppes of Western Mongolia. In the seventeenth century they travelled through the Kirghiz steppes into Russian territory and settled near the Volga. They were Buddhists, nomads who kept sheep and cattle and moved all the while to find grazing.

The Russian authorities allowed them to remain and gave them land on both banks of the Volga, then began to try and turn them into Christians. They were a brave and warlike people and the Tzars used their cavalry against the attempted Moslem invasions of southern Russia. But the pressure to give up their religion increased to such an extent that those on the East bank of the Volga decided to return to their homelands. The Chinese Emperor and the Dalai Lama secretly encouraged them.

In 1771 they burnt their villages on the East bank and began the great return march. A horde of three hundred thousand started out on the two thousand mile march. Fewer than a hundred thousand reached their destination. First the

Russians slaughtered them, then they were attacked by every tribe through whose lands they moved. It took them more than a year and many of those who did not die by the sword and the spear collapsed in the summer heat of the desert or died of cold in the freezing winters. It was said that for many years their path could be traced by the skeletons of the dead.

The Russians had prevented the Kalmucks on the West bank of the Volga from leaving and had forced them into a tribal reservation, a sandy desert below sea level with its administrative capital at Astrakhan.

Occasionally groups up to a hundred strong would break out of the reservation and make their way across the Kirghiz steppes, through the Tien Shan Mountains, to join their people in their original homeland. Some were Christian, some Buddhist. It didn't matter. Their drive was to escape from life on a reservation. Not all of them reached their goal, and Prasolov told me that the inhabitants of the valley were the descendants of one such group of refugees.

The 1917 Revolution almost wiped out those remaining on the Volga. Their flocks and horses were requisitioned and many died in the great Volga famine that followed.

I asked Prasolov why the four horsemen had saved Wynter and why, if they were as poor and wretched as they seemed, they had not simply cut his throat and robbed him. He could not answer.

Of what had happened next to Wynter, he had only heard at second-hand. Wynter had come into Kashgar when he had recovered. By that time rumours were already circulating that he had tried to sabotage a fellow-competitor in the race. Prasolov knew that he had gone back to England to clear his name, that this had apparently proved impossible and that he had returned to the valley.

Prasolov told me that when he himself had first come to Kashgar in 1919 Wynter was hardly seen. People spoke of him living remotely in the mountains and occasionally some of the inhabitants of the valley would come into market with wool or skins. Occasionally Prasolov would be asked to order goods from either Russia or India. I asked him what they were but he smiled and changed the subject by asking me if I thought there was going to be war. I tried to bring him back to the subject of Wynter but he rose, begged to be excused and I found myself out in the street where my driver was waiting. From what I could gather though, trade had increased over the years and that in itself was something of a mystery.

[4]

The Bulldog-Saxon stood like an ancient religious artefact left over from a forgotten civilisation; something that had been worshipped, or built, like the Easter Island statues, for reasons no longer known.

Daniel, Julie, Victoria Hollande and Chris Parker were grouped around the dais on which it stood, in the middle of the big room in the Hollande Museum in Highclare. It was massive, much bigger than Daniel could ever have imagined, and it was flanked by the General's other historic motors used in his active life: there was the E.R.A. he had driven to victory in one of the Brooklands trials; the Sunbeam he had used for hill climbs; the chain-driven Wolseley in which he had nearly died on the Pendine Sands when he had been trying to take the World Land Speed record from Harry Wynter: the half-track Citroen which he had used for an expedition to the Cameroons. In the other rooms they had seen the canoe in which he had voyaged down the Congo River; his dog-sled, the tents he had used in the Antarctic, those he had taken with him to South America, his compasses, his books, his pressure lamps, his sleeping-bags, his cooking utensils, his boots, his anoraks, his ice-axes; there were many photographs of him, some in cars, some standing by dead game, some in deserts, some in African villages, some standing by light aircraft in remote parts of the world – the memorabilia of life of adventure and achievement.

The Bulldog-Saxon was something far beyond the rest and it dominated the museum's largest room.

Chris walked around it, stroking the dark green, highly-polished metal. 'It was designed by McGillvray, who'd worked for the Argyll Company in Scotland,' he said.

Daniel was aware of Julie watching Chris with a fascination that had been growing throughout the tour as they listened to him: a professional who knew his facts and had himself been to most of the places in which the General had travelled – and a good few more.

'It was based on their 20/50 model,' he said. 'Designed for rough work.' He moved to the front of the car. 'Front wheel brakes. One of the first cars to have them. Look at this bodywork. See how it's been modified behind the scuttle. That was the General's idea.'

The superstructure was about eight feet long and four feet wide, widening out to six feet at the top, and across it were fitted hoops to carry a covered-wagonlike hood. Daniel could barely imagine this massive machine negotiating the Nankow Pass.

'Look at the wheels.' Chris touched the clean black tyre-covers. 'Nearly four feet in diameter. Gave it a huge clearance.'

Daniel said, 'I was talking to an expert the other day who said the Abbott Special was the better car.'

Chris turned and again Daniel experienced the sudden shock of his deep blue eyes and black hair. He was wearing a white roll-neck sweater and black hopsack trousers. He opened his mouth as though to challenge the statement, then paused and said, 'He might be right. Trouble is, we'll never know.' He turned to Victoria. 'My God, if we had the two of them, wouldn't that be something! We'd upstage Lord Montagu. They'd be worth a fortune.' He smiled. 'Rather like having two diamond ear-rings. One is valuable by itself if the stone is good, but a pair is worth more than the sum of the jewels alone. And with all the history of that race. . .'

'What do you think they'd be worth?' Julie said.

'Difficult to say. I think you can just go on adding noughts. They'd be among the most sought-after cars in the world.'

'Let's go, it's freezing in here,' Victoria said. 'Once Chris gets onto his favourite subject . . . I mean, the Bulldog . . . it's difficult to get him away.'

Parker's face became suddenly shadowy with irritation at

the implied criticism but it cleared instantly. 'It's true. I sometimes come just to look at her. And when you think of what she went through – apart from a few dents, she's as good as new.'

'Does she go?' Julie said.

'Yes. They all do.'

'That's Chris's work.' There was more than a hint of pride in Victoria's voice.

'They don't make 'em like that any more.' Daniel's irony was not lost on any of them.

'Lunch, I think,' Victoria said quickly.

It was obvious that she had set out to charm them from the moment they arrived, as though to wipe out the memory of the last two encounters. They had sherry in a room which had once been used by the General as his study. It was book-lined from floor to ceiling with travel books. Daniel saw *Hakluyt's Voyages*, *The Worst Journey in the World*, Cook's biography. A log-fire burned brightly.

They went through to lunch. The dining-room's tall windows overlooked a terrace that dropped away to a ha-ha. A herd of Friesian cows stood below it as though posing for their photographs. 'We run our own farm,' Victoria said. 'It makes a terrible loss, but we have our own fresh vegetables and milk.'

Lunch started with a smoked salmon which Chris had caught on the Oykel, followed by pheasant –which Chris had shot – and a lemon sorbet. With it they drank a Mercurey which Daniel decided was one of the best he had ever tasted. He checked himself from inquiring if Chris had made it.

Conversation was general, punctuated only by the snap of the Bouvier des Flandres' jaw as it lay at Victoria's feet and fed off scraps which she dropped from time to time.

They talked incessantly about the General. Julie, who seemed to have completely forgotten her dislike of Victoria, asked her about the Hollande family and how long they had been at Highclare.

'Well over a hundred years,' she said, 'but we are newcomers compared with the Wynters.' She pointed to a hill which they could see through the windows. 'They lived on the other side. In fact, they once owned Luscombe Park. The relationship between the two families started with the Crimea when my great-grandfather saved General Wynter's life. That's when the fortunes of the families changed, too. General Wynter was so grateful he put my great-grandfather in the way of making a lot of money. He bought up all the remounts and artillery horses at the end of the War – borrowed the capital, of course – and sold the meat to the starving Russian Army which had withstood the siege of Sebastopol.'

'That's an achievement,' Julie said. 'First you fight them, then you do business with them.'

'That was the beginning of his fortune. The Wynters' fortunes had already begun to decline so my great-grandfather bought Luscombe Park from them.'

They had coffee round the fire in the study and it was then that she said, 'I have a confession to make. I didn't only ask you to lunch to make up for my bad behaviour. There's an ulterior motive.'

She was standing in front of the fire, holding her coffee cup. She was dressed in oatmeal whipcord slacks, a tan silk shirt and a pale yellow V-neck sweater, with a few pieces of chunky gold jewellery. It was amazing, Daniel thought, how someone so small was able to dominate the room as she did. There was no doubt it was her territory: the General had dominated here before her and she had inherited his strength and personality.

'Chris and I have been talking, and I've been doing a lot of thinking,' she said. 'I realise I've been both a prig and something of a fool. You were right, Daniel, when you accused me of hypocrisy – I know you didn't use the word, but that's what it amounted to. I think your point was that truth was what the Hollande Trust was based on, yet I wasn't prepared to seek it out about my own father.' She paused to sip her coffee. 'It took some self-examination, but I decided you were right. If there is anything that can shed light on a pretty murky incident, it's our duty to shed it.'

She stopped as though expecting a comment, but Daniel and Julie looked at her in silence.

'I don't think you understand what this is about,' Parker

said. 'Victoria means we'll help. We have the infrastructure and the logistical capability. It's the sort of thing we do all the time.'

'Just a moment,' Daniel said. 'Let me get this straight. We're talking about going to the valley?'

He nodded. 'We want to go too, and we can organise it for you.'

'You say you want to help, but that sounds as though you want to take over.'

'Have you had any experience of making films?'

'No.'

'Or trekking in high mountains?'

'No.'

'You'd need a Nagra Sound Recorder. Know how much they cost? About fifteen thousand pounds. You'd need the small Arriflex. You'd need film, batteries, insulated bags –'

Victoria said, 'Chris has made half a dozen documentaries for *The World About Us* and *Fragile Earth*.'

'We'd go to Channel Four on this. It's a natural, too, for P.B.S. in America.'

'Hang on . . .' Daniel said.

Victoria smiled at him. 'I realise this must have come as a surprise, but Chris and I have discussed it. I couldn't live with myself if I kept out of your expedition. The financial aspect could be thrashed out later. The Trust itself would invest and I don't think we would want to make a profit out of anything we discovered. I have to say one thing, though: I believe in the General and the most important thing in my life is his Trust. The very word implies justice and truth.'

'Infrastructure! Logistical capability! Christ, those were the jargon words they used in the Navy!'

Daniel and Julie were on the Kingston by-pass on their way home, and traffic was thickening. He snatched a glance at her and saw she was staring into the dark of late afternoon. They had hardly spoken since they left Hampshire.

He said savagely, 'Chris caught the salmon. Chris shot the pheasant. Chris mended the Bulldog-Saxon. We're being hijacked. To hell with them. It was my idea. You know, there must be Kalmucks left in the valley. I mean, what happened to them when my grandfather died? There's no record of them leaving. If we found them, we'd know what happened in his last years.'

'We'd never do it by ourselves.'

'Why not?'

'Money. Time. Lack of experience.'

They cleared the Robin Hood roundabout and went up the hill to the traffic lights.

'Chris Parker *has* made films,' she said.

'Victoria wants to come, too. And she's in her sixties!'

'She's probably tougher than you are. Anyway, it'd be her money.'

'It'd be the Trust's.'

'Same thing.'

As they turned into Roehampton Lane he pulled into the kerb. 'You've done nothing but play Devil's Advocate,' he said. 'Why?'

'I want you to understand what you'd be getting into, that's all.'

'No, it isn't. You're trying to put me off. You have been from the start. It sounds as though you'd like me to hand over the whole project to them. Why?'

She was silent for a moment, then she said, 'Because, well, I've got my own thing to do.'

'Whether I accept their offer or not, I want you to come with me,' he said. 'Whatever problems there are, I think we can manage. The two of us. I want you to come, but if you decide to stay here. . . .' There was a heartbeat's pause. 'I'll go anyway.'

BOOK THREE

The Valley

[1]

Daniel felt a tap on his knee. The pilot swung the Cessna in a graceful curve and pointed downwards. 'Karakorum Highway,' he said.

Daniel saw the line of the road snaking up into the snow-capped mountains. Julie, Victoria and Chris leant over to look.

'You could almost drive all the way to Sahr,' Billy Mahindra had said. 'Or take a bus.'

As Daniel looked down he could indeed see a bus, like a child's model, climbing slowly towards the Khunjerab Pass. Central Asia was so different from what he had expected that he had to tell himself that this was where the caravans of yaks had climbed, where wolves and bears had roamed, where the post-runners had fought the blizzards and the cold of the mountains to bring through the mail, where his own anonymous post-runner had died with a bag full of letters.

Nothing had prepared him for what he had found in Kashmir. His picture of India and the north-west, the mountains and the people, had come from novels and films, fossilised by history, seen through a romantic haze. But in the last few years that picture had been shattered. The Dal Lake and Srinagar reminded him of the Amsterdam canals where, if you fell in, you would want to have your stomach pumped immediately; where houseboats were hung with the drying laundry of American and European hippies; where faceless businessmen met for conferences at the Centaur Hotel. Dead cows still floated down the Jhelum River, but the shops by the Third Bridge were now expressly for the tourist trade, full of cheap saris, toy tigers, 'genuine' walnut carvings mass-produced in factories, cheap carpets made in Kashmir but called Persian and even cheaper ones manufactured in India and called Kashmiri.

They had been met at Srinagar by a beautiful young man in a pale green silk suit who had driven them to the extraordinary house near Gulmarg. With its steeply-pitched roof and wide balcony on the first floor, it seemed to have come directly from Switzerland, but it overlooked one of the great views of the world, the Vale of Kashmir with the Ladakh Range as a backdrop.

They had been there for three days, part of a perpetual house-party with guests arriving at Srinagar every day while others were leaving. They were all chic Indians from Bombay or Calcutta, wealthy, young, dressed by Gucci and Hermes, Cartier and Ted Lapidus. Daniel had been introduced to them but was never able to separate one from another in his mind. Billy Mahindra himself had spent most of the daylight hours on the huge balcony looking through a telescope at anything that moved in the valley, and all the time a large Sony short-wave radio had relayed a cricket Test Match from England. It had been strange, in this place, to hear a voice talking about 'opening the batting'.

Billy was in his thirties, owlish in appearance, but said to be brilliant. He had been educated in England where he had used Luscombe Park as a second home in the short holidays, and had then gone on to the Harvard Business School. A few years ago he had inherited his father's textile empire and moved up among the top twenty of India's millionaires. Victoria had known him since he was a baby, and he called her 'aunt' unselfconsciously. She had met the Mahindras through the General when she herself had been a child and had climbed with Billy's father in the Himalayas before the war. It was his aeroplane in which they were now flying. Billy wore a crew-cut about twenty years out of date and used a great deal of prep school slang.

He was one of a series of contacts, some Victoria's, some Chris's and some Julie's, who had smoothed their path in the past few months. It seemed to Daniel that somehow he had been lifted by the seat of his pants and hurled into a series of arrangements which he could hardly have imagined six months before. He had learned how to use sound-recording equipment from a friend of Julie's and had done a crash course in camera technique to back up Chris if necessary.

He had been made chiefly responsible for travel arrangements and the deeper he plunged into them, the more the romance faded as he discovered the remorseless inroads of the tourist into once-remote corners of the world. He had first become aware of this when he had gone to the Chinese Tourist Bureau off Baker Street and found that it was possible to travel from Pekin to Urumchi, even to Kashgar, by train and bus. He had picked up leaflets which advertised Red Arrow Express tours through the Gobi Desert: 'After breakfast we depart for the station and board the weekly Chinese train proceeding through the Gobi Desert,' one of them had started. The Silk Road was now a bus road. There were special train tours for railway buffs, garden tours for flower fanatics, there was even a cycling tour in Manchuria: 'While participants will need to be reasonably fit, no previous cycle touring experience is necessary. . . .' It all sounded like the Home Counties on August Bank Holiday.

But there was one major difference: it was not permitted to travel unaccompanied and there was not the remotest chance that they would be allowed to take in their lightweight cameras and recording equipment.

That was where Billy Mahindra had become involved. Describing the expedition as 'smashing fun', he offered his plane so they could take everything they needed into Sahr undetected. When he heard about their plan his eyes had flashed with delight behind his thick-lensed spectacles.

As they had prepared to leave, his other guests came and went. The cricket Test Match had drawn to its conclusion, and storms had swept down the Vale of Kashmir in black squally showers. They had watched the lightning crackle and had heard the thunder and Billy had said, 'Tasand is angry. He is our thunder fiend. Every now and then he comes from his cave to stir things up.'

'Not for us, I hope,' Victoria had said.

He had poured a glass of freshly-made lemonade and had passed it to her. 'You'll be okay, Aunt Vicky.'

Sahr's situation was never far from Daniel's mind. It was

now much more complicated than the pawn-like role it had played in the nineteenth century.

He had done his homework and discovered that it was one of those curious countries that sometimes crop up in remote parts, an enigma, a kind of no man's land, existing – if it could be said to exist at all as an ethnographic entity – because it had become a vacuum and no one wanted it filled.

It had always been on lists of the world's poorest countries. It had no trade, no quoted revenue, no balance of payments surplus or deficit. Most economists found difficulty in making any statements about it at all.

At the end of the nineteenth century it had been ruled by a Mir and had a population of less than 2,000. In the last few years of the century it had been struck by two tragedies. The first came from outside: a British anthropological expedition which had come to study the inhabitants brought with it a virulent measles virus. Isolated as they had been from the mainstream of the world's diseases and without the anti-bodies to cope, the people had died like flies. It was thought that the epidemic had wiped out nearly half the population. This catastrophe was followed by a famine which put paid to many of the remainder. By the beginning of the twentieth century the Mir had led what was left of his people into India, where they had been settled near Dharmsala, later to be the location where a far greater people – the Tibetans – had established their government-in-exile.

For some years the small abandoned kingdom was home only to the *markhor* and the Siberian roe, the wolf and the bear – and a few surviving Kalmucks. In the mid-thirties, fearing that Russia was about to make a move into Sahr, the Chinese claimed it. The British Government, as rulers of India, took China to the Permanent Court of International Justice at The Hague. By then China herself was under pressure from Japan in Manchuria and waging her own civil war. She made no attempt to defend herself; Britain won the case and Sahr remained a vacuum.

No one was sure exactly when a splinter of the Kalmuck Horde had settled there, but it was probably about 1905, and it was to their valley that Harry Coles Wynter had been brought.

With the Second World War, Sahr, like most of that part of Central Asia, disappeared behind a bamboo curtain. No one could be sure what was happening there. Rumours held that the Kalmucks had been driven out by the Chinese, but these were unconfirmed. The only thing known for sure was that when Chinese troops over-ran the Indian border posts in 1962, and the world held its breath as Asia teetered on the brink of full-scale war, at least one Chinese division had passed through Sahr on its way to the Indian border. Almost imperceptibly, it seemed, the world had accepted that the mountain kingdom had become a Chinese protectorate.

But recently, according to what Daniel had discovered in London, facts which Billy Mahindra expanded, the situation had changed dramatically.

The aggressive pressure of the Chinese under Mao, when they were playing their brinkmanship games in the Karakorums and along the length of the Himalayas, had ended. Since Mao's death, as part of their new image and their wooing of the West, the Chinese had pulled back from the positions they had taken. Neither India nor Pakistan now felt threatened by them. The Karakorum Highway had been built by Pakistan and China in co-operation. There was a new feeling of relaxation between the countries and any tension that did exist in the area was generated by Russia in Afghanistan. China's image was benefiting by comparison, and everyone seemed to have decided to forget her invasion of Tibet in 1950.

Sahr was still inaccessible by road, but wealthy Indian sportsmen had, in the past few years, been able to get permission to over-fly territory now 'under Chinese administration' – as the maps had it – and use the shooting grounds in Sahr. It was because of this that Billy Mahindra had been able to help them.

'It's a good time to go,' he had said. 'The Chinese want to be pals with India and pals with Pakistan, and they're having talks with the Russians at this very moment because they want to be pals with them, too. As usual, they're blaming everything that happened in the past on Mao and the Gang of Four.'

'You can't be pals with Russia *and* America at the same time,' Daniel had said.

Billy had glanced at him shrewdly. 'They're doing their best.'

'When were you last in Sahr?' Victoria had said.

'Just before Daddy died. Ram took us in in the plane and left us for a week. We never saw a living soul. The place is stiff with game. Daddy got the best *markhor* of his life with the last shot he ever fired. Nice, don't you think? I hope you've brought a decent rifle.'

'Three seventy-five magnum,' Chris had said.

'It's a bit on the heavy side, but it'll do.'

'Have you ever been into the Golden Valley?' Julie had asked.

'I don't even know exactly where it is. Never heard of it until Aunt Vicky mentioned it.'

When the storms abated they had taken off and put down at Gilgit to refuel and get the latest weather reports. They had wandered through the trinkety town, then stood in the clear mountain air and watched a tourist bus approach on its way into the Karakorums. *Tartary Safaris: Genghis Khan Tours* was stencilled on the side. Young faces peered out, from behind the steamed-up windows. Soon, Daniel thought, as travel became more comfortable, those same windows would be filled with blue-rinsed hair and Hawaiian shirts.

Chris said, 'Before the war the only motor vehicles ever to reach Gilgit were the caterpillar tractors of the Haardt-Citroen Expedition. And they had to be taken to bits and carried.'

'Progress?' Daniel nodded at the bus.

'You can't stop it.'

'So there'll soon be a car-park at the top of Everest and a Kentucky Fried Chicken stand in every village.'

'If it wasn't for progress we wouldn't be here. We wouldn't have cameras or sound equipment. We wouldn't even have an aeroplane.'

Ram met them at the airfield. He was of middle height, running to fat, and had once, according to Billy, worked as a pilot for Air India. 'You're lucky,' he said, consulting a sheet of paper. 'Weather's all clear for three or four days at least. But you know what that means?'

'Cold,' Victoria said as they climbed aboard the aircraft.

'Brass monkey weather. Hope you've got your woolly undies.'

They took off into brilliant sunshine, flying west of north. They had changed seats, and Daniel was sitting with Victoria in the rear of the aircraft. Julie and Chris were up front. Every now and then Chris would turn and talk to her. Sometimes she responded, sometimes she only nodded. She had spent a good deal of time with him before they left England, but that was natural. So, indeed, had Daniel. They were working as a team. But once or twice he had come back to the flat and she and Chris had been there together. He had not liked that and they'd had a blazing row.

Since leaving London there had only been one row. It had blown up the day after they landed in Bombay. She had not been in her hotel room when he called and later he found she had gone shopping with Parker. He had told her flatly that he didn't want her going off like that again.

'Chattel slavery was abolished in the eighteenth century,' she had said angrily. Was Parker the reason she had come, he wondered. She had made a sudden decision, almost too sudden. He would have to watch Parker very, very carefully.

As though aware that he was thinking of her, Julie turned to look at him, and smiled. Half-seriously, he found himself wondering whether his uncompromising attitude in Bombay had impressed her – a victory for the treat-'em-rough school of male behaviour?

Next to him, Victoria was studying a map. Accustomed himself to dealing with naval charts, he had been impressed by her professionalism. She was using an American Air Force operational navigation chart which had been prepared by the Defence Mapping Agency Aerospace Centre in St. Louis. She had cut the large sheets into manageable squares, pasted them on card and covered them in plastic. Every few moments she looked out of the window, tracing their route.

From the moment they started to plan the trip – Parker called it 'the expedition' – she had drawn on her enormous experience. Stores had been one of her responsibilities and as far as Daniel could tell they were going to live on spartan rations, though they would be healthy enough. Everything had to be light and concentrated, for everything would have to be carried in on their backs. She had mixed muesli and bought supplies of dried milk, slabs of dark chocolate, cubes of Maggi soup, which took his mind back to the rations used by his grandfather and Eric Burten. She had bought dried fruit and, through one of her contacts, had managed to lay her hands on dried meat – *biltong* – from southern Africa, which had the highest protein levels of any food. But although she impressed him, his emotions were not engaged by her, perhaps because she herself was so cool. The only emotion he had detected in her apart from her initial anger with himself and Julie, was her warmth towards Chris. Daniel was unable to judge him without bias and had to recognise that, even without the complication of Julie, the chemistry between them was wrong. One irritation was that Chris seemed to have been everywhere and seen everything. At one of their planning meetings he had mentioned the possibility of shooting a young *markhor* for the pot.

'What's a *markhor*?' Julie had asked, looking at Daniel.

He had never heard the word before but Chris had said, in a slightly superior tone, 'Asian mountain goat.'

It was that tone which had become increasingly annoying. Later when he had mentioned it to Julie, she had said, 'He *has* been everywhere. And he *has* done everything. And he *does* know a lot. Which is why we're going with him.'

The thrum of the engines was making him sleepy. The first few days at Gulmarg, which lay between two and three thousand metres above sea-level, had acted on him like a stimulant. Now the reaction had set in, though Gulmarg, at least, had helped their acclimatisation for the hard slog into the valley that lay ahead.

He woke from a light doze to find Victoria leaning across him, looking down at the ground.

'Sahr,' she said.

The plane banked and began to lose altitude, flitting like a bird along the flanks of the mountains, in and out of the shadows cast by the peaks. He could see a yellow-brown landscape, bisected by the thin line of one of the Chinese

154

military roads rushing up to meet them. The landing-strip had been put in by the Chinese in 1962 and he hoped that it was still in reasonable condition. A bump . . . another . . . and they were rushing along the ground in a cloud of dust.

[2]

Daniel held up a cardboard square on which the lettering *Sahr Expedition. Scene One* had been chalked, and Chris focused the camera and started shooting. Julie and Victoria lifted their packs and struggled into them.

'Start walking now,' Chris said. 'You too, Dan. Get your pack on and follow them.'

Daniel hated being called Dan, but did as he was told. The three of them moved along the valley floor with Chris using a wide-angle lens in the lightweight camera to give the effect of three small figures in the vastness of the landscape.

It was early afternoon and the heat in the valley was intense. It seemed impossible that the temperature would plummet to crackling, freezing cold as the sun left the area. The aircraft, and Ram's hand waving goodbye, was only a memory.

The landscape was much as it had appeared from the air, tawny, dry, treeless except for an occasional stand of birch. An ice-blue stream flowed down the centre. Nothing seemed to gain from the water, for its banks were hard gravel and sterile.

The mountains of the Sahr range towered around them, now, in early summer, streaked by snow almost down to the valley floor. Much of the snow was dirty where the wind had blown dust. It was not a prepossessing place, but at one time people had lived here and the evidence was all around them. The valley might once have been green but, as Billy had told them, it faced east, the direction from which almost no rain fell in summer. That, combined with overgrazing by goats and sheep, had turned the place into semi-desert.

They walked away from the landing-strip, itself no more

than a dusty, level stretch, heading north-east. They passed what had once been a village of stone houses. The roofs had long since gone and frost had cracked the stone, so that they were beginning to resemble natural phenomena. One day dust and mud would cover them completely and they would become simple bumps on the valley floor.

'That must have been the Residency over there,' Chris said.

He swung his camera towards a kind of Victorian villa which had clearly been built in the British Colonial style. Once the home of the British political officer, it too was a ruin. It had been built of larger blocks of stone, dressed by masons, an altogether more robust construction than the other houses, but even so the walls had collapsed into piles of rubble.

They picked their way into what was left of the building while Chris continued shooting. They had decided to make a film of the complete expedition so that if they found nothing in the Golden Valley, and had no natural story-line, the trip itself to this little-known corner of Central Asia would be of interest.

'Look at this.' Julie smoothed a piece of paper out in her hand. It was covered with Chinese characters.

'Cigarette packet.' Chris raised the camera. 'Hold it up.'

Daniel picked his way through the old building. The wood, if the floors had been wooden, had gone long ago. Fires had been made on the ground in the shelter of the standing walls, perhaps by nomads, perhaps by other expeditions passing through.

Victoria said, 'We shouldn't waste too much time, we've a long way to go.'

They formed a line and began to move up the valley, Victoria leading. She was confident of her directions and seemed completely orientated.

The exact whereabouts of the Golden Valley was something about which Daniel and Julie had talked at length when they had first discussed the trip. Finding it had seemed a major obstacle. But Victoria, through her contacts at the Royal Geographical Society, had been shown an account from the Society's archives in which the pilot of a World War II

156

aircraft described how he had flown low over Sahr trying to beat a storm. In a remote valley he had seen smoke and also figures. His navigator had pin-pointed the area and Victoria had the map-reference.

By mid-afternoon, the sun was off the valley and suddenly the temperature began to fall. The cold seemed to come flowing across the valley floor. Daniel had been drenched in sweat one moment, the next he was shivering.

They made camp about four o'clock. A wind had come, and as darkness fell they were glad to retreat into their tents. Daniel felt physically drained and in the light of the small lantern he could see that Julie's face was drawn.

'Would you like some tea?' he said.

She shook her head. They were sharing one tent. Victoria and Chris had one each.

'Sorry you came?'

'No. Are you?'

He thought for a moment, then said. 'Not now.'

She did not need to ask what he meant.

As the night wore on, the cold grew more intense; in the distance they could hear sounds like pistol shots as it cracked rocks high up the mountains. Occasionally, not too far from them, there was a slight thud as a splinter landed in the valley. He had read of climbers being killed, or seriously injured, by this hailstorm of stones that broke away in the cold. So far, they were sufficiently far out into the valley to escape.

He hardly slept and by the muffled coughing and restlessness of Julie next to him he knew that she, too, was having a bad time. He longed to turn towards her and take her in his arms, but separate sleeping-bags in freezing conditions were not conducive to such fancies. By morning he was so stiff he could hardly move.

They heated a mixture of dried milk and water and spooned down muesli standing up, not talking, clouds of steam coming from the milk and their breaths. Even Chris seemed subdued. The small stream beside which they had camped was frozen when they woke yet, within an hour of the sun striking the valley floor, it was flowing again.

*

They climbed steadily for two days towards the north-east col and when they reached it Chris estimated the height at between ten and eleven thousand feet. Snow lay all around them and the sun, blazing from a cloudless sky and reflected from the snow and the rocks, began to burn so that they had to cover their skins with cream.

On the col they made tea and lay on their packs in the sun.

Julie sipped and said, 'This is when I want a cigarette.'

Chris said, 'I didn't know you smoked.'

'I don't.'

'I'm glad.'

Julie did not reply.

Victoria rose and said, 'I'm going to reconnoitre. I'll be back in an hour.'

'I'll come with you,' Chris said.

'No.'

She left her pack, but took her parka and an ice-axe which she used as a climbing stick. Daniel watched as she swung away to her left and began to traverse the side of the mountain. Soon she was lost to view.

They were surrounded by massive peaks and he could not see where another valley might lie, yet there had to be one if Victoria was right. It was said to lie parallel with the main valley, but mountains seemed to hem them in, peak upon snowy peak. What kind of valley, he wondered, could lie at the dark, shadowy base of such monsters.

He was staring up at a tumbled moraine on the side of the mountain to the north when he caught a flash of light. It disappeared, then came again.

'Someone's watching us,' he said.

Chris turned to follow the direction in which he was pointing.

'See it? The kind of flashing light you get on the lenses of binoculars or a telescope.'

'Probably ice flare.' Chris lifted his own binoculars. 'Or a patch of crystals catching the sun.' He studied the moraine for some moments, then said, 'Nothing there.'

Daniel lay back on his pack and closed his eyes. At that

158

moment, drowsy in the sun, he could not bring himself to argue.

But the sun left the col early and he woke shivering. The wind had come up, but all around the peaks were still bathed in brilliant sunshine and the sky was cobalt.

As they waited for Victoria, Chris was writing in his log-book.

'Do you think she really knows where we are in relation to the valley?' Daniel said.

'She knows exactly.'

'I don't see how the valley can be near here.' He pushed himself up and stamped his feet. 'If it is, it must be in perpetual darkness.'

He walked to the edge of the col and looked north. Again he saw a flash of sunlight on the moraine opposite. The ground did not drop away more than two or three thousand feet before rising again into the side of the next mountain. He did not know the mountain's name, or even if it had one. On the maps they were simply numbers. The Sahr range was one of the least-explored of the chains of mountains which joined the Karakorums.

Standing in the bitter wind he felt as he sometimes had in the Navy when the sea stretched out all around him, knowing that if his ship went down there would be at least a thousand miles of water between himself and land in any direction. Now, as peak after peak rode towards the horizon, he wondered what would happen if they got into real trouble; what if one of them fell and broke a limb, if Julie had sudden appendicitis? Then he saw clearly in his mind's eye her small white scar running to the top of her pubic hair and suddenly her whole, naked body was in his mind. He turned and walked towards her. Chris was showing her his log-book and their heads were close. Daniel stopped, hating him. The small figure of Victoria showed itself on the skyline, first as a tiny dot that grew larger as she approached.

She led them off the col, traversing westwards and slightly downhill. They were in deep shadow. Already the snow was beginning to freeze, but this did not seem to bother her and Daniel marvelled again at the steely quality in her. He and Chris were carrying the heaviest packs, but hers was not much lighter. They turned one of the ridges on the flank of the mountain and were faced by huge grey cliffs rearing up ahead of them, blotting out the snow-covered peaks, making the greyness more intense. Victoria pointed at the cliffs with her ice-axe, though the direction looked to Daniel like a cul-de-sac. It seemed, if they followed her, that they must bump into the wall itself. He knew that they could not climb the cliffs, even if they had been prepared for rock.

As they moved further down the mountain, he realised that there had been an optical illusion. The mountain had seemed to present one unbroken cliff face, but there were, in fact, two cliffs split by the volcanic eruption which had formed them. The split could only be seen from one angle. It was not more than a few feet wide, just comfortable enough to move through with their packs. It was a narrow, dark defile, but above them, through the gap in the cliffs, which seemed constantly to be about to close in over them, they could make out the navy-blue of the sky. The wind, trapped in the twisting corridor, whistled by them, making conversation impossible.

They continued for nearly an hour before the cliffs began gradually to lean away from them on either side. The light grew stronger, the wind weaker. Soon they came out on another col. It was bathed in warm afternoon sunshine. They stood at the edge and looked down. Below them was a valley dappled in sunlight. There were stands of trees and green grass; a stream twinkled down the middle. A few hundred feet above the valley bottom was a band of rock a mile, or more in length, which glowed golden in the sunlight.

The valley seemed to be in the shape of a banana for, after a few miles, it swung south-west and was lost to view. It was so beautiful and so unexpected after the main Sahr valley that it left them speechless.

'The Golden Valley,' Victoria said.

They went down a rocky path, watched by a troop of *markhor*.

'Hang on!' Chris said.

As he unslung his rifle Julie said, 'You're not going to kill one!'

'Be quiet! Get down.'

The *markhor*, the males with twisted horns and small beards, the females with their kids, were about two hundred yards away, tense, uncertain.

'Go away!' Julie shouted. 'Go away.'

In a flash, they were gone.

Chris said nothing, did not look at her, but put the rifle back into its cover.

'We may be sorry you did that,' Victoria said.

Julie looked defiant and there were angry red spots on her cheeks.

As they descended, the wind dropped away and the air became almost balmy. They reached the valley floor and the sun was still on it in patches. It was warm enough to wash at the stream, although the freezing water tasted bitter. It rushed over a white stone bottom in a flood but Daniel knew this would soon stop as the melting snow on the high ground froze for the night.

'I've never seen anywhere like it,' Julie said.

'I could take you to a glen in Scotland between Carrbridge and Inverness and you could hardly tell the difference, except for the mountains.'

'Let's have a look around!' Her exhaustion had gone for the moment.

'Perhaps you'd like to help make camp first?' Victoria said. 'There'll be plenty of time to look round.' It was like being suddenly reprimanded by a headmistress.

The flood in the river dropped rapidly and that night they listened to its soft gurgling as it spilled and eddied over the stones. Daniel lay awake for a long time before he realised that the noise had stopped and that the river must have frozen. There was total silence, except for the occasional crack of splitting rock. He felt lonelier at that moment than he had ever felt in his life before. He removed his hand from the sleeping bag and touched Julie lightly. 'Are you awake?' he whispered

She turned. He heard a soft groan and then the even breathing again. She was sleeping heavily.

The morning was blue and gold and the air like a knife. After their usual breakfast of hot milk, muesli and tea, they began to walk down the valley. They stopped once and Chris warmed up the camera in its 'barney' – a kind of small overcoat – and he did a piece to camera while Daniel filmed and Julie made the recording. Only Victoria seemed to want no part in the making of the film. She walked on steadily with short, rapid strides, a slight figure dominated by her huge pack.

The sun quickly warmed the air and it grew hot, but this was not the desert heat of the Sahr Valley, it was more like the warmth of a Scottish glen on a blazing summer's day. The grass was not thick, but it was grass. Once or twice there was a sudden pungent smell as they walked through and crushed a patch of wild onions. On the slopes above them the trees were silver birch, dwarf juniper and some scattered pine, but on the valley floor and along the stream there were willows. They saw wild roses and wild clematis, forget-me-nots, gentians, columbines and jasmine.

They followed the river down in a wide loop. The valley gradually changed. From the eastern end, where they had entered, it had been narrow and deep; now it began to open out and they saw what looked like the remains of stone walls. There were several of them and they appeared to be the remains of corrals for sheep or goats. Chris filmed, then he made notes and did another short piece to camera, and by that time Victoria had disappeared. They went on for a mile or more without seeing her.

'She'll be all right,' Chris said. 'She's probably the toughest of all of us.'

The golden cliffs ran parallel to them along the valley. The river was flowing again, widening out now and becoming shallower as the valley itself widened. Mountain ridges came down into it to break its level surface and it was only once they had rounded each one that they were able to see the vista ahead.

About noon they came round a bend in the river and knew they had reached the end of their long journey.

It was a surprising end. Their physical goal, in Daniel's mind, had always been shadowy. He had imagined some kind of village and, having read of the round tentlike structures called *yurts* in Harry Wynter's diary, he had first built up pictures of a community of these dwellings. Then, having studied accounts of the hill tribes in Hunza and Ladakh, he had been more attuned to the ruined walls of the Sahr Valley, and small stonebuilt houses. To a certain extent, his imagination had been accurate. There were ruins of such houses. But they were dominated by a single unexpected structure: a monastery.

The golden cliffs here were not more than a hundred yards from the river. They towered above it in a bluff, and beneath the cliffs nestled the village, reminding him of cliff villages along the Dordogne in France.

The monastery seemed part of the organic structure of the cliff itself. The sun was striking it now and it glowed golden like the cliffs. It had a warmth, almost a textural feel, as though he was looking at a painting. Eagles soared above it.

What was unmistakeable was that it was in a state of massive ruin. Great blocks had fallen away and rolled down towards the river. Walls had collapsed outwards. Where there had once been window holes there were now large rents in the fabric. But there was still a great deal standing. It was as tall as a five-storey building with a frontage that he estimated at about a hundred and fifty feet. The three of them stood, awed.

'It's like a medieval castle and those little houses are the dwellings of the villeins,' Julie said. 'Where did they all go to? And why?'

'Like the *Marie Celeste*,' Daniel said.

'Don't let your imaginations run away with you,' Chris said. 'You'll find the explanation is more prosaic than that. Untenable weather conditions or *force majeure* is what usually causes this sort of decay.'

On the outskirts of what had been the village they could see the low stone walls of animal byres and they passed something which, to Daniel's eye, was a reminder of his youth. It was an oblong trough in the ground, lined with stone, one end of which was cut vertically, the other a more gentle slope.

'Looks like some sort of grave which has been opened and robbed,' Chris said.

'It's a sheep dip,' Daniel said.

'A what!'

'You push the sheep into the deeper end and they swim along and come out up the slope.'

They went on. Then Chris stopped and pointed to two holes in the cliff face above the monastery. Black streaks above one disfigured the rocks. The holes were about thirty feet apart and the cliff was sheer beneath them. 'Monks would have lived up there,' he said. 'They climbed up on long ladders, then pushed the ladders away. I've seen places like this before. They led lives of utter solitude. Food was passed up in baskets on the end of long ropes.'

They separated and took their own paths through the village towards the monastery. Daniel heard Julie call. He skirted a ruined house and found her looking at an old broken cart.

'Where are they all?' she said. 'If they're dead, there should be graves. People don't just vanish.'

Occasionally in what had once been a garden they saw stunted trees, but whether or not they had ever borne fruit they could not tell, for most were dead or blown over by winter gales. There was an air of sadness about the place, an eeriness that made them shiver.

She said, 'When we came in yesterday I thought the valley was a kind of Shangri La. But now. . .'

'Shangri La's not a place, it's a state of mind,' he said.

As though she was experiencing the same need he had felt during the night, she put her hand on his arm. He tightened his arm against his body. trapping her hand.

Chris was standing some little distance away, frowning at them. 'Have you seen Victoria?' he said.

'No, but there's her pack,' Julie said.

The pack was lying on the broad flight of stone stairs that led up to the monastery's entrance.

Chris turned towards the building and called. The echo bounced off the cliff walls.

They walked through the main doorway and picked their way over rubble from broken walls and fallen ceilings. In some places they could look up through two or three storeys to the sky above. The place had once been a maze of corridors and small, cell-like rooms. Now many had collapsed into each other. They found themselves in a large, cavernous room that must have been, Daniel thought, some kind of meeting-place, perhaps a communal dining-room. But its floor was cracked in places and heaps of rubble lay about. The ruin was too great to have beem caused by the passage of time. Daniel said, 'There must have been an earthquake.'

A strange and unpleasant smell hung over the building. 'Sort of old-cheesey,' Julie said.

Another voice to their left said, 'Rancid butter.' and Victoria stepped out from another room amd came towards them. 'The monks would have had butter lamps, and they put butter in their tea. The smell gets into the stone of a place like this. You get used to it.'

'I thought we'd lost you,' Chris said.

'I found this.' They stared in silence at a length of rubber-coated electric wire about six inches long.

'Wynter's?' Chris said. 'What on earth did he want it for? He couldn't have had a generator, could he?'

They searched the building for half an hour but found nothing more of interest except for blackened stones where fires had once been made.

The sun was still shining when they went out.

'Wynter probably lived in one of the houses,' Julie said.

'We'll have to go through each one,' Chris said.

'He may not even have lived here,' Daniel said. 'There could be another village farther down the valley.'

'No,' Victoria said. 'We've arrived.'

There was a shingle beach below the village and they pitched their tents on rising, gassy ground above it. Daniel bent to move a piece of wood so that he could drive in one of the tent pegs, and found it was nailed to a second piece.

'Look at this,' he said to Julie. 'It's like a kind of trestle.'

'There's another one,' she said, pointing. 'And some planks.'

'How the hell did they get planks here?'

'We'd better tell Chris. He may want to film them.'

'While you're filming I'll go back into the monastery,' Victoria said. 'This evening we'll work out a plan on how to search the area methodically.' She walked up what had once been a village lane, and disappeared.

*

Daniel woke with a start. It was a little after two o'clock in the morning. Bright moonlight penetrated the dark blue nylon, making the inside of the tent glow. The river had frozen and the valley was silent. His heart was hammering in his ears as though he had been having a nightmare, but he knew he had not been dreaming. Some noise outside had caused him to wake. He lay back, listening. Then he heard what sounded like a footstep. Chris or Victoria? He doubted it. In this cold you made sure you didn't have to get up during the night to relieve yourself. What if there were people living in this valley? People that no one knew about. Nomads? Bandits?

Still in his sleeping bag, he opened the tent-flap and looked out. He could see nothing except the brilliant ice flare of the river. The sound came again, as though a boot was scraping on a stone. His own boots were in the sleeping bag beside him and he quickly put them on and drew on his parka. The night was bitter and clear as crystal. The moon was three-quarters full. The sound was coming from the village and, carefully picking his way along one of the lanes, he walked towards the monastery. He thought for a moment he saw a figure or a shadow on the steps, then it was gone.

Softly, trying to step on tussocks of grass, he followed. He climbed the stairs. The entrance loomed in front of him. Through the broken walls and roof streamed bars of moonlight and he could see the large room in which they had been that afternoon. He stopped and listened.

There was something lost and other-worldly about the place. The smell came at him like a miasma. He thought of saffron-robed monks eating *tsampa* and drinking butter tea at long tables; he thought of the prayer-wheels that must have decorated the monastery; the great horns that sounded over the valley and the great gongs that clashed; and wondered how many monks had died when they were overtaken by the earthquake.

At that moment, like a sudden flash of sunlight on a mirror, he saw a glint of light. It came from somewhere in the depths of the monastery itself and flashed for less than a second. Then he saw it again, and softly he made his way forward.

As he moved into the interior of the building the smell of old butter seeped more strongly out of the stones. He followed

166

the jinking light until he reached a point where he could go no further, for the moonlight ended abruptly and the dark began. He was now somewhere near the rear wall of the monastery where it abutted on the cliff. The light came and went as though someone was moving a torch from left to right. It disappeared entirely, but after a minute or two it returned. The angle changed abruptly as it was pointed upwards and for a moment he saw a face. It was Victoria's. She was staring intently at the rear wall, holding the torch with one hand and feeling the stones with the other. Then the light moved and she disappeared and all that was left to his eye was the small circle of light dancing on the stones above her.

He watched for nearly half an hour, then began to freeze and went softly back to his tent. He had congealed in the monastery and was unable to get warm. He lay awake until the sun struck the tent. He spent the wakeful hours fretting at what he had just seen. It made no sense. Victoria had all the time in the world during the day to examine the monastery; even if she was suffering from insomnia, a night search made no sense.

The following morning, while they were sipping their tea in the early sun and watching the river begin to thaw, he said, 'I heard noises last night.'

'What sort of noises?' Chris said.

'Footsteps. It must have been about two o'clock. I couldn't sleep and I heard the scrape of a boot.'

'Probably rock fall,' Victoria said. 'Splitting in the cold up on the peaks.'

'You didn't hear anything then?' He looked directly at Chris and Victoria, who were standing together.

'Not a thing,' Chris said.

'I slept like a baby,' Victoria said.

'Must have been a ghostly monk,' Julie suggested.

They postponed the search of the houses because Chris wanted to do as much filming as possible while the clear weather lasted. Daniel was recording and it was some time before he had an opportunity to talk to Julie about what had happened.

They stood in an alleyway under the ruined wall of a house while he described what he had seen. She frowned, first in bewilderment, then in disbelief.

'Are you sure you weren't. . . ?' she began.

'Of course I'm sure. I nearly froze to death in the bloody place.'

'But why should she. . . ?'

'Precisely. Don't you get the feeling that her behaviour is odd, as though she knows something we don't?'

'She seems so certain she's right all the time.'

After they'd had their mid-day meal, they began to search the ruined houses, looking for anything that might connect the present with the past of Harry Coles Wynter.

Chris had drawn a rough map of the place and divided it into sections like an archaeological dig so they could work methodically. Daniel bided his time until each was hidden from the other by the walls of the houses they were searching. Then he moved quickly up one of the grass-grown alleys, up the steps and into the monastery. From the shadow of the entrance he looked back but could see no one, and hoped that no one had seen him.

Sunshine was pouring in, lighting the dusty interior. He went directly to the wall at the rear. It was about twenty-five to thirty feet wide and about ten feet high and part of it was illuminated by a yellow band of sunlight coming through the broken walls above it.

He looked at it for some minutes, then he began to run his hand over it, as Victoria had done the night before, but without knowing what he was looking for. The wall was just a wall. He moved along it, his fingers trailing over the rough stone surface, his nails picking up dry mud from the mortar between them. Then, towards the far end, where the sun did not shine and he had to examine the surface by touch alone, his fingers told him he had found something, or rather, that he had *not* found something. He felt again. What was missing was mortar. He strained his eyes in the gloom but could not see well enough. He found a box of matches in a pocket and in the sudden light he could see he had been right. There was an area about ten feet wide and stretching to the top of the wall where the stones had been laid without mortar. He noticed, too, that those at the top were not dressed as well as those at the bottom and some did not meet accurately. There were gaps where his fingers could go in. He wondered what he would touch if he poked a stick through. The cliff-face, of course. Or would he? His heart began to race. Was there a cliff-face behind the wall, and if there was, why would one go to all the trouble of building one when the cliffs themselves would act as a wall? He remembered the cliff sanctuaries along the Dordogne and some cliff dwellings near Granada. There the cliffs had been used as part of the building. He reached up as high as he could and placed his hand against the wall. A faint draught of cold air touched his palm and there was also a bar of light which must have come from the other side of the wall. If he could get up near the top he might be able to see through the gap between the stones. He looked for something to stand on, but there was only fallen masonry. He began to carry rocks to the base of the wall and soon had built a shaky mound about three feet high. It was unstable but, as he climbed on it, he decided he could hold his balance long enough to examine the gap. He had just steadied himself when a voice, echoing through the broken building, said: 'What are you doing, Daniel?' It was so unexpected that he automatically turned. For a fraction of a second he glimpsed Victoria, then the stones under his feet moved. He fell forward, saving himself by thrusting his hands against the wall. He felt it shift and threw himself backwards. As he did so, a section of the wall fell away from him with a roar.

Dust swirled around him as he got to his feet. The entire section of the unmortared wall had given way into what looked like a cavern. The dust was so thick that he was unable to make out anything other than the fact that there was a hole in the top of the cave through which sunlight streamed.

He was aware of Victoria standing next to him, but so great was their surprise that neither spoke. Then he heard running feet and Chris, followed by Julie, came through the outer room.

'Are you all right?' Chris said. Then he stopped. 'Jesus!'

They stood in the gap staring at a scene which, as the dust cleared, sharpened and refined itself like the image of photographic printing paper in a developing tank. Then, with great care, they picked their way across the rubble and moved into the cavern. The smell of rancid butter was much stronger.

The cave swelled out on either side of the wall into a chamber about thirty feet wide and twice as long, disappearing into dark shadows where dust veils hung. There was enough sunlight streaming in through the vent above for them to see what lay around them.

It was as though they had walked into a museum. To their right against the rock face and beneath the vent was a series of stone-built fireplaces and several brick ovens. Old black pots still hung on iron hooks above them and old utensils lay on the dusty floor. There *was* a *Marie Celeste* quality about what they saw, for in one of the pots was the remains of something that had been cooked but which had become petrified by time, and unidentifiable. Above the cooking area the cave's wall was covered in furry black soot where the smoke had made its lazy way up to the natural flue.

What faced them on the left-hand side of the cavern was even stranger. It was a kind of store-room with artefacts belonging to a more recent period. For a moment, Daniel saw in his mind the farm shed in which his uncle had stored what he called his 'bits and pieces' and where he had taught Daniel his manual skills. He could also have been looking at the back store of a small engineering company or a country garage. Everything was placed neatly in piles as though awaiting a storeman to disinter a piece of equipment on request. There was a large circular saw bolted onto its wooden frame, all set up with its drive belt. Next to it were four tree axes. Then there was a water pump and several more trestles similar to the ones they had seen near the river. There were lengths of planking nailed together longwise in a V-shape and alongside these were rolls of hosepipe, perished now and seamed by tiny cracks. There were boxes of nails and screws and bolts. There were shifting spanners and ring spanners and coils of wire. There was a rack on which hung saws and planes. There was what looked like a hammer-mill and a number of rolls of meshed wire, from fine to large. There were shovels and picks and coils of rope. Separate piles of drive belts lay against the wall. They were of varying lengths and widths, some had been used, some were still unmarked. There were three-pound hammers, some without shafts, and lengths of iron piping. There was a small forge with its charcoal still intact and its large bellows lying next to it. One section of the cavern seemed given over to agricultural implements, with fag-hooks and shears, bags of salt, ploughshares, chains, yokes, half-a-dozen hoes.

'For God's sake!' Julie whispered. 'What does it all mean?'

Victoria said, 'There's some kind of passageway at the back.'

She shone a torch into the back of the cave. They moved forward in a group as though unwilling to become separated.

The passage penetrated the rock for some yards then opened out into a second chamber. It was somewhat smaller than the first and the cold was intense. Around the base of the walls were several sealed drums and in the centre of the floor was a huge mound covered by a blanket of sheep- and goat-skins, some grey-white, some brown, which had been sewn together.

They stared at it for a moment, then Daniel and Parker each took an end of the blanket and began to pull it back. Daniel found himself suddenly afraid of what they might find, something which had been hidden, undisturbed, for so many years. But nothing in his imagination could have matched reality. As they pulled back the blanket a car was revealed. In its livery of black and green it stood in the middle of the cavern like some arcane god-head whose secret place this was. It glowed in the light of Victoria's torch, its brasswork shining dully through the layer of grease that covered it. The tyre-covers had gone from its back wheels and been replaced by iron tyre bands of the kind used on wagons. Its front wheels and axle were missing and it was propped up on two petrol drums, giving it the look of a great beast that had been wounded, a modern minotaurus awaiting its victims. They stood gazing at it as the minutes passed, unwilling to believe its existence. Then Parker walked slowly towards the front end, hesitated for a second and lifted one side of the engine cowling. Victoria directed the beam of her torch into the vital organs. 'It's the Abbott Special,' he whispered, and even the whisper echoed from the chamber walls.

They crowded round him. The engine was coated in grease. Victoria played her torch over the wheel hubs and bent to shine the beam on the gearbox and finally the underbelly of the car. Everywhere, on every nut and bolt, every joint, on every piece of bare metal, there was a coating of grease. The car was in a state of perfect preservation.

They continued to inspect it as though hypnotised until, after a while, the fierce cold drove them out into the sunshine, where they stood in a silent group, unable to take in the significance of what they had discovered.

Then Daniel said, 'He went back to fetch it.'

'How on earth did he get it here?' Julie said, remembering the tortuous route by which they had entered the valley.

'In pieces,' Parker said. 'But what a hell of a job!'

Daniel was watching Victoria. Had she known? Was this what she had been looking for? Or had she simply sensed that there was something not quite right about the wall?

'But why go to all that trouble?' Julie said.

'To preserve it, obviously,' Parker said.

'Here? In the middle of nowhere? What'd be the point?' Daniel said.

'It's worth a fortune,' Parker said. 'He may have thought. . .'

'It wasn't worth a fortune then. It's only *now* that it's valuable.'

Julie said, 'Anyway, supposing you're right, and he brought it here in pieces and reassembled it. He was just going to

172

have to take it to bits again to get it out. It doesn't make sense.'

'It does in one way.' Victoria had hardly spoken and her voice startled them. She was suddenly looking older; not a well-preserved woman in her forties, but her true age, drawn and pale.

'In what way?'

'It helped him to create a world for them.'

They waited for her to explain, but she turned away and walked back into the cavern.

During the remainder of the afternoon they made an inventory of everything in the two caves. Victoria kept to herself, studying the artefacts, lifting them, returning them to their places, shining her torch into dark corners as though convinced there were further discoveries to be made. But they found nothing more.

Parker discussed how he would film the caverns. He decided it could be done only with available light when the sun struck squarely on the air-vent, but there was no sunlight in the rear cavern to film the car. He took a roll of flash shots of every aspect of it, explaining that it would have to be moved into the light before they could record it on videotape.

They could only work inside for short periods because of the cold. When the sun left the monastery and the temperature dropped even further, they gave up for the day.

The sun shone in the valley and everything was still in the warm, golden light. Parker brought a bottle of whisky from his tent and said, 'Celebration time! Come on, Julie, let's find some firewood.'

They went to the shingle beach to fetch some of the old trestles and planking. Among it Parker found a frame on which wire mesh had been nailed. They paused briefly to study it, but could not decide what it might have been. The mesh itself had rusted, and crumbled to nothing as it was touched.

Soon flames were crackling and leaping through the old, dry wood. They stood around the fire, drinking the whisky.

Parker and Julie could talk only of the film they were

planning: both professionals, both judging, knowing they had something unique.

'Finding the Abbott makes our story ten times as good,' Parker said. 'We've got material now for a two-parter, and I can't see any reason why it shouldn't go world-wide.'

'We still haven't a clue why he did it;' she said. 'Nor what happened. We need to know that. I mean, they built that wall as though they were deliberately hiding all those things, including the Abbott. It's as though they meant to come back. So what happened to them?'

Victoria said, 'I checked with the Royal Geographical Society before we left. There's no record of the Kalmucks leaving the valley.'

'People don't just disappear.'

'They were nomads,' Daniel said. 'After my grandfather died they might simply have moved on. Don't forget, they'd spent hundreds of years moving on. The fact that there's no record in London doesn't mean anything.'

'Wouldn't they have taken some of their belongings with them?' Parker said.

'And why wall up the cave?' Julie said.

'To preserve the car?' Daniel suggested. 'Maybe they thought it was a God. Like the Cargo Cult in New Guinea.'

The whisky took effect quickly. Perhaps it was their excitement added to the altitude , for soon Daniel felt light-headed. He knew that Julie and Chris were feeling the same, for they were laughing more than usual. Only Victoria seemed unchanged, for she had hardly touched her drink.

They discussed what they had found, over and round the subject. Then suddenly Chris leapt up and began to dance on the sand, clapping his hands above his head. Julie joined him and, laughing, they began a shuffling flamenco, crunching their feet on the shingle, as Parker sang a wordless *cante jonda*. They whirled faster and faster until Julie tripped and sprawled on the shingle and he allowed himself to fall half on top of her. It was clumsily done, unsubtle, and Daniel was gripped by the rage which had been lying dormant in him since the day he had first met Parker.

Parker had his arms round Julie and she was still trying to laugh, but at the same time struggling to get away. Abruptly,

Daniel leant forward, gripped him by the collar of his heavy plaid shirt and yanked him backwards.

'For Christ's sake, stop pawing her!' he said.

Parker came up like a cat onto one knee and his hands were suddenly in front of him like weapons. The laughter was gone. There was a sinewy coldness and the look of a predator about to attack. But Daniel's anger was so great that he welcomed what he knew was about to happen, bracing himself, tasting the projected violence.

Victoria came between them. 'Stop it! Stop it! You're like children.' Her voice was harsh with contempt.

Daniel's rage died and his body began to shake with reaction. Slowly, Parker stood up. They looked at each other for a moment over Victoria's head. Julie rose, her face white.

'Try to behave like adults,' Victoria said. 'We're a long way from home. We only have each other to depend on. If we can't do that, we may very well not survive.' She turned and walked away along the river bank.

Daniel said, 'I'm sorry.'

Parker stared at him for several seconds, then bent to pick up his fallen glass.

Shivering, Daniel fetched his heavy parka from the tent and walked up through the village. He was still angry, but forced himself to push it to one side. Victoria was right. This was not the time nor the place. All his naval experience had taught him that the only way to survive in danger was to be part of a team and to carry out your own part as well as you could. On the other hand, that was why he had left the Navy. He did not like being part of a team. He found himself at the monastery and climbed up the steps, making for the car.

He stood in front of it, playing his torch over the bodywork. More and more it resembled an amputated animal. *Had* those people worshipped it? Had it become some kind of idol? He thought of Harry Coles Wynter struggling through the desert with the dying Eric Burten and being tracked by the four Kalmuck horsemen. Harry Wynter had got it wrong from the start. They hadn't wanted to kill him, or they would have done so in the desert when he was alone and sick and on foot. What *had* they wanted, then? And why had they brought the car into the valley? He thought of the immense task it would have been to take it to pieces and carry each part through the narrow cleft in the cliffs. It simply didn't make any sense. The engine block alone would have weighed half a ton. He prowled round the car. The grease had hardened into a sticky substance and was mixed with dust. As he examined it, an idea, amorphous and fragmented at first, began slowly to grow in his mind like an amoeba.

'Daniel?'

Julie came through the outer cavern and stood beside him. She slipped her hand through his arm. 'I'm sorry. I shouldn't have played his silly games. I want you to know I didn't mean anything by it.'

'Is he why you came?'

'No.'

'Sure?'

'Yes, I'm sure.'

'Why did you?'

She paused, then said. 'It's simple. I didn't want to lose you. You know what they say about kids: the only way you'll ever keep them is to let them go? Well, it doesn't work quite that way with grown-ups. We've both had the same sort of experience: you being away from Jo for long periods; Freddie and I always saying good-bye.'

For a moment he was out of his depth, then he remembered that Freddie had been the actor with whom she had lived.

'The more successful he became, the more he was away,' she said. 'Finally, he just didn't come back. I kept thinking this would happen to us if you went back to sea or Dubai or wherever.'

'Glasgow?'

'Yes, Glasgow. So I tried to stop you. Tried to put you off. But when this trip came up, I knew that if I put you off, I'd lose you – and yet I was too scared of letting you go alone. So . . . well, now you know.'

'I thought you might have come because of Chris.'

She touched his face in a characteristic gesture, and smiled. 'No, Dan, no!'

'For God's sake, not Dan!'

'I'll stop calling you Dan if you stop being silly.'

'If I wasn't so bloody cold I'd. . .'

'Not now. Not in front of the Abbott.'

He put his arms around her. 'As we were?'

'More so. You?'

'Much more so. I've been afraid – I thought I might have lost you.'

'I've followed you half-way round the world. Fat chance of you losing *me*.' She indicated the car. 'We've come about as far as he did.'

He said, 'I keep wondering why they brought it. Think of the effort involved. And I keep on wondering why they didn't kill him.'

'Why should they? They weren't Khazak raiders. They were Kalmucks and they were half-starved.'

'That's true. But in the *Diaries* he himself thought he was in danger from them.' He was still looking at the car and voiced the thought that had now reached maturity: 'God, if only we could get it out!'

'Out of the monastery?'

'Out of the valley. Out of Central Asia. It's worth a fortune.' Abruptly, he turned and led her back into the first cavern. He played his torch over the implements in their boxes and on their racks. 'Everything's here. Every spanner and wrench. Every tool one would need to get her going again. Even petrol.'

'Everything except the front wheels,' Julie said.

That night they ate their meal together as usual, building up the fire and sitting round it. But there was no communication. As the crackling cold descended, it gathered in the river bottom and soon the mist began to rise. They went to their tents. The sexual tension between Daniel and Julie was overwhelming. As their lips met he felt a surge of blood in his abdomen and the kiss became almost an act of violence as though two carnivores were tasting each other in preparation for a feast.

Their tent was thirty yards from the other two, but no matter where it had been, nothing, at that point, could have stopped them. All control vanished. They ripped at the zips of the sleeping bags and formed one large envelope and then, pulling and fumbling at each other's clothes, they undressed.

177

The tent began to shake. Various cooking implements hanging from the roof pole knocked together, sounding like a dozen bell-wethers.

It was quickly over for both of them, and in spite of the cold, Daniel was sweating. Every muscle was flaccid, as though shot with novocaine. They lay, held in each other's arms, and he fell instantly asleep.

He slept more deeply than he had since the journey began and when he woke in the early dawn he felt more peaceful than he had for a long time. In their sleep they had adjusted their bodies so that they lay in their familiar way, her bottom in his stomach, his knees in the crook of hers, his arm over her, enfolding her and drawing her into him.

He thought that this was how it should always be: Julie and himself, together, married, with children. Yet he knew it could not happen yet, that his own pride and stubborness would not let it happen until he was his own man again, with a job and money in the bank and a future. The film might make the difference and yet . . . it wasn't really *his*, no matter what anyone said. If the film world was to be his future he would like to enter it on his own terms, with his own money and his own equipment. It was not too far away from his original idea of life, apart from a desk or an office. But he was aware of his need to lead – egotistical as it might seem.

Since the start of the expedition he had seen what equipment was necessary and learnt how much cameras, recorders, film would cost. All were beyond him. What he needed was a massive injection of money or a job that would interest and fulfil him, or both. The real irony was that here was his chance. The Abbott Special was valuable. It might be worth fifty thousand pounds. Or double. Or treble. It was worth what someone would be willing to pay. And historic cars were excellent investments and big business. For a few moments, he fantasised. Say the car had not been taken to pieces; say there was another exit from the valley and it had been driven here. If it could be driven in, it could be driven out. There was no doubting its toughness. It was built like a tank and had already got through the Nankow Pass and across both the Black Gobi and the Takla Makan before it had been set against the mountains.

There might have been times when movement under its own power was impossible and the Kalmucks had carried or pulled it. Now there were military roads all over the Sahr range. They were primitive tracks for the most part, built for self-propelled guns, half-tracks and personnel carriers, but if they could get along such roads there was no reason why the Abbott couldn't.

But – and this was the final big but – nothing could be done without the wheels. He could not imagine why they had been removed. What was the point? Perhaps they had been so damaged on the trip into the valley that they had been irreparable. But that didn't make sense. The rest of the car was immaculate. If his grandfather had damaged the wheels he had certainly had enough time to replace them or have others made, and that would have been in keeping with the general picture, the care which had been taken of the car. What was the point, after all, of preserving something so perfectly when you could not ever expect to use it? Unless . . . unless the wheels had been used for something else, a temporary expedient, something like. . . .

He rose swiftly. Julie half woke and he kissed her on her temple.

'Where you going?' she mumbled.

'Outside.'

'Come back.'

'Yes.'

His boots had hardened in the cold and he had to force his feet into them. Finally he got them on and laced up. Julie had drifted into sleep again.

The mist had thickened during the night and he could not see the other tents or the river. Occasionally he could hear the crack of splitting rock, but nothing more. It was a dead, silent world, withdrawn behind its mist. This was how Harry Wynter must have seen it on countless mornings. And just for a split second he had a vision of the houses, roofed and inhabited, orange fires glowing, smoke mixing with the mist; the sound of animals; women calling to children. They seemed to be all round him: voices, shadows. And deep in the monastery the smell of old butter, the monks moving, the throaty sound of the horns, the clashing of brass cymbals, the

179

fluttering of prayer wheels. The two layers of inhabitants fused in his mind and he stood still in the mist as their ghosts passed him by. Then the vision vanished and he picked his way through the ruined alleys, past broken walls and smashed chimneys. God knew what fearful event had overtaken these places. A second earthquake?

He searched for more than an hour. He lost his bearings in the mist and once had to go down to the ice-covered river to reorientate himself. From the river he worked up again towards the cliffs, tracing and retracing his steps through each alley. At last he found what he was looking for. He came upon it suddenly, almost bumping into it, for the grey wood of which it was made blended with the grey of the mist. It lay on its back, its gaunt wooden ribs rising up like bones. It had not been a very large cart, but it must have made a difference to the lives of the people. He touched it. The wood was not rotten like that of the old trestles, but had been smashed by whatever had smashed the houses and the monastery. It had a single shaft that had partly broken away from its base and he assumed that two bullocks yoked on either side would have drawn it. But drawn it on what? That was the point of his search.

It lay next to a ruined house. All that remained of the house was part of a side wall and the empty interior where the floor had once been laid. This was overgrown by a tangle of wild clematis. He stepped into it and forced the trailing stems aside. For a moment he was fearful that in the dense bush he might suddenly come upon a snake, but told himself that in this cold no snake would be active.

He continued to search until he cracked his shin on something he knew was not wood. He bent, pulling aside the matted tendrils, until he found what he had guessed, but hardly dared to hope might be somewhere near the cart; its wheels. He examined them. The hickory spokes were badly scarred, but they were still intact. Iron tyre-bands had been sweated onto specially-made felloes. He knew now what the small forge had been for. The hubs still had their caps and he brushed away the mud and dirt which had gathered on them. Underneath he read the words, 'Abbott Motor Co.,

London, England.' So the front axle of the car, with its two wheels, had been used to create a second vehicle, the cart.

If they could get the axle and the wheels refitted, and if they could get the grease-covered engine firing again, then . . . then why not?

'Why not?' Victoria said. 'Because it's impossible, that's why! You can't go anywhere in a car without front wheels!'

They were standing on the shingle beach. The mist had been burnt away and the early sun was warm. The stream was beginning to trickle again.

'I'm saying if. *If* we could find the front wheels?'

The hypothesis obviously irritated her.

'How would you get it out?' Parker said. 'Take it to pieces again with a screw-driver?' He laughed.

'Not necessarily. I don't think it ever was taken to pieces. I think there's another way into the valley. I think he drove it in. And if it could be driven in, it can be driven out.'

'Even if it could, what then?' Parker said.

'Use the military roads. Travel at night. Try and get it to the Karakorum Highway.'

'Suppose we can't?'

'Get it as close as we can to the border so that we could reach it with a helicopter. At the Falklands the big Sea Kings picked up much heavier loads than the Abbott.'

'D'you think the Chinese would tolerate something like that?'

'We'd be gone before they knew.'

'What we really need is Chitty-Chitty-Bang-Bang to fly it out,' Julie said.

But Parker had been staring at Daniel in a different way. Slowly he said, 'It might be worth a try. I mean, if we could get it out it'd be worth a fortune. Especially with its history – and especially matched with the Bulldog-Saxon.'

Victoria threw the dregs of her coffee onto the ground and said, 'It's an interesting hypothetical situation, but since we don't have the front wheels, the whole thing is. . .'

'But I do,' Daniel said. 'I know exactly where they are.'

It was as though he and Parker were suddenly alone. The hostility between them still crackled like electricity but there was something else now, a shared interest, a masculine emotion, a special knowledge of what might and what might not be a reality.

Victoria seemed to sense that events were rapidly building over which she had no control. 'This is ridiculous!' she said.

But Parker took no notice. 'We'd need the axle.'

'I know where that is, too.'

Victoria said, more vehemently, 'Don't be silly, Chris!'

He turned to her: 'Can't you imagine what this would mean to the Trust? Having both cars. Why, we could sell them. . .!

'The Abbott isn't *your* car,' Daniel said.

Parker laughed. 'You think it's an inheritance?'

'Why not?'

'You can't be serious.'

'I'm serious enough to make problems.'

There was a pause, then Parker said, 'Do you think you could manage to put it together by yourself?'

'No.'

'I could.'

'Maybe.'

Victoria said, 'Chris, I forbid. . .'

He took her arm and marched her several paces away. They talked in fierce whispers, Parker's hand stabbing the air for emphasis.

Julie said, 'You must be mad, Daniel! This would jeopardise everything. We have a film nearly made and you'd. . .'

'Why should it? You and Victoria could film while we worked on the car. You both know what to do. You could film us at work. And if we got the car going. . . Christ Almighty, we'd have a much better film than the one we've got. *And* we'd have the car.'

Parker came back to them, his flat Slavic face triumphant. 'All right. We'll do it together. Only one condition: the car comes to the Trust.'

'Victoria said the Trust wanted nothing out of this. We have contracts.'

'Nothing about cars in the contract. Read the small print.'

'You do it then,' Daniel said. 'That is, if you ever find the wheels, and if you've got the time and the strength.' They stared at each other. 'You see, you can't do it without me, just as I can't do it without you.'

Parker nodded, as though he had been prepared for this. 'Okay, but there's still a condition: if we ever get her out, the Trust buys her from you.'

'How much?'

'Ten thousand.'

'She's worth five or six times that!'

'Of course she is. At Sotheby's. In London. Intact.'

Victoria was standing some little way off. Her face was cold, as though she wanted to disassociate herself from the haggling.

But Julie, emotions near the surface as always, turned on Daniel. 'How can you! How can you bargain like this? We came here to discover whether your grandfather was the victim of. . .'

'We came here to make money,' Daniel said flatly. He turned back to Parker. 'All right. Ten thousand and all rights in the documentary. We'll write a contract now.'

Parker shrugged, but his eyes were excited. 'If that's what you want.'

[4]

'Jesus, what a mess!' Parker said.

He and Daniel cut away the wild clematis and revealed what lay beneath to the bright sunshine. A curious armistice had formed between them. Below it, the old hostility remained, but now they needed each other.

After a trip up to the monastery to fetch tools, Parker said, 'We'll be able to bolt the axle directly onto the road springs. It'll be bumpy, but you·could build a tank on that chassis. I've never seen anything like it.'

'What do we do first?'

'First we get the axle and the wheels onto the car, then we bring her out of the back cave into the front one. We can work in the sunlight, and Julie can film.'

'How long d'you reckon it'll take?'

'God knows.'

They had five days before the plane was due to pick them up in the main Sahr valley. Five days in which to get the Abbott Special going again and to find a way out of the valley. The plan was to rendezvous with the aircraft, which would take out Julie and Victoria after which the two men would try to find a way with the car through the mountains to reach the Karakorum Highway.

There would come a point of no return when a decision would have to be made, when the whole project would have to be abandoned and they would have to walk out the way they had come in.

It took them most of the first morning to transport the axle and the wheels up into the monastery where they could bolt them onto the car. This last was surprisingly easy, for like everything else the original bolts were intact and had a coating of grease. It was as though, in the back of Harry Wynter's mind, had always been the thought that one day the Abbott might be reassembled. But it was the only easy job.

When the front wheels were fitted, they inspected the rear wheels.

'At first I thought that was the rim,' Parker said, touching one of the iron tyre bands that had been fitted to the four wheels. 'But it isn't. The originals were special tyres. He'd never have got them again. Easier to make something permanent, or else get new wheels entirely, and that would have been a problem here. These old cars needed blacksmiths as often as they needed mechanics.'

It was late in the afternoon before the Abbott stood squarely on its own four wheels and the two men were exhausted and half-frozen. They pushed the car slowly and gently through the connecting passageway into the comparative warmth of the outer cave. Iron wheels crunched on the stone floor.

The next day, they tackled the engine itself.

Julie, still angry at what she considered a kind of treachery on Daniel's part, nevertheless did what she could to film their work. Victoria, unwillingly, explored the lower portion of the valley to search for an exit, but found extensive marshy ground. There were doubts about the fuel. 'It's been here for more than thirty years,' Parker said. 'Petrol loses its combustibility if it's in contact with the air over a long period.'

There were more than forty square, five-gallon tins. Some contained kerosene, some oil, but most were petrol-cans. Each would have been brought into the valley by pony or yak from the Russian merchant in Kashgar. They were marked with Cyrillic printing which neither Daniel nor Parker could read, but they assumed that they had come from refineries at Baku.

Whoever had filled them had done a good job. The caps were still sealed. Parker shone his torch over them. Only a few had areas of rust and these they put aside to discard.

'Let's open one,' Parker said. They carried one of the rustless cans outside, holed it and poured a little petrol onto the stone floor, then put a match to it. There was a moment's pause, then the flame caught and the petrol ignited.

They drained the fuel tank and refilled it, then drained the engine sump and refilled it. Finally, with some of the petrol, they began to clean the grease from the engine. This was a long and tedious job.

The following morning, as soon as the sun lit the outer cave, they began on the engine, but not before Parker had had a row with Victoria. He had asked her to go down the valley again and search for a way out. She had said, 'There is no way out! And this whole scheme is ridiculous!'

'There has to be a way. I agree with Dan. Wynter drove it in.'

'*All right*! He drove it in!' Suddenly she was on the edge of hysteria. From this cool, enclosed, elderly woman, it came as a double shock, as though she was suddenly exposing some flaw in her psyche that she had kept well hidden. 'Things have changed! It was more than fifty years ago!' She was trembling now, and turned away. They watched her go off into the ruined village, then Julie followed her and they disappeared behind a collapsed house.

'What caused that?' Daniel said.

'I don't know. If we can get that engine to fire today, one

of us can go down the valley tomorrow and find a way out.'
Parker paused. 'I've not seen her like this before.'

They climbed up into the monastery and started work. 'If
this was a modern car, we wouldn't have a chance,' Chris
said, fitting the big starting handle to the front. 'But then
there isn't a modern car that could stand the hammering this
one has.' He turned the engine over very slowly and there
was a sucking noise. 'Right. Now let's have a look at the
magneto.'

They unbolted the magneto, which was about the size of
four of their fists. He handed Daniel a lead to hold. 'Hang
onto that. If you feel anything, let me know. Anything at all.'

There was a coupling on the front of the magneto which
he turned by hand in a series of jerks. 'I'm doing what the
starting handle does. Feel anything?'

'No.'

'These things pick up damp, no matter how dry the atmosphere is. We'll cook it. Fetch up some of that wood.'

Daniel hesitated. The order had been so peremptory that
it had jarred his hostility to the surface again. But he told
himself that this was not the time for injured pride. He
collected some pieces of dry planking and they made a fire
in one of the monks' old cooking areas and hung a black pot
over it in which they placed the magneto, covering it with a
lid.

'While that's drying we'll take out the plugs and clean
them,' Parker said.

Daniel removed the plugs and washed them in petrol,
taking care not to damage the sparking gap. Parker worked
on the back wheels. 'Well, that's a bugger,' he remarked
suddenly. 'No brakes. None on the front nor the back. Looks
like they've had these back wheels off before and never refitted
the brakes. We'll just have to use the gears.' Julie came in
and he looked up at her. 'How's Victoria?'

'Better.'

Julie was filming their work now whenever the sun in the
cave was bright enough, getting as much as possible on tape
for editing later.

After several hours they took the magneto out of the pot

and let it cool, then Parker asked Daniel to take the leads again as he twisted the coupling.

'Anything?'

'No.' Then suddenly both his arms jerked up into the air and his body felt as though someone had hit him at the base of the neck. 'Wow!'

Parker turned the coupling again and again Daniel's body jerked as the current passed through it.

'We're in business,' Parker said.

They refitted the magneto and he showed Daniel how to operate the advance and retard levers on the steering wheel. Then he went to the front of the car. 'Well, here goes!'

He gripped the starting handle and swung it. The engine gave an asthmatic wheeze. He swung again. And again. He swung until his arm began to cramp. Then Daniel took his turn. Each time the engine coughed and wheezed and stuttered, but would not come to life. Both men were sweating.

'We'll check that magneto again,' Parker said. He unfastened one of the leads and held it near the engine block. 'Swing!'

Each time Daniel swung a long blue spark crackled from the lead, arcing towards and making contact with the engine metal.

Parker refastened the lead and stood, deep in thought. 'These engines are dead simple,' he said. 'If you've got fuel and it's coming through, if the spark plugs are clean, if you've got a magneto and it's pushing out a spark, then, damn it, you should get it to fire. Try again.'

They swung and swung, but the engine only wheezed and spluttered. Eventually they stopped and stared at the Abbott Special, hating her.

In the silence, the scream was very loud.

'Victoria!' Daniel was already running and the others followed.

The scream had come from the area of the monastery which had been most severely damaged by the earthquake, where walls and upper storeys had collapsed onto the ground floor. It was a mass of rubble and stone blocks and reminded Daniel of pictures he had seen of Cologne and Hamburg at the end of the war.

'Where are you?' he called.

'Here!' The voice was quite close, but he could see no way through the rubble and thought for a moment that she must have fallen. He climbed over several large, broken slabs and saw an opening on the other side. He lowered himself to the ground and found himself in a passageway they had not previously seen. He moved along it and suddenly came into a third cave which, like the first, was illuminated by rays of sunshine from an opening above. Victoria was standing there, staring at its contents.

It was smaller than the other two caverns and had obviously been used as a living area. There was a wood and canvas camp bed against the right-hand wall. The wooden pieces had been smashed and the canvas was in strips. Alongside it was a wooden chest and this, too, had been smashed. A broken lantern lay beside it. Nailed onto the rock wall above the bed were three old posters issued by British railway companies. There was a picture of Ilfracombe behind a locomotive from the Great Western Railway. Another showed the Lake District and a third the Scottish Highlands. They had been torn in places and were covered by dust. On the ground, where it had fallen, was an old *Country Life* calendar. Beyond the chest, lying on its side, was the remains of a Zenith Trans-Oceanic radio. It had been broken by something heavy and its back had burst open, showing the old batteries. Their acid had long ago leaked out and they were covered in white, encrusted powder.

But these were not the objects that had provoked Victoria's scream. The reason for that lay along the left-hand wall. There were perhaps twenty of them, still clothed, lying in the strange, abandoned attitudes in which they had fallen: whitened skulls, feet with long, tapering bones. Some even retained remnants of their skin, parchment-coloured, with the texture of crisp, old leather.

'Oh, my God!' Julie burst out.

They were all swept by the horror of the discovery. They turned away, searching for somewhere else to look, and the shock was reflected in all their eyes. Julie groped her way towards Daniel and he put his arm around her shoulders.

'Who are they?' she whispered.

'Don't you know?' Victoria said. 'Can't you see?'

She pointed to one of the skeletons but her arm was shaking so wildly that at first they could not make out what she was pointing at. On its feet, still in place after all these years, was a pair of English mountaineering boots with ridges of nail heads on the soles and heels. Daniel felt his insides turn to water. He knew, with utter certainty, that he was looking at what remained of his grandfather.

Parker said, 'They must have been caught by an earthquake.'

For a moment, it seemed the only explanation, then Daniel said: 'But nothing's collapsed on them. They would have been safe here.'

'Why is the furniture broken? The bed and that chest?'

'Could they have been brought in? Could this be their tomb?' Julie said.

'Look at them more closely,' Victoria said.

Daniel crouched next to one of the skeletons and saw a small loop of wire around its wrist-bones. Several other bodies had the same attachment. He understood what Victoria had already seen. 'They weren't killed by an earthquake. They were murdered. They were tied by the wrists first and then killed.' He straightened and looked at the rock wall behind the bodies. It was pockmarked by bullets. 'First they were tied up, and then they were herded in here and shot. But there are only about twenty. What happened to the others?'

Parker bent down and picked up several empty brass cartridge cases. He examined them in the shaft of sunlight. 'Russian,' he said, passing one to Daniel.

As Daniel looked at it, he felt a tremor, a kind of fluttering inside his chest. It grew more severe and they heard the rumble of a rockslide. They looked round in panic.

'Earthquake!' Daniel shouted, and grabbed Julie by the arm, pulling her back along the narrow passageway and forcing her ahead of him through the gaps in the rock slabs. Parker thrust Victoria after them. The whole mountain seemed to be coming down on top of them. Dust lashed through the air, making it impossible to see. Daniel expected at any moment that the great blocks would dislodge themselves and block the entrance. They fought their way back into the open. Briefly, he was deaf and blind, then his senses cleared and he knew what the noise was: thirty feet above them hovered a helicopter.

It was making an appalling din and churning up dust with every sweep of its rotor. Then it suddenly swung past them and landed on the open space at the bottom of the monastery steps.

It bore Chinese markings, and after some minutes a door in the side opened and a man in military uniform jumped down. Julie and Daniel had come to the front of the monastery, and they were joined by Victoria and Chris Parker. They were all covered in dust and shamefaced after their panic.

'How do you do?' The Chinese officer came up the steps to meet them. He was about twenty-seven and wore a padded coat and a round fur cap on which a bright red insignia was fastened. He was smiling, and when he reached the group he looked first at Julie, then at Victoria. 'Miss Hollande?'

Victoria said, 'I'm Miss Hollande.'

'Major Liu.' He consulted a sheet of paper, spoke each of their names in turn, and shook hands when identity was established. He had a smooth olive complexion and the smile never left his lips. On the right side of his mouth he had a single gold tooth.

'Have you had good fortune?' he said.

For a moment they did not comprehend then, abruptly, Daniel realised they were being asked about their ostensible purpose for being in Sahr. 'Not so far,' he said.

'I heard there were many *markhor*.'

'We saw some coming in, but couldn't get a shot.' Parker said, catching on quickly.

They took him down to their camp, where he accepted coffee.

'How about your pilot?' Julie said.

'He does not drink coffee.'

Daniel noticed that the helicopter door on the pilot's side was partly open and he thought he saw, beyond it, the snout of a machine pistol.

'I have shot many *markhor*,' Liu said. 'I am excellent hunter.' He spoke English well enough, but with the artificiality of someone who has learned it as a foreign language from a teacher who had also been taught.

'More coffee?' Julie said.

'It is excellent. Yes, please, thank you very much.'

They talked about the hunting, or the lack of it, for some minutes, then he suddenly said, 'May I see your papers, please?' After the friendliness of their meeting, this was said with undisguised authority. But he kept on smiling even as he glanced at their passports and their permissions to overfly Chinese territory.

'Thank you, thank you,' he said, bowing and handing the papers back. 'Where have you been hunting?'

'Up and down the valley,' Daniel said.

'Ah so. And no good fortune?'

'No.'

'Such is hunting.' He threw his coffee dregs onto the shingle. 'Did you hunt in main Sahr valley?'

'Isn't this the main Sahr valley?' Daniel said.

Major Liu smiled. 'No, Mr. Wynter, this is not main valley. Main valley is over mountains.' He pointed back the way they had come. 'Your permissions are for main valley.'

'Permissions? What permissions?' Victoria said. 'We don't need permission to hunt here. This is Sahr.'

'Sahr under Chinese protection.'

'Since when?' Julie said.

'Since long time.' He smiled.

Daniel said hastily, 'We didn't realise that.'

'We got all the permissions we were told we needed,' Parker said. 'They were for overflying. No one said anything about Sahr. As far as we're concerned, this is no-man's-land.'

'No-man's-land?' Major Liu's smile grew wider. 'How can that be? This Chinese territory. It has been so for more than thirty (he pronounced it "serty") years.'

'We apologise,' Daniel said, cutting across Parker. 'We didn't know.'

'I must ask you to return to main valley.'

'Yes. We'll go back tomorrow.'

'That is good. Unfortunately there is no monastery to explore in main valley.' His gold tooth blinked in the sunlight, and he lit a cigarette. Daniel realised they must have been under observation since they arrived. 'You found that in monastery?'

'Found what?'

Liu pointed to the cartridge case which Daniel's fingers had been twisting. He held out his hand for it.

'This is not for *markhor*,' he said.

'No.'

'Please, Mr. Wynter, inform me where you found it.'

Daniel hesitated for a moment, but there was no way he could prevaricate. He led the way up through the ruined village. When the others began to follow, Major Liu turned to them. 'Wait here, please.' The friendly tone had gone, so had the smile.

Daniel led him away from the cavern which housed the Abbott, showing him the path through the fallen slabs to the passageway that led into the rock tomb. Liu stared impassively at the piles of bones.

'They were shot,' Daniel said, indicating the bullet marks on the rock. 'Look. Their hands were wired behind their backs.'

Liu did not answer. He touched one of the skeletons with the toe of his fur-lined boot. It was a knee joint and the bones collapsed into the dust.

Daniel was unable to restrain himself. 'For God's sake! Can't you leave them in place!'

'Why so?' Liu said. 'They are probably bones of Tibetan monks. Do you care?'

'They were murdered and I suspect if those ruined houses were searched we'd find more of them.'

'What has it to do with you, Mr. Wynter? Why you come here? You have no permission for this valley. You do not hunt. You spend all the day in monastery. Why?'

'We came to shoot *markhor*. We didn't know there was a monastery here.'

'Why you tell untruths?' Again he touched a skeleton with the toe of his boot, and the bones came apart. 'What does it matter who they were? They are dead.' He picked up several more brass cartridge cases, then went over to look at a poster and the camp bed. Daniel picked up the *Country Life* calendar.

192

There was something touching and precious about it. It was dated 1950 and seemed to hint at a less complicated world.

Major Liu was examining the cave. At last he said, 'Thank you, Mr. Wynter.'

Daniel followed him out. The day was changing rapidly. Racing clouds were moving along the valley from the east. The sun was gone and the wind was rising. The helicopter squatted at the bottom of the steps, the rotor moving slowly round and round.

The others walked towards them.

'What happened in there?' Julie said to Liu.

'Who can say?'

'It was a massacre,' Victoria said.

'The bullets are Russian,' Parker said.

'Yes, Russian,' Major Liu said.

'Why would the Russians come in this far?' Victoria's voice was filled with disbelief. 'There hasn't been a Russian in this part of the world for eighty years or more.'

'Who can say?' Liu repeated. He bowed to Julie and then to Victoria. 'I go now.' His manner had changed once more. He smiled, but the smile was thin, the bow merely a jerk of the head. 'You stay.'

'We can't stay. We have to rendezvous with our plane,' Victoria said.

The smile vanised again. 'You stay. Tomorrow I come back.' It was an order. 'Your rifles please. They will be returned to you.'

Chris gave him the Magnum.

'You have only one?'

'Yes.'

He turned and then, as though remembering his manners, said, 'Thank you for the coffee.' He ran to the helicopter and climbed aboard. Moments later it had swirled up and was disappearing eastward, gaining height all the time.

No one spoke until it had vanished. The valley was no longer golden, but grey and freezing, and everything had suddenly changed for them.

[5]

It was Julie who broke the silence. 'The more he smiled, the more I hated him,' she said.

'What do you think?' Parker said to Daniel. In that moment, there was a subtle change in their relationship, for it was as though for the first time he was acknowledging the need for some sort of guidance.

'I think we have a problem,' Daniel said slowly.

'I've travelled in places like this before and I know the mentality of these people,' Victoria said. 'They're basically bureaucrats, like the military everywhere. Something has happened for which they haven't planned, have no terms of reference. Major Liu will go back to his headquarters, wherever they are, and they'll discuss the situation and form some sort of plan. Then they'll send him back with a few men and they'll escort us back into the main valley and wait with us until our plane comes. It happens all the time, whenever one crosses a hostile border.'

'I don't think so,' Daniel said. 'Look at it from the Chinese point of view.' (Suddenly he was remembering a planning meeting in *Sirius* when someone had said, 'We must look at it from an Argentine point of view.') 'It's their territory – or at least, they say it is, and we come in and discover something very strange and horrible.'

'What's it got to do with *them*?' Parker said. 'No one knows what really happened. The massacre could have been carried out by Kazaks or Turkis, anyone.'

Daniel pulled the old *Country Life* calendar from the inside of the parka. 'I found this. See? 1950. Someone – my grandfather, probably – had been marking off the days up to the end of September and the first couple of days in October.'

'Was anything happening here then?' Julie said. 'I mean, revolution or war lords fighting, or anything like that? What else would cause one group of people to tie up another and then shoot them?'

'I remember 1950 very well,' Victoria said reflectively. 'It was a bad time for the General. He was ill. Chest trouble. It always became worse in the autumn. I remember he was in bed and I used to read him *The Times* every morning after breakfast. Sometimes I wouldn't even have my own breakfast. He'd ring his bell and I'd have to stop everything. Sometimes he had the radio on and I was reading at the same time. I remember that *The Times* carried stories every day about the flight of the Dalai Lama.'

'That's it!' Daniel said. '*Must* be it! The Chinese invasion of Tibet!'

Victoria said, 'They invaded early in October, 1950. A couple of years ago I went to a lecture at the R.G.S. when they showed smuggled slides of what the Chinese had done to the Tibetan monasteries ... just heaps of rubble. I remember the lecturer said that they'd attacked Tibet in six different areas. . .'

'And they came through here! They murdered my grandfather and the Kalmucks – or some of them at least – and smashed their houses and then went on their way.' He paused, trying to reconstruct in his mind what might have happened. 'They never found the Abbott, because it had been walled up by then, which probably means my grandfather had been expecting them.'

'He had the radio,' Parker said. 'Those Trans-Oceanics were the most powerful short-wave receivers on the market at the time. And the news was probably on every B.B.C. World Service broadcast.'

'It was all over the world,' Victoria said. 'Everyone was told how the Chinese were advancing and no one could do anything to stop them.'

Julie said, 'He would have listened. He knew he and the Kalmucks were in danger, so he hid the Abbott and their other belongings behind the wall. And then ... and then somehow they were trapped, perhaps while they were trying to get out of the valley.'

195

'And there never was an earthquake,' Parker said. 'After they'd been shot, the Chinese blew up the monastery just as they wrecked the others.'

'But they were Russian bullets, not Chinese,' Victoria said.

'Russia supplied arms to the Chinese for years. They equipped half their army in Korea,' Daniel said.

They stood in the bitter cold, feeling for the truth, trying to build up the picture of what had happened.

'Why would they need to kill them?' Julie asked. 'They were harmless people.'

'Because they were there.' Daniel remembered some of the television specials he had seen about the invasion of Tibet. 'The Chinese used German blitzkrieg tactics. As they came through they blew up monasteries, villages and killed everyone in their way.'

'Suppose we're right?' Parker said. 'How does the scenario go on now?'

'What I don't think will happen is that Liu will come back tomorrow and escort us into the main valley and put us politely on a plane and tell us not to be naughty and don't do it again, as Victoria suggested. We know too much. We've got it all on film. . .'

'How do they know that? Liu didn't see our cameras or equipment,' Julie said.

'They know everything we've done since we arrived. That wasn't ice flare we saw on the col at the entrance to the valley. That was a reflection of sunlight on binoculars, or a telescope. They've been watching us from over there.' He nodded across the valley to the mountains. 'I'll bet they're watching us right now. They've seen us filming, all right. That's why they whistled up the helicopter.'

'Then why didn't the Smiling Major mention it?'

'He caught us out with his talk about hunting. We lied when we said we'd been hunting up and down the valley, and he knew it. He came to find out exactly what we've been up to and now he knows that we have a most unpleasant story on film, implicating his country in a cold-blooded massacre of God knows how many harmless people. We'll probably find even more corpses. Look, China's been putting all its propaganda efforts into showing a new face to the West. Now they're having talks with the Russians – Major Desai mentioned them in London. America sees the talks as dangerous. For years she's used the hostility between Russia and China as a basis for her foreign policy. The last thing she wants is detente between them. So you can imagine what the American propagada machine would do with this.'

'It's years ago. It's no longer important,' Victoria said.

'Perhaps it's just important enough for them to want to keep it quiet. Why rock the boat if it can be avoided? Don't forget, to the Russians the Kalmucks are Russian.'

'Then our Major Liu's information will go to Pekin for a decision,' Chris said. 'I don't think we should be around to discover what it is.'

'Don't be hysterical,' Julie said.

'Chris is right,' Daniel said.

'They'd take us to Kashgar, perhaps. Keep us somewhere until the talks are over. Put us in gaol for illegal photography . . . spying . . . force us to sign statements that we had been guilty of acts against the Chinese People's Republic. There are a lot of things they could do. And we'd certainly lose all our equipment and film.'

'Or they could simply do what they did to Harry Wynter and the Kalmucks,' Parker said. 'It would be the simplest of all. We just disappear. A search is made. Nothing found. Too bad. Accidents happen in these mountains all the time. Bears still roam here, so do wolves. . . .'

They were suddenly silent, chilled by what he had said even more than by the bitter wind. They looked to each other for denials, confidence, optimism, but none was forthcoming. If the sun had been shining and the cliffs had been golden and the stream had glinted, there might have been some. One of them might have suggested that they were letting their imaginations run away with them. But their discovery of what lay in the cave, allied to the leached-out look of the valley, the stream that was already freezing over, the wind that was flapping the tents, the knowledge that men with guns were watching them from across the valley, all combined to heighten their anxiety. They could tell themselves they were over-anxious, but Daniel and Parker *might* be right. And always in their minds were the bodies: the skeletal limbs, the parchment skin, the empty eye sockets, the stainded teeth — and the English mountaineering boots with hob nails.

'We've got to get out,' Daniel said.

'We can't leave in daylight,' Parker said abruptly. 'And we can't go back the way we came. If Dan's right, that's where they're watching and, anyway, I wouldn't trust myself to find that defile in the dark.'

'We have to go down the valley,' Daniel said.

They were almost whispering in their urgency.

'What about that marsh?' Julie said.

'We don't know how deep it is. We'll have to try it, it's the only way. We're going to have to leave the tents. At least that'll give us time in the morning before they realise we've gone. If we can't get through the marsh, we'll have to climb out.'

He looked at the mountains that crowded in on them, with the snow streaks, coming down almost to the valley in places. They reared up into the sky between ten and twenty thousand feet. He thought, *God help us if we have to go up there.*

'The main valley lies to the south of this,' Victoria said. 'Our plane's due in two and a half days.'

'We can make it,' Parker said. 'In the meantime, we must act normally. We had a fire yesterday. Let's build another one. At least it'll give them something to look at.' He turned to Daniel: 'It's a damn shame about the car.'

Daniel himself had already experienced a feeling of bitterness at its loss, which even overshadowed the distress of discovering his grandfather's body. Not a nice thing to find out about oneself, he thought, but there it was: venality awaiting the right temptation to surface.

Almost as though she was reading his thoughts, Julie said, 'Do you think we should bury him?'

She was talking to Daniel, but Victoria answered. 'No! Leave him where he is. Don't disturb him now. That's where he lived. His spirit's more comfortable there.'

Daniel was surprised at her vehemence, but he nodded. 'He's had more than thirty years there. It would do no good to move him.' He paused, then said, 'I'm going to have one last look for the *Diaries*.'

'Haven't you found out enough?' Victoria said. 'Why can't you let it go at that?'

'It's what we came for!' Julie said.

He went back into the monastery for the last time. He stood in the cave that had become a tomb, looking at the bones of the grandfather he had never known, the man who had buried Eric Burten in the Takla Makan and had lived in this remote place, an outcast from a society that had vilified him. This was where he had made his life, and this is where he had been murdered.

He realised there was nothing further to be found in the cave unless he moved the bodies themselves, and he was not going to do that. He took one last look and climbed back through the fallen blocks of stone. Then he stepped in through the broken wall and took his final look at the Abbott. He thought how magnificent she was, even with her strange, iron-shod wheels. For a second or two he allowed his mind to project him back to England, the owner of this car. Would he really have sold it to Parker? Somehow it meant more than money to him.

He looked around for some memento, some souvenir of his grandfather that he could take with him. There were the great brass Marechal lights, but it would take time to remove them, and then they would be too heavy to carry. Anyway, he did not wish to mutilate the Abbott now that she had been made whole again. There was nothing small, nothing that he could simply slip into his pocket. He glanced in the toolbox on the back, but even the tools were too bulky. He turned and made his way to the top of the steps. The wind was blowing a gale and the day was dying.

The first thing he saw was Julie running towards him. She had been down near the frozen river. Her voice was faint and the wind whipped it away like a sea-bird's cry. He saw, past her in the distance, well past the shingle beach, two figures. One was on the ground, the other was bending over it. He jumped down the steps and raced through the ruined houses, meeting Julie as she plunged up one of the alleys. 'It's Chris!' she said. 'He's been shot!'

They ran back along the flat, tussocky river bank. He

registered, first, the blood, secondly, Victoria's face, which could have belonged to a woman of ninety. She had managed to rip away part of Chris's left trouser leg and her hands were covered in blood. He was groaning in pain.

She looked at up at Daniel. 'We were collecting wood. I saw him fall.'

Parker's left thigh looked as though someone had taken a meat cleaver to it. The last time Daniel had seen anything like it was when the Exocet had burst in *Sirius*. The for'ard gun turret had looked like a butcher's shop. He could not imagine that such a wound had been caused by a single bullet, unless it was soft-nosed. He tied a tourniquet above it and as he did so he felt something embedded in the hem of Chris's parka. It was a sliver of rock about six inches long and shaped like a dagger. He showed it to the women. 'This is what did it. The bullet must have sliced it off one of the rocks and it came like shrapnel.'

They helped Parker to his feet. He tried to hobble a few steps, but collapsed into Daniel's arms.

'I'll have to carry him. Help me to get him onto my back,' Daniel said.

It was about three hundred metres to the tents and before he reached half way his legs began to buckle and he had to rest. Parker was groaning as the pain hit him in waves. They reached the tents in stages and by the time they arrived Daniel was exhausted. They had brought first-aid dressings and a few ampoules of morphia. Daniel bandaged Chris's leg from just above his knee to his crotch, then gave him a shot of morphia.

'It should be stitched,' he said. 'What actually happened?'

Parker said, 'I'd gone down to get wood. One of those long planks. It had been carried downstream well below the shingle beach. I was cold from all the standing about and I thought I'd run. I was nearly there when it happened. Funny, I didn't feel it for a second. It was as though someone had given me a sharp slap on the thigh. A second later I heard the shot and when I looked down I saw the blood.'

Daniel looked over at the mountains on the opposite side of the valley. Where were they, he wondered? Above the cliffs? In caves? It was a narrow valley, less than two thousand metres across at its widest. Sniper's rifle, telescopic sight. Piece of cake. 'You were running?' he said. 'That probably did it. It might have been a warning shot. Maybe they thought you were trying to make a run for it, and they didn't actually mean to hit you.'

'We must wait for Major Liu to come tomorrow,' Victoria said. 'We have to get him to a doctor.'

'*If* he comes tomorrow.'

'How about a doctor in India?' Julie said. How do we get him out?'

A thought crept into Daniel's mind: they could leave him. They could leave him to wait for Major Liu, in his sleeping bag, with food and morphia and the syringe, while they took out the film. In wartime, wounded men often had to be left behind enemy lines. Well, they were now, in a way, behind enemy lines. . . .

As though reading his silence, Parker pushed himself up into a half-sitting position and said, 'For God's sake, don't leave me!'

Victoria knelt beside him. 'Of course we won't!'

'We can't carry him,' Daniel said.

'I'll walk,' Parker said. 'I'll get a stick. Don't worry about me. I'll manage.' There was panic in his voice.

But Daniel knew he couldn't walk ten yards and he also knew neither he nor the women could carry him without a stretcher.

'We could make a litter,' Victoria said. 'We have the wood and enough tools and nails.'

'How far would we get? Could we carry him across the marsh or up the slopes?'

'We could try, damn it!'

'We wouldn't even get half way to the marsh before those chaps over there caught us up. They're not going to be fooled by the silent camp for long.'

'All you've done so far is think up objections!' Victoria's voice was rising. 'He's badly hurt! Can't you be more positive?'

Daniel's mind went over every possibility, probing at each, but each time coming to a dead end. 'We'll have to stay,' he said at last.

'There's got to be a way,' Julie said. 'Can't we find a yak or a mule or something? Some sort of transport to carry Chris.'

'Don't be asinine! Where would we get a yak or a mule?' Victoria snapped.

But the word transport had triggered the computer in Daniel's mind. 'What about the Abbott?' he said.

It was like dropping a stone into a still pond. The ripples reached each of them in turn.

'But there's the marsh,' Julie said.

'It had to come in that way,' Daniel said. If my grandfather drove it in, we can drive it out. Maybe the marsh is shallow. Maybe somewhere there's a hard surface a few inches under the surface.'

Victoria said, 'Aren't you forgetting something? You haven't been able to start it.'

Daniel bent over Chris.

'Yes?' The voice was fainter.

'Is there anything you can think of that we didn't try?'

'You could cook the plugs.' The voice was hardly audible now. 'That's the problem: getting a cold engine started after all this time.'

'They built a fire under it in the desert. Harry Wynter wrote about it in his *Diary* of the race.'

'That was to thaw out the water in the engine. Try that now and you'll blow the whole thing sky high with all the petrol vapour in the cave.'

It was almost dark and they lit the little gas lamps. Chris was barely conscious.

'What do you mean about the plugs?'

'You heat them and . . . then you could. . .'

'Then you could what?' Daniel shook him. 'And then what?'

But Chris had lapsed into unconsciousness.

They took him into his tent and Victoria stayed with him.

Daniel said to Julie: 'Come on. At least we'll have a try.' Starting the car, he realised, had become the *only* alternative.

Julie sat in the driving seat. He had shown her what he had learned from Parker about the lever on the steering wheel which advanced or retarded the spark. He had lit some old kerosene lanterns and the cave glowed in the dim light.

'Ready?' he said.

'Yes.'

'You've checked she's in neutral?'

'Yes.'

'Because if she starts when I swing she'll flatten me.'

He wound the starting handle and he heard again the sucking noise as the engine took in air.

'Right,' he said. 'Here goes.'

He swung, and heard the same slurping, asthmatic wheeze the engine had made earlier in the day. He swung and swung until he felt his right arm was tearing from the shoulder joint.

He paused. 'Advance a little more.'

He swung again.'

'More!'

He swung again.

'Push the choke in a bit. More!'

'There isn't any more,' Julie said. 'That's it.'

Again he swung. And swung. Each time it sounded as though the engine might fire, but each time the noise dissipated into nothing.

He leant against the wall of the cave.

'Are you sure you put in the right fuel?' Julie said. 'From one of the sealed drums?'

'Yes.'

'It couldn't have gone off since you poured it?'

'No!'

'There couldn't be a key missing?'

'No.'

'Or any wires that need to be joined?'

'For Christ's *sake*!' He could feel the sweat dripping into his eye-sockets.

'I'm sorry.'

'We'll have to start again. Come and hold this.'

He loosened one of the leads as he had seen Parker do and made her hold it near to the engine block. He returned to the starting handle and swung. A crackling spark leapt from the lead onto the engine metal.

'That means the magneto's okay.'

He took out the plugs, cleaned them and heated them as Parker had suggested, then he told Julie to retard the spark and began to swing again . . . and again . . . and again.

He knew he did not have much strength left. It was draining away on each attack. He had tried to use his left arm, but it did not have the power.

He stopped. 'I don't know what else to do,' he said.

'You can't give up now!' Victoria was standing by the collapsed wall.

'What the hell do you know about it!' Then he made a supreme effort, and collected himself. 'Is Chris awake?' He thought that any tiny suggestion might help.

'No.'

In a rage, he swung the starting-handle, and then childish anger flooded through him. He kicked the Abbott's wheel and felt the pain go up through his foot and leg.

He realised that Julie and Victoria were looking at him almost with fear, because he was their only hope. Tears came into the back of his eyes: a mixture of exhaustion, doubt, frustration and self-pity.

He saw himself suddenly at thirteen or fourteen, when his uncle had sent him out into the cold Spring weather to give the lawn its first cut of the year.

'Come on, Daniel,' his uncle had said. 'Time to get the place looking shipshape.'

The mower was green and squat. He remembered pulling . . . pulling . . . pulling on the starter just as he was swinging at the starting handle now. His young biceps had become tight and painful. He was in a rage by the time his uncle had come out and said, 'You're never going to start it like that, chum. But I can show you a trick or two.'

Could it. . . ? He tried to recall exactly what his uncle had done. It might work. Both machines were internal combustion engines. They both exploded petrol in a chamber to produce energy. Why not?

He pushed himself away from the wall of the cave, went to the front of the Abbott, raised the engine cowling and took out several of the spark plugs. This was how he had done it on the mower for several years and it had always done the trick. Using the cap of the petrol drum he threw a teaspoonful or two of petrol into the hole from which he had removed the plugs, then he replaced them and their leads.

'Ready?'

'Yes.'

'Try advancing the spark.'

He swung. There was an explosion and a cloud of blue smoke shot out of the rear of the car. The backfire spun the starting handle, which caught him a glancing blow on the arm. He staggered backwards, falling among the tool boxes. For a moment he thought his arm was broken. He stood rubbing it. The anger left him. Instead there was a feeling of cold resolution. 'Retard,' he said, then he swung again. He heard a strange noise, as though the cave was filled with sewing machines. He ran to where Julie was sitting, grabbed the air control and moved it slightly. The engine note deepened and became more regular. The Abbott Special was running again after more than thirty years.

It should have been a time for jubilation, but he was so exhausted and so frightened that the engine would wheeze itself out, never to start again, that he went into immediate action, loading fuel and ropes and a spade into the back of the car. He made Julie sit at the controls while Victoria went to see to Chris. Then he cleared a path through the rubble and, with a rope attached to a heavy block of stone which acted as a drogue, the Abbott, like some great animal emerging from its lair, came slowly out into the fitful moonlight and bumped down the shallow steps of the monastery. The wind tore at them, the temperature was well below freezing, but they seemed not to feel it as badly as they had earlier. Every part of their muscles and their minds was directed at the car and the problem of keeping it going. They squeezed it through the alleys of the ruined village and brought it down to the tents. They packed what gear they could then, between them, they managed to get the half-conscious Chris into the back, where Victoria held him. Julie sat beside Daniel.

The Abbott's lights didn't work, there were no brakes and they could only select first gear. But the engine drove the back wheels, and that was enough.

'Right?' Daniel said. 'Then here goes.'

The car, built so long ago in London by a man who had soon afterwards killed himself, set off down the bank of the river on its iron-shod wheels, grinding along at four miles an hour.

The wheels were a problem. On this mixture of grass and sand, some of it hard, some soft, they sank into the sand easily. Soon Daniel was leaving the car so frequently to dig them out that Julie took over the driving, holding the huge wooden steering wheel as a drowning sailor clings to a lifebelt.

In the rear, Victoria tried to protect Chris from the worst of the bumps, using her own body as a shock absorber.

Lightened by the absence of Daniel's weight, the wheels did not bog down so often. He spent much of his time walking ahead of the car, for whenever the moon went behind clouds the silvery landscape was blotted out as though a curtain had been drawn. No one talked. No one thought of anything other than the immediate task: keep the car moving at all costs.

Around midnight the wind began to die and the clouds disappeared into the north-west. Stars blazed down and the setting moon gave them light to see by. The wind had been a blessing, Daniel thought, for it had carried the engine-noise away from the Chinese soldiers. He wondered if they were far enough down the valley now for the noise not to reach them. It was impossible to tell how many miles they had come, or what speed they were making, for the car spent almost as much time stationary as moving. Occasionally they came to patches of sand where a hundred yards might take half an hour and others where on a hard surface they might reach their top speed.

The sky began to lighten. Daniel looked back through his powerful glasses. The valley appeared very different from this angle. They had come in a wide semi-circle. The monastery was no longer visible. Now the mountains seemed to be leaning away from them as the valley widened. Nothing moved.

They went on, this strange slow-moving convoy, each in a cocoon of his own thoughts; Chris coming in and out of consciousness and in pain again as the morphia wore off; Julie clinging to the wheel, her face sharp with tension, her eyes staring into the greyness, looking for rocks or patches of sand, holes that might break a half shaft; and Victoria, grey-faced but iron-hard, enduring.

The sky gradually became navy blue, then light blue as the sun touched the peaks, turning them shell pink. The colours intensified. Some slopes were still dark, black in the shadows, others crystalline, so bright the reflection hurt their eyes. Soon the air began to grow hot and Daniel knew that this was the vital time. Now binoculars would be trained on their tents. When no one emerged . . . what?

The river widened in sympathy with the valley, and it was already melting. Daniel was thirsty, he wanted coffee. But there was no time to make it.

Crash. Bang. Crash. Bang. The wheels hit stone, fell off, hit more. The engine growled and back-fired, sometimes seemed to weaken to a point when he thought it must cut out. Then it picked up again. It had been like that all night and his body had become attuned to its beat. Each time it slowed, he held his breath. But always it gathered itself.

Suddenly they came to the marsh. Daniel saw it as a stretch of brilliant water, shining in the sun, almost blinding him. Julie brought the car to a stop. He examined the area through his glasses. It consisted of a sheet of water broken by reeds and tussock grass and was framed on either side by outcrops of rock, like reefs at sea, making it impossible to take the car round it.

He walked ahead to investigate. At the edge, where the water was at its shallowest, the ice had already melted, but as he stepped out into it, he realised that where it was deeper only a few millimetres of water at the top had melted. The rest was solid ice. But would it be thick enough to bear the car's weight?

He walked out onto it, probing ahead of him with the spade. He jumped up and down. It held.

When he came back to the car, his eyes were alight. 'This is how Harry Wynter brought her in!' he said. 'He drove her over the ice. It's all ice-bound here in winter and spring. Even now the river freezes every night.'

Victoria's face was clouded with worry about Chris. She hardly seemed to register what he had said.

'You go ahead,' he said to Julie. 'I'll give you about thirty yards and then follow. Watch for cracks, and warn me. Victoria, you go with her. I want the car as light as possible.'

Julie walked out onto the ice, turned and waved him to come on. They had no idea how big the marsh was, except that about three miles farther on the valley became narrower again and the chances were that it would be squeezed into a river. He drove the Abbott gingerly forward. Its metal wheels crushed the thin ice at the edge, then it heaved itself up onto the thicker ice and began to churn its way across, surface water spinning from its wheels, the droplets making rainbows in the sunshine.

Julie walked between the tussocks and the reeds, searching always for cracks or thin areas. The surface ice was melting rapidly now for the sun was blazing down. What was below? Was there a hard surface a few centimetres down? Was the water deep? Or would there be quicksands that would suck her under? He was terrified for her, hating himself for what he was asking her to do, but there was no other way.

He was drenched with sweat in the heat and the reflection was dazzling. He felt the Abbott lurch and then come crawling on. One of the wheels had cracked the ice. The car balanced for a moment, then slithered forward as the back wheels recovered some traction, onto a thicker surface. He looked at Julie and realised that her feet were now nearly covered in water. Then he saw something else: the fluffy tuft of a broken reed was moving slowly past her legs. There was no wind, so there had to be a current in the marsh. That meant that the sun had melted the stream above and it had started to flow. Soon the sun would bring down melt water in greater and greater quantities from the snow on the slopes above them and the river would rise as it did every day. They were clearly crossing the river's main channel through the marsh, the part that would melt more quickly.

Away to his left the marsh was in deep shadow where the sun was hidden by the tip of a peak. He signalled to Julie and Victoria to lead him in that direction. There the ice was, as he had hoped, still frozen and they were able to continue for more than a mile without mishap.

They had been on the ice for more than an hour and had

passed the halfway mark. The valley began to narrow. Here there was no shade.

Julie and Victoria plunged ahead through the water. As Daniel had hoped, the narrowing valley caused the marsh to return to a river channel. There were wide banks just as there had been at the monastery. As the women reached them, and turned, he felt the Abbott pitch forward and stop. One of the back wheels had gone through the ice. The engine stalled and the Abbott lay like a sleeping drunk.

Daniel left the car and inspected the disaster. The wheel had gone in up to its axle, but the other wheel seemed firm enough. 'It must have hit a thin pocket of ice,' he said. 'There's probably a current flowing beneath it. We'll have to unload her. We'll get everything off, then try to get her going.'

They lifted Chris down and Victoria gave him another shot of morphia. His face was flushed and he was feverish. Daniel handed Victoria his binoculars and said, 'Keep an eye out for any movement. Julie and I can unload.'

They made neat piles of the fuel and the oil and their own belongings on the ice. Finally they came to the big wooden tool-box which was bolted onto the back of the car. Daniel opened the lid and began to lift out the heavy wrenches and spanners. The pile grew larger and larger. At last there was only a piece of canvas lining covering the bottom of the empty box. In one corner he noticed a raised area, as though a couple of tiles or a thin box had been placed beneath the canvas. He pulled it aside and looked down at two leather-bound books tied together with twine. The cover of one had once been embossed with gold leaf. Most had worn away but the indented letters were still legible. He traced them with his finger. They said: *Harry Coles Wynter, Pekin–London, 1910.* He scooped up the books and was turning in triumph to the others when Victoria's voice cut the stillness like a knife.

'Here they come!'

He looked for somewhere to put the *Diaries*, then stuffed them inside Chris's parka. He took the binoculars from Victoria and looked across the marsh and up the valley. He could see nothing at first, then made out a series of white dots bobbing up and down. At first he thought she had made a mistake and that they were *markhor*. Then he realised that the light colour was white snow tunics. He was looking at eight Chinese soldiers running towards them.

'Tell me when they reach the edge of the marsh,' he said. The hot engine started again and he tried to ease her gently forward, but the wheel on top of the ice went round and round, unable to find traction. He gave Julie the controls while he went to the rear and tried to push – like a Sunday motorist on the Kingston by-pass, he thought. His feet slithered out beneath him and his strength was nothing compared to the weight of the Abbott.

'They're there!' Victoria said.

Through the glasses, he saw that the Chinese had bunched together and were hesitating. By this time, he thought, all the thin ice would have melted. They came on, wading in the shallow water and reached hard ice again. They wouldn't take long to reach the car.

He ran back to see if there was anything among their belongings that might help to move the car. The sleeping bags. He undid two and laid them under the good wheel, using them like desert mats.

Now!' he called.

Julie accelerated. The wheel spun, slowed, spun, slowed, and then gripped. The Abbott lurched forward. But with a crunching noise, the other wheel began to dig itself deeper.

'Stop!' he yelled.

He grabbed another sleeping bag and fed it under the second wheel. 'All right!'

The car swayed even further over to one side, then the second wheel gripped and the Abbott came out of the hole like some ancient reptile emerging onto dry land. 'Keep her going!' he shouted.

'They're still coming!' Victoria said.

The Abbott was less than fifty yards from the shore when, with a splintering crack, all four wheels went through the ice. Daniel experienced a sensation of total despair. There was nothing they could do now.

She seemed to be floating. Then he realised she was still moving, her wheels still turning. She must be on some kind of hard bottom. With a grinding, grating noise, she moved slowly forward, breaking the ice as she did so, her huge wheels keeping the body just above the surface of the water.

He heard a shot and then a ripple of shots as though from a machine-gun. At that distance they sounded like small fire-crackers, crisp and brittle. The Abbott was trundling up the sandy bank out of the water. He could see some of the Chinese standing in firing positions. He and Victoria lifted Chris between them and carried him to the bank. They heard the ricochet of a bullet as it struck the metal of the Abbott, then Julie drove her on into the safety of a hollow.

Daniel and Victoria went back onto the marsh to bring back fuel cans and sleeping bags. The gunfire intensified. They took what fuel they could and abandoned the rest.

As he went back for the last time, bending low to try and give as little target as he could, he slipped and fell, slithering across the ice, face down.

He found himself looking into the empty eye-sockets of a skull. He reared up in fright. All around it, trapped in the ice, were other bones. He saw a whole rib cage, smaller skeletons, skulls, human and animal. Wherever he looked, there were bones, and he knew he had found the second graveyard. The Kalmucks must have been coming out of the valley, the whole tribe, women, children, goats, sheep, trying to escape; trapped here in the marsh and slaughtered where they were.

He rose to his feet and picked up the last of the gear. As he did so he felt a blow that jerked his arms forward. He looked down and saw that a hole had appeared in the sleeping bag where the bullet had hit. The Chinese were only a couple of hundred yards away, still coming forward. Then suddenly, one went down, disappearing as though he had fallen into a hole. A second fell. The rest stopped and helped them out. Came on carefully. A third went down. This time, they did not come on.

Daniel ran for the car. 'They can't come through today,' he said. 'It'll be midnight before the marsh freezes again. We've got twelve hours.'

It was twenty-four hours since they had left the marsh. They lay among the ruins of one of the old houses in the main Sahr Valley, huddling against the standing walls, trying to escape the wind. It had started snowing in the night, flurries of fine powder snow sweeping down the valley from the east. They had driven throughout the previous day without stopping, too frightened to pause in case the car's engine stopped, never to start again; with no idea whether the Chinese were pursuing them. They had found that the valley opened out and the landscape became more arid. It made the going easier, for the gravelly surface was firm under the wheels.

They had swung gradually from east-west through south-west to due south and found a military road which the Chinese had built in 1962, which took them up over a pass where snow was still lying. From the top of the pass they had looked down at the western end of the Sahr Valley and by nightfall had reached it. But they were now at the far end and it had taken them most of the night, first in half a gale, then in the driving snow flurries, to reach the point where they were due to rendezvous with the pilot, Ram.

All the time they had been watching for the white dots that might be Chinese soldiers, or the sudden eagle shadow of a swooping helicopter. They saw neither. They had been alone in a vast wilderness.

The flight from the Golden Valley had become a question of will, for they were almost beyond exhaustion. It would have been easy to give up. But ironically, it was the car itself that had kept them going. To Daniel, the Abbott Special had become more than the sum of its parts. It had developed its own personality. In human terms it was very old, yet it was indomitable. It never gave up. Its wheels grew more battered, its body worn and scraped, its engine note became ragged. But it never stopped. It ran on and on like an old traction engine, noisy, smoky, appallingly uncomfortable, but somehow indestructible. It was this quality of resilience that had given him strength.

Now, from the ruined house he looked out at the bleak prospect before him, the dun-coloured landscape, the dusty landing strip, the snow flurries that came hissing down, cutting visibility, and he wondered how on earth Ram would find them. He had parked the Abbott at the back of the old house. It was the best place he could find. He wished there were bushes or trees he could cut to hide it, but there was not even enough wood to make a fire to keep them warm. I'll come back, he told himself. I'll come back for her one day. He pulled the sleeping-bag up to protect his face from the snow and thought about the possibilities. Billy Mahindra might help. It would be the sort of escapade to appeal to him. They could hire a big helicopter to winch it out . . . but that was in the future, and any future would depend on whether they got out.

He imagined Ram trying to bring the Cessna through the Sahr range and the snow. Or would the Chinese helicopter, with Major Liu, arrive instead? He looked at his watch. It was nine o'clock in the morning and Ram was due at noon.

Chris moaned. His head was on Victoria's lap and she was trying to shield him from the worst of the snow. The hood of his parka was up but even so snow was riming his eyebrows. She wiped it away with a lover's care. Could Julie have been wrong about them, Daniel wondered. *Were* they lovers? There had been stranger attractions between men and women. Or was it a case of the rich woman buying her pleasures? There was no question that Chris would have been successful with younger women. But there was always the lure of money. No one was immune from that.

Chris twisted and groaned again and his gloved hand went out to touch his thigh. Without discussing it, they were all aware that he could not survive much longer without medical attention. Victoria caught his hand and held it in hers. Daniel

213

saw tears in her eyes but was not sure whether they came from emotion or the biting wind.

She moved Chris gently into a more comfortable position and as she did so Daniel remembered the two books he had retrieved from the Abbott's toolbox and slipped into Chris's parka. He had been so preoccupied at the time – for that matter, ever since – that he had not thought of them. Now he reached over and unzipped the parka.

'What are you doing?' Victoria said angrily.

He held up the top book so she could see the indented printing.

Again, as on their first meeting, he admired her control. Her face was already grey and frozen in the dirty light of morning, but her mouth became a straight line. 'Where did you find those?' she whispered.

'In the Abbott's tool-box.'

'You didn't tell me.'

'No.'

'May I have them, please.' It was an order, rather than a request.

'No.'

Her face hardened and there was a look of contempt in her eyes. 'All right,' she said. 'How much?'

Julie had pushed herself away from the wall and crawled over to them. 'Are they. . . ?'

'My grandfather's *Diaries*. I found them as we were going across the marsh, just before we saw the Chinese.'

'And now he wants to sell them,' Victoria said.

It had not occurred to him, but the thought mushroomed in his mind. Could he sell them? What did it really matter to him, all this digging up the past? He had told her in London that his grandfather meant little to him. That was not quite true now, for he had journeyed a long way with Harry Coles Wynter, half way round the world and across the Black Gobi. And finally he had found those pathetic bones in the cave. Even so. . . . His mind went back to Blacker at the shipping company, the Team Leader's job he had been offered; the dole office; the weekly queue for his State handout. . . .

Perhaps this *was* his opportunity. Perhaps this was the only chance he might get.

'Have you thought of a figure?' Victoria said. 'Can we start bargaining? Or shall I name one and we'll take it from there?'

'God, you disgust me!' Julie said. 'You people think that anyone can be bought. It was *Daniel's* grandfather who died in that cave. It was *his* grandfather who suffered all these years from an injustice.'

'How do you know it was an injustice?' Victoria said.

'If it wasn't so, why do you want the *Diaires* so badly?'

Daniel felt that he had been dragged back from the edge of a precipice.

Then, suddenly, he realised that a pattern was forming in his mind. All the pieces had been there, yet he had not been able to put them together.

'These are why you came, aren't they?' he said slowly. 'It had nothing to do with truth and justice and honour, those conceptions you said our generation didn't understand. You came here for the *Diaries.*'

Julie built on his thoughts. 'You came to find them before we did. Maybe destroy them. The film didn't mean anything ... neither did Harry Wynter or the Kalmucks ... or anything except finding the second part of the *Diary*. You already knew what was in the first.'

'Keep your voice down!' Victoria said.

'Chris can't hear. Even if he could he's past caring.' Then Julie said something so brutal that even Daniel found it hard to accept. 'If he dies, you killed him.'

Victoria flinched as though she had been struck. Then slowly her face crumpled like paper. She leaned forward, resting her head against Chris and this time Daniel knew they were real tears coursing down her cheeks.

But Julie was not impressed. 'He doesn't know, does he? You never told the truth: not to Chris, not to us, not to anyone.'

'I couldn't.' Victoria spoke more to herself than to them. 'I couldn't.'

Daniel realised that the truth had been there all along, but masked by other 'truths'. 'You've been here before, haven't you?' he said. 'Here in Sahr. In the Golden Valley?' She didn't answer. 'Christ! I should've guessed! 1939!' It was one of the first dates he had seen in the reading room of the Westminster Reference Library, in a newspaper cutting which described General Hollande setting off to find a 'lost' city in Amazonia. One line had said that his daughter was going to climb in the Himalayas. 'You didn't go to the Himalayas, did you?'

'No.' Her reply was hardly audible, whipped away on the wind.

'You came to Sahr. And *that's* what you were afraid of. That you'd be in the second part of the diary. The part you hadn't known about. The part about the Golden Valley.'

She shook her head. 'He wouldn't let me in,' she said. 'He turned me back.'

Then she began to talk. At first her speech was soft and disjointed, the words flung about by the wind, but gradually her voice strengthened and the words flowed, checked, and flowed again.

Harry Coles Wynter had been part of her life as long as she could remember. His name always seemed to have lurked like some ghost in the Hollandes' attic; some mad relative locked and chained in an upstairs room; always there, but never mentioned by her father. It cropped up among his friends in conversations she only half-heard; the maids talked about him; the gardeners talked about him; before Percy Preece had gone off to start his car-hire business, he had talked about him.

Once, in the early thirties, she had seen Mary Wynter, a cold, remote beauty, at a house-party in London. 'You know who that is?' someone said to her. 'She was married to the man who tried to kill your father.'

The General had been in some far part of the world and unable to be questioned, her mother was dead. She had asked the servants and the story had gradually built up by accretion, each knowing a few details. Then, some months later, her father had returned and she had asked him. He had said, 'We don't listen to gossip. Harry Wynter was a friend of mine. Leave it there.'

She had not, of course, left it there, or at least, it had not left her, for every once in a while Wynter's name would crop up. Wanting to discover more, she had preceded Daniel to the newspaper libraries and read published letters which had come from him in Sahr, protesting the injustice of the charges made against him. There were also the reports of the race and its aftermath. The more she read, the more she came to admire her father, for it was plain that Harry Wynter had tried to destroy him, yet his honour was such that he never blamed him in public, nor even to her in private. The General was a taciturn man, but to his daughter, his actions spoke for him. Her mother had died when she was a baby and he was all she knew of both father and mother. At her most impressionable age, she saw him being feted in England, a man in the classic mould of soldier-explorer that the British love, and, on top of it, in founding his Trust for the benefit of young people, a visionary. He was mentioned in the same breath as T. E. Lawrence. Always, at the back of her mind, was the resentment of what Harry Coles Wynter had tried to do.

As she grew older and was able to understand more, she had realised that perhaps the situation was not black and white. There were people who said they didn't believe the story and suggested that Harry had been a man whose honour was at least as profound as her father's. She heard women describe him as one of the most attractive men in England. She heard men, on the other hand, call him a homosexual.

She saw her father and Harry as two medieval knights who should have been bound by fealty and honour. What had caused the corruption of one and not the other? These were romantic questions put forward by a romantic nature corseted by the conventions of the time and her upbringing, and held for the most part in check.

She had married young, a colonel in her father's regiment who was nearly twenty years her senior. It was a disaster. The qualities she was used to in her father, and for which she had looked in her husband, were missing.

To escape, she went climbing in Central Asia, as part of a team that had mounted an attack on Mir Samir in Nuristan. When the others returned to England she, unwilling to take up her marriage again, had stayed.

There was no coincidence in her meeting with Harry

Wynter. Over the years, her curiosity about him had grown. In Gilgit, on the North West Frontier of India, she had asked about him. The story of the Englishman who had lived for years in a remote Sahr valley with the remnants of a tribe of Kalmucks was well-known on the Frontier. Her certainty about her father did not waver, but she found that she wanted to see for herself the man who had attempted to kill him.

Travelling under her married name, she had gone in search of Wynter as her father went in search of the source of rivers. He had become an object of discovery himself and, without realising it, she had followed the path Archibald Preece had taken a few months before. Harry had turned up in Kashgar, to pick up supplies. She had managed an introduction through the British Consul. Daniel had Preece's picture of him in his mind: a good-looking man, thin, fit, suntanned, in the prime of his life, lonely. And Victoria: small, slender, attractive, her body like whipcord, with a will to match. Also lonely.

Almost before she realised what had happened, they had become lovers.

As Daniel listened, he realised it was almost impossible for her to describe the intensity of their affair, but he was able to imagine, to read between her spoken lines, to begin to understand the passion that had grown up between them: between this man, rejected by his own society, and the woman young enough to be his daughter. It was plain that it was Victoria who had fallen most deeply in love. He by that time was battle-scarred, wary, protective. She, emerging from an unhappy brush with marriage, was ready for the love she had not previously discovered.

'It was as though everything before had happened in a different world,' she said, choosing her words with care. 'Once I'd met him and talked to him it wasn't so much that I didn't believe the stories I'd heard, it was as though they were immaterial, had no value, simply didn't matter any more. There was a magic about the place and that time and about his house that seemed to mask everything else.'

Daniel remembered the house that Preece had described, with its fig-tree and its cool fountain and the strange, wild-looking Kalmucks lounging in the courtyard. He visualised

Harry and Victoria lying together in the upstairs room in which Preece had talked to Harry and he found himself envying his grandfather.

At first, Harry had hardly spoken of his background to her but then, as though he had found an audience to answer a need – just as she had found one now – he told her the truth about the race, about what had happened later. He spoke of his wife, Mary, not knowing that Victoria could put a face and figure to the name. He described Victoria's father and the British newspapers that had pilloried him. He spoke as though he was telling her about some remote historical event, but she could hear bitterness still, and sadness when he spoke of his son. When he started to tell her about his valley and the Kalmucks, his whole physical appearance seemed to change. His thin, ascetic face lit up with enthusiasm, and she had listened spellbound to the story of his life there.

It had begun with his rescue in the desert by the four Kalmuck horsemen. One of the riders, an old man, had returned to Russia secretly some years before to try to bring out the remnants of his family. During his journey he had seen a steam-driven threshing machine. It had been the most amazing and memorable sight of his life. When he had come upon the Abbott Special in the desert it did not occur to him that it was a form of transport. To him it was simply an engine which could be moved from A to B on its own wheels and could be of immense value to his people.

Some weeks later when Harry Wynter had recovered from his illness and could make sense of his surroundings, the Abbott was already in the Golden Valley. The Kalmucks had gone into the desert with their ponies and their yaks and had dragged it up into the mountains and across the frozen marsh. They had not cut Harry's throat for one very good reason: he understood how to make the engine work.

As soon as he had grasped their thinking he realised that they had taken a major step towards their own survival. They were on the very edge of extinction. Years of living from hand to mouth had reduced their numbers to fewer than three hundred men, women and children. If crops failed, they starved; if they didn't, they barely survived.

The Abbott was to be their salvation. The front wheels

went to build a cart. During the months that followed he was able to show them how to take off the back wheels and use the back axle as a driving shaft to drive the belts which, in turn, threshed, and pumped water, and spun a circular saw. He demonstrated that they had, in effect, the best donkey engine in the world.

Daniel, in spite of the cold and the misery of his present position, felt the kind of excitement his grandfather must have known as he began to understand the uses to which a car could be put if the last thing one wanted to do was drive it.

So the Abbott had become the Kalmuck's prize possession, their saviour, and Harry Wynter had become a kind of king among them. The car re-vitalised them, changed their lives. It enabled them to buy a few animals, a little seed corn, build stone houses, eat, keep warm.

Nevertheless, Victoria had wondered aloud how that remote valley, with its bitter climate, could continue to support nearly three hundred people. It was some time before Harry had revealed to her the inner core of their existence: a secret he had shared only with her, the woman he had come to love. The valley contained gold.

Daniel heard Julie's indrawn breath above the sound of the hissing snow. 'I thought it was the golden light on the cliffs that gave it its name,' she whispered.

'It's always been known there was gold on the Tibetan plateau,' Victoria said. 'It's been panned there for hundreds of years. The rivers that flow off the plateau also contain it. Not much. Very little, in fact. It was never worthwhile trying to win it manually. But once Harry adopted the Kalmuck's philosophy towards the internal combustion engine, he knew he could pan on a large scale. He bought a water-pump which could be driven by the engine, pumped water up into a cistern in the monastery, then used a flume to take it down into a dolly and wash the spoil. It's the oldest form of alluvial mining there is. It's the way they did it in California and the Klondyke.'

Daniel said: 'The shingle beach! That's where they would have washed for the gold. The shingle was the spoil they dug out of the river. And the trestles and the wooden planking we found must have been part of the flume.'

The quantities they had found were small, but they were enough. Harry Wynter sold the gold dust through Prasolov in Kashgar and with the proceeds was able to import fuel for the engine, clothing and harnesses, blankets and food. Life in the valley became worth living, not something which had to be endured. When he described it to Victoria, Harry was already toying with the idea of somehow adapting his own life there so she could share it with him.

She stopped.

After a long pause, Daniel said, 'What happened?'

'He found out who I was. There was a cable from my father which reached the Consulate. He used my maiden name. It wasn't long before everyone knew who I was.'

'And?'

'He did what he did to Archie Preece. He simply disappeared. He was there one morning. I left him to go to the bazaar. When I came back the house was shut and there wasn't a soul about.' She looked past them, her eyes seeing a different world and a different time. 'I followed him. I found out where the valley lay. It was summer, and blindingly hot. Half a dozen of his men turned me back at the head of the valley where the defile is. We couldn't speak each other's language, but they made it plain enough. Harry had given the orders. I went round by the main Sahr Valley and tried to get in at the other end. I thought no one could stop me but, of course, the marsh did. I suppose I could have climbed around it, but by that time I was finished. I had heatstroke. I gave up and went back to Kashgar.'

Again she was silent and Daniel wondered whether to prompt her, but she picked up the thread of her thoughts. 'I waited there for several weeks, hoping he'd come back, but he didn't. So I went home to England. The war was about to begin.'

'And you said nothing?' Julie said.

'That's right. I said nothing. The General had been nominated for the Gold Medal of the Royal Geographical Society. Do you understand what an honour that is? The Trust had blossomed. He was back in harness. How could I have sacrificed him? I had loved and respected him from my earliest moments. I would have destroyed him.'

'So you believed what Harry had told you about the race?'

'I probably did. I say probably because the whole relationship with Harry began to take on an air of fantasy. Once I got back, I wondered if it had all been real, or just a dream of the high mountains. But eventually, when father became old and senile and sick and I nursed him, he told me the truth, too. It had all happened exactly as Harry said. He couldn't stop talking about it. He'd sit in his wheelchair, smoking and coughing, talking of the race until I grew to hate him. And Harry. And everything about it. I only wanted it forgotten.'

'So when you heard there was a second *Diary*, you decided to get rid of it,' Julie said.

'Only once I knew you were set on coming here to make your documentary. It had lain here for more than thirty years. It might have lain for thirty more, except for. . .'

'Us,' Daniel said.

'Yes, you.'

'Did you block Archie Preece's book?'

'Its publication would have damaged the Trust, the General's memory, me, everything I've lived for, and. . .' As she looked down at Chris, they heard the thrashing sound of a helicopter's rotors. It came up the valley from west to east, thudding in the air. Daniel felt it in his chest cavity again as he had in the monastery, but in the snow flurries they did not see it, even though it seemed to come very close. Gradually, it passed them by and went on up the valley, its noise growing fainter.

'He'll be back once the snow stops,' Daniel said. 'Then he'll spot the Abbott.'

'Maybe the snow won't stop,' Julie said.

'Maybe not. Maybe Ram will get in, but again, maybe not.'

They were quiet for a while, huddling down against the broken walls. Daniel knew there were still questions to be answered.

'What happened to the note my grandfather left at the fuel dump?' he said.

'My father destroyed it. He put it in his pocket and later destroyed it.'

'And Percy Preece did all the rest, as your father knew he would. My grandfather said there was plenty of fuel left, but by the time Preece and your father got there, most of it had drained away. How did that happen?'

'I don't know. Harry thought the taps might have been opened by Kazaks.'

'Could it have been your father?'

'I don't think so. I believe he would have confessed it when he told me all the rest.'

'So all he had to do was keep quiet. He didn't even have to accuse Harry Wynter of anything.'

'People like to believe the worst. The General was a good judge of character.'

'And Harry was neither homosexual nor bisexual.'

'The opposite, if anything.' She looked past them again, remembering. 'Once you start, you have to keep on.'

'Start what?'

'Lying.'

'You and your father destroyed him,' Daniel said.

'If I had rehabilitated him, I would have destroyed my father. And please don't talk to me of justice. At the time I thought and thought about it until I couldn't think any longer. Now *you* think of something: think of all the young men and women who were helped by the Trust, whose lives were changed for the better, who looked up to my father and tried to follow his example.' She stared down at Chris, and suddenly it did not seem so much the look of a lover.

'My God!' Daniel said, as he glanced from one to the other.

'It's not what you think. He's not my son. This isn't *East Lynne*.' She brushed the snow off Chris's eyebrows again. 'He's my half-brother. It was another thing the world could never know about the General. He had the . . . problem some men have in middle-age, especially when they are single.'

'Who was the mother?'

'A young girl on the estate called Valerie. A relative of Eric Burten's, strangely enough.' For a moment it meant nothing, then Daniel saw in his mind's eye blonde hair, and remembered one of the interviews Archibald Preece had had with Eric Burten's mother in Pear Tree Cottage. He had described

223

a young blonde with a baby. She was Eric Burten's niece. He did a swift calculation. It fitted.

'His mother died when he was a child. He grew up in the Trust. He doesn't know about his father. He never will. But eventually, he'll take over the Trust.'

As though knowing they were talking about him, Chris groaned, grinding his teeth in pain. Victoria's eyes were stricken. 'Is there nothing we can do?'

As she tried to shelter him from the snow, Daniel opened Chris's trousers and took off the bandage around his leg. The material was already crisp with dried blood and the wound gaped open like a rotten mouth filled with suppuration.

He remembered that when *Sirius* had been hit there had been men with such wounds and they had been taken aboard the carrier for surgery. When he saw them again, some had lost an arm, some a leg, some their lives.

He said, 'We've no choice now, we must take the first transport that arrives.'

They did not talk after that, but crouched against the wind, waiting in the light snow for the helicopter or the Cessna: China or India.

Noon came and went. Either Ram had had to turn back, or he had never started. Another hour passed. Then, faintly above the wind, Daniel thought he heard the sound of an aircraft, but it was so far away he could not tell whether it was the helicopter or the Cessna. In either case, it would be impossible for the pilot to spot them through the increasing snow. He had already made up his mind what had to be done. He pushed the *Diaries* into Victoria's hands and stumbled through the wind towards the Abbott. He unscrewed the heavy steel petrol cap, tore his handkerchief into strips and tied them together, dipped one end into the fuel tank, trailed the other end as far as it would go to make a fuse; then he lit it.

He sprang backwards, flinging up his arms in front of his face. The pressure wave from the explosion slammed him into the ruined wall of the house. When he opened his eyes, the Abbott was an inferno. Flames were leaping up and black smoke was pouring into the sky. The interior burnt away and then the paintwork began to bubble and crack and blacken.

The wooden steering wheel became a static catherine wheel, the wood in the wheels caught, the engine cowling buckled, the great Marechal lamps twisted drunkenly in the heat. He felt tears at the back of his eyes and found he could look no longer.

The noise of the burning car was so great that it was some moments before he heard the aircraft. It came ghosting through the snow, a single-winged Cessna, and he could see Ram's pale brown skin and his upraised thumb.

They took off into the wind, bumping and lurching, and finally they were airborne. No one spoke, or smiled, or cracked a joke. As Ram banked to turn south-east Daniel looked down through a gap in the snow squall and saw the Abbott, a charred black mass covered by oily black smoke. It was a beacon all right. It had carried his grandfather from Pekin almost to Kashgar, then it had kept alive the last remnants of a broken people, and lastly it had carried them to safety over roads only a modern tractor might have managed. There was something Wagnerian about its end, as though it had found its own Valhalla. Better than ending up in the air-conditioned garage of some wealthy collector.

He felt a touch on his sleeve and looked at Victoria. She held the *Diaries* out to him. 'What do you want me to do with these?' she said.

His mind was blank. He looked across at Julie. She lay in one of the seats, her mouth half open, unconscious with exhaustion. She was the only part of his future of which he was quite, quite certain. At that moment, he didn't give a damn about anything else. He knew there would be decisions to be taken, arrangements to be made, plans to be discussed. There was Chris, there was their film, there was. . .

He said, 'Whatever you like.' Then he closed his eyes.

AUTHOR'S NOTE

Motoring enthusiasts will know there was no Pekin–London race in 1910. But there was a Pekin–Paris race in 1907, on which mine is based. There was no such car as the 'Abbott Special'. It is a reincarnation of the famous Itala, which won the 1907 race, driven by Prince Scipione Borghese.

My thanks for their help goes to David Johns, Dick Slater and the Technical Services Department of the Shell Company.